PERFECT SINS

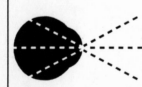 This Large Print Book carries the
Seal of Approval of N.A.V.H.

PERFECT SINS

JO BANNISTER

THORNDIKE PRESS

A part of Gale, Cengage Learning

GALE
CENGAGE Learning·

Farmington Hills, Mich • San Francisco • New York • Waterville, Maine
Meriden, Conn • Mason, Ohio • Chicago

GALE
CENGAGE Learning·

Thorndike Press® Large Print Crime Scene.
The text of this Large Print edition is unabridged.
Other aspects of the book may vary from the original edition.
Set in 16 pt. Plantin.

LIBRARY OF CONGRESS CATALOGING-IN-PUBLICATION DATA

Bannister, Jo.
  Perfect sins / by Jo Bannister. — Large print edition.
    pages ; cm. — (Thorndike Press large print crime scene)
  ISBN 978-1-4104-7677-7 (hardcover) — ISBN 1-4104-7677-4 (hardcover)
  1. Missing persons—Investigation—Fiction. 2. Policewomen—Fiction. 3. Large type books. I. Title.
  PR6052.A497P47 2015
  823'.914—dc23   2014045900

Published in 2015 by arrangement with St. Martin's Press, LLC

Printed in Mexico
1 2 3 4 5 6 7 19 18 17 16 15

PERFECT SINS

CHAPTER 1

Stephen Graves remembered the name well enough. But he wouldn't have recognized Gabriel Ash if they'd passed in the street. He'd struck Graves as a big man when they first met: tall, big-boned, powerful of build and of intellect. The man before him now seemed entirely shrunken. He even seemed shorter, thanks to a slight apologetic stoop.

Graves ushered him to a chair, quickly, as if afraid he might fall down. But his anxiety was unwarranted. Ash was in better shape than he looked. He was in better shape than he'd been for years.

With his visitor safely seated, Graves called his PA and asked for coffee. Ash waited politely, aware that these days his host's time was more important, or certainly more expensive, than his own.

Finally Graves overcame his surprise enough to open the conversation. It wasn't difficult to guess why Ash was here — there was only one issue that concerned them both. "I imagine it's the same matter you want to discuss."

Ash nodded. Thick black curls fell in his eyes. Graves doubted he'd spent proper money on a haircut since they'd last met. Only the suit was the same, and though clean and pressed, it now hung from Ash's cadaverous frame. "Some things have come up. Queries. I hoped you could cast some light . . ." Graves didn't interrupt him. The sentence just petered out, as if he'd lost interest in it.

The CEO of Bertram Castings took a moment to realize he'd finished. "Yes," he said. Then, keenly, "Yes, of course. Anything. If I can. If there's anything I haven't already told you. But first" — he bit his lip — "can I say how sorry I am about what happened? When I heard . . . I couldn't help feeling . . . guilty, I suppose. If you hadn't been trying to help us, perhaps . . . none of it . . ." It was his turn to run out of words.

Ash smiled. It was an oddly innocent smile for a man of forty, apparently without bitterness. "I was just doing my job. If I hadn't been doing it here, I'd have been doing it somewhere else. The consequences would very probably have been the same."

Whether or not it was true, the manufacturer appreciated him saying it. He'd assumed that Ash had been hating his guts for the last four years. It would have been understandable. "Has there been some news?"

"No," said Ash quickly. "At least, nothing" — he sought an appropriate adjective — "reliable. But someone said something, in a different context, and he was probably just winding me up, but I didn't feel I could let it go without at least trying to be sure."

"Who?" asked Graves, almost holding his breath. "Said what?"

"It was a policeman. A senior policeman, who might well have heard things that weren't public knowledge. But who also had a good reason for wanting me to think he could help me." Ash swallowed. "He said — he gave me to understand — that he knew what had happened to my family. And I think — I *think* — he was saying that my sons are still alive."

Graves took a steadying breath and let it out slowly. "That would be wonderful."

"Yes, it would," agreed Ash. His voice was gossamer-thin. "If it's true."

"You said a policeman?"

"But not a very good one."

"You mean, you think he's lying?"

"He could have lied."

Graves frowned. "How can I help? Surely the one you need to be talking to, or someone needs to be talking to, is this policeman — to establish whether he actually knows anything or not."

"You're right, of course." Ash nodded. "Unfortunately, he's dead."

The man across the desk froze. "Who killed him?"

"A criminal. It's a long story," said Ash tiredly. "Before he died, when he was anxious for my help, he said he knew where my boys are. He might have meant where they were buried, but that's not what he said. Before I could ask him to explain, he died in front of me. And now I don't know, and don't know how to find out, if he was telling the truth."

It was a much abbreviated version of that desperate day's events, but it was accurate and it was as full an account as a peripheral player like Graves would need. Being a weapons manufacturer didn't make him an expert on gang culture. The whole of the arms trade is so ringed about by regulations that he couldn't have sold weapons to gangsters if he'd wanted to. He was an engineer by training, a businessman by choice, a pen pusher by necessity. The government inspectors cast such long shadows over his trade that he'd once found himself photocopying his wife's birthday card, just in case.

"Gabriel, I don't know what to say." The use of his visitor's first name didn't come naturally — they'd never been on first name terms — but it felt more awkward still to call him Mr. Ash when the man had stripped his soul in front of him. "Tell me how you think I can help."

Ash smiled again, gratefully. "In all honesty, I'm not sure you can. I just couldn't think where else to go. The thing is, this policeman had been working in Norbold, where I live, for the last eight years. Before that he was up north somewhere. He was never in Africa. If he knew anything about Somali piracy, he heard about it while living and working in England. And that's what he said — that he heard it from a local criminal. In fact, the one who shot him.

"And if he really did know something, if it wasn't just a bait he was dangling in front of me, I think that had to be true. I'm pretty sure he didn't get it from an official source. I've been to Whitehall — I still know people there — and what they told me is that they've learned nothing new about my family in the last four years. I believe them. If there'd been anything to report, my old boss would have told me, with or without his minister's approval."

Ash had worked for Philip Welbeck for five years. He'd known he was a good boss. He hadn't known how good a friend he was until his world fell apart. Admittedly, Ash had broken Welbeck's nose in a highly public brawl in Parliament Street, and Welbeck had had him committed to a psychiatric institution, but both these acts had long ago been forgiven. Ash had been far from rational when he took a swing at his superior. And Welbeck had been absolutely rational, as cool and clinical as always, and totally focused on the safety of Ash's family, when he called the men in white coats.

There was no knowing if Cathy and the boys were still alive when Ash, insane with worry, stormed down to London, demanding to know what was being done to find them. But if they were alive, it was to keep Ash from returning to his job in national security and hunting down those responsible for the hijacking of British-made munitions. This was what he was good at, what he was perhaps better at than anyone else. It had taken the pirates some time to recognize the fact. But when they did, they had moved quickly to neutralize the threat he posed. Holding his family hostage gave them control of Gabriel Ash.

After the scene in Parliament Street it was impossible to pretend he hadn't disobeyed Welbeck's instructions by returning to London. All Welbeck could do to salvage the situation was make it clear that Ash wasn't working, on his family's abduction or the acts of piracy that preceded it, because he wasn't fit to work, and quite possibly never would be again.

That was then. This was now. Ash couldn't use official channels to pursue the search anymore. This was what he was doing instead: picking up the threads of the investigation that had cost him everything and trying to find out if they still led anywhere.

He was grateful Graves had agreed to see him. Ash wanted him to understand that, though he had little in the way of new evidence, he wasn't just raking over the same old coals. "If this policeman was telling the truth, he learned what happened to my family from a Norbold drug dealer. And that means that everyone involved in these hijackings isn't half a world away in Somalia. There's a local dimension. Someone here is involved."

"Here?" Graves's eyebrows shot toward his hairline. Although he was no older than

Ash, his hair was gray and he kept it clipped short to teach it a lesson. He did spend proper money on haircuts.

"Sorry," said Ash hastily, "I don't mean here at Bertrams. I mean here in England. And I found myself wondering — you're going to think I'm crazy," Ash interjected with the painful wryness of someone who knew what it was like to be thought crazy — "if there was any chance that someone you work with could be selling information on your shipments. Not necessarily one of your employees — it could be an auditor or a tax inspector, or someone from Health & Safety, someone who comes and goes without exciting much interest. But someone who has access to your shipping details, so the pirates know when you're sending munitions in their direction, what aircraft you'll be using, and which airfields you'll be putting down at."

Graves was obviously taken aback. His company had lost a small fortune in goods hijacked en route to their end users in Africa, but the general understanding had been that that was where the problem lay — in Africa, with the customers' security arrangements. Five times in four years it had happened, and it wasn't just the munitions that had disappeared each time but

14

also the aircraft and the crew. People had died trying to deliver his goods, and the only consolation was that the British police had looked at Bertrams's security protocols and told the CEO there was nothing more he could have done to protect them.

Now Gabriel Ash seemed to be telling him something different. "How would I know?" he asked, concerned.

"Maybe you wouldn't. Maybe there was nothing to notice. But maybe there was someone who showed just a bit more interest in your shipping arrangements than seemed natural. Who asked where aircraft would be refueled, or which carrier was carrying which shipment, or how crew were recruited. Something like that. Or something quite different, but still not quite what you'd expect. Not quite right."

Graves was trying to think, but this had been sprung on him. He'd had a couple of hours' notice that Ash wanted to call, none at all that this was the reason. His face creased with the effort to remember. Finally, regretfully, he shook his head. "I'm sorry, nothing's coming to mind. But can I have some time to think about it? I'll go through the records, see who was in the office in the days before each hijacking. See if any pattern emerges. Give me your number. I'll call you if I come up with anything."

Ash gave him the number of his new mobile. "Call me anyway. It doesn't need to be a concrete suspicion. If you think of anyone with access to the relevant information, I'll talk to the other firms that lost shipments and see if the same name comes up again."

Graves pulled over a notebook and wrote some names and numbers from memory. "Talk to Bob Simpson at Gaskins. I know they lost a shipment of assault rifles not long ago. And Sandy Pierson at Viking. That's Ms. Pierson, incidentally," he added with a nervous grin, "don't get off on the wrong foot by asking for Mr. Pierson. They've both become involved since you . . ." Another unfinished sentence. This time the missing words were *Went doolally.*

Ash nodded his thanks and folded the paper carefully into his breast pocket. "I suppose it's a pretty small world, arms manufacture — that you all know one another?"

"In some ways," agreed Graves. "In others, of course, it's global. But anyone in the industry will help you if they can. We need to get on top of these hijackings. Somali pirates are making a quarter of the world almost a no-go area for weapons exports."

"Which begs the question why you continue selling a sensitive product to such a volatile region."

Graves shrugged. "Because it's our business. Because volatile regions are where arms are needed. We couldn't stay solvent by selling what we make to the Isle of Man. And then, don't we have an obligation to support Third World countries that are trying to make a go of the democratic model? They wouldn't get far if all the demagogues and tyrants around them could march over their undefended borders."

It was a valid point. Besides, Ash wasn't here to do battle with the arms industry. His mission was much more tightly focused than that. "I need to be candid with you, Mr. Graves. Tackling piracy against British citizens, British carriers, and British goods is the job of the British government. It used to be my job, but it isn't anymore. My only interest now is in finding out what happened to my wife and my sons.

"They disappeared because, when I *was* part of the government investigation, I got close enough to the pirates to worry them." Ash's deep, dark eyes were hot with the memory: at how clever he'd been, and how stupid. "For four years I believed my family were dead. Now there seems just a small chance that they aren't — that if I can work it out, I can find them. I may be fooling myself. But I don't want to mislead you. If finding my family means destroying these people — in Somalia, in England, wherever they are — then I will if I can. But that's not my priority. If you help me, you have to understand that I may not be able to help you much in return. If the pirates offer to buy my silence with the only currency I'm interested in, nothing — not honor, not duty, *nothing* — will stop me from taking it. Nothing matters to me as much as finding my wife and sons."

"I understand that," said Graves, rising and offering his hand. "Bertrams will help in any way we can."

CHAPTER 2

There were two people waiting outside for him. Using the term liberally. Hazel Best was behind the wheel of what was, after all, her car. The white dog beside her moved obligingly into the backseat when Ash returned.

"Any luck?" Hazel glanced at him and then quickly away again. It was plain from his face that he'd learned nothing. She wouldn't have dreamed of saying "I told you so," and he knew her better by now than to expect it. But she didn't want him thinking she was thinking it, either.

"He said he'd give it some more thought, get in touch if anything occurred to him. He gave me a couple more names — firms that have been hit while I was off the scene." He looked at her. "He thinks I'm on a fool's mission."

Hazel gave a tiny nod. She was a lot younger than Ash, and she wasn't his girlfriend, but she was honest with him. "You always knew the odds were against you. You knew before we came here. It was just something to try. It might have led somewhere. It still might."

"But probably not," admitted Ash.

He made an effort to put the disappointment behind him. It wasn't that he'd been expecting a miracle. Most crimes get solved within the first forty-eight hours or not at all. This one was four years old. In his heart, where he didn't allow himself the comfort of irrational hope, he knew it was too long. That anything Chief Superintendent Fountain had known — if he'd known anything, if he wasn't just dangling bait — had died with him. Cathy and the boys were gone, and there was no longer a trail to take him to their killers. But that was also true yesterday. Today's failure added little to the sum of his unhappiness.

He looked at his watch. "Almost twelve. Do you want to stop for lunch, or shall we press on and take your dad out for a late one?"

Hazel had called her father while she was waiting for Ash. "He's got something in the oven for us. Don't get your hopes up — he's not much of a cook. All I can promise is that it'll be nice and brown."

Ash managed a smile. He hadn't done much cooking recently, either. "A bit of gravy covers a multitude of sins." Two months ago he hadn't even done much eating. Now he found himself sufficiently cheered by the prospect of a proper sitdown meal at his friend's home to be tolerant of a piece of overdone meat.

"Not on fish, it doesn't," said Hazel grimly, starting the car.

Alfred Best had been a color sergeant in the British army, and the ability to make tomato water lilies is not a significant survival skill. Such cooking as he had done in those days was of the one pot, open fire, "If it doesn't kill you, it was a success" variety. And then, Hazel's mother had been a good cook. It was only since her death that he'd had to teach himself about such things as oven temperatures and timings. Anyway, he'd always rather liked food that bit back.

As Hazel turned through the wrought-iron gates and he glimpsed Byrfield House down the avenue of sycamores, Ash wondered if there was something she hadn't told him. He tried to remember what she *had* told him. Her father was in the army — she'd grown up in the country — she'd had a pony and dogs and climbed trees. . . . She *hadn't* said she was a daughter of the aristocracy, but perhaps that was more a second date sort of conversation.

But then he saw the man standing at the open door of the gate lodge, wearing an apron that bore the legend *Soldiers do it AGAIN and AGAIN until they GET IT RIGHT,* and the world settled quietly back into place. There was nothing wrong with being a daughter of the nobility. But if she had been and hadn't said, he'd have wondered why not.

And that was silly, too, because they hadn't known each other very long and they didn't know each other very well. She'd saved his life a couple of times, but apart from that . . . She didn't owe him any confidences. The fact that he'd had to share most of his life story with her, including — no, especially — the grim bits, didn't put her under the obligation to reciprocate.

The man in the apron raised a hand, and as soon as Hazel had parked she was out of the car and throwing her arms around him. He wasn't a big man — Hazel was taller — and where she was fair, he was faintly ginger. But he radiated that quiet capability that doesn't need to be shouted about. There are two kinds of soldier: those who yell "Charge!" and those who say "Follow

22

me." Alfred Best was the latter kind.

Hazel disengaged from the hug and introduced them. The two men shook hands. "Come inside," said Best, "have a beer while dinner's finishing off."

Hazel went to the cupboard under the stairs. "Home brew or the real stuff?" she asked Ash.

Gabriel Ash wasn't a serious drinker, but he knew there was only one answer to that which wouldn't make a man an implacable enemy. "Can I try your home brew?"

During lunch — the cod, despite Hazel's misgivings, had developed only a thin layer of crackling — Best asked how long the drive had taken. Hazel flicked Ash a glance before answering. "We came the scenic route. Gabriel had some business in Grantham."

Best was too straightforward a man to pretend not to know what she was talking about. Of course Hazel had told her father about the events of the last two months. Of course both Gabriel Ash's part in them and the history it sprang from were known to him.

He regarded Ash levelly. "I was sorry to hear about your family, Mr. Ash," he said somberly. "Are you getting anywhere with your inquiries?"

Before he met Hazel, for years the only one who had spoken to Ash about his tragedy was his therapist. It still felt strange to have it discussed in the course of a normal conversation. Strange, but better.

"Thank you," he said. "No, I don't really think so. I'm not sure there's anything new to find. I thought so — at least I thought there was a chance — but the harder I look, the more I feel Hazel was probably right. That what I thought was a clue was only a diversion, something to channel me in a way that suited the man who dropped it. I'm going through the motions mainly so that I don't wonder later if I missed something."

"If that's all that comes of it," said Best, "it'll have been worth your time."

Over what Ash thought was crème brûlée but turned out to be blancmange, Best said to his daughter, "Pete says will you drop by his place before you leave. I told him you were coming. He's been digging again — got something to show you."

Hazel saw the slightly puzzled look on Ash's face and grinned. "Not vegetables — archaeology. He's putting together a history of the big house."

"Pete is," Ash said carefully.

"Lord Byrfield. But if your name was Peregrine," said Hazel, "wouldn't you try to

24

keep it a secret?"

"Nearly as much as if it was Gabriel," said Ash glumly.

They walked up the long drive after lunch. In the June sunshine the white lurcher flashed among the giant trees like a ghost on speed.

"It's the rabbits," explained Ash. "It's in her blood."

As she passed them, the dog paused just long enough to give Hazel a slightly embarrassed look, as if she knew chasing rabbits was less than cool but she just couldn't resist.

Ash said, "I hope your father doesn't mind having me and Patience to stay. It's asking a lot, when your daughter turns up for a visit with not only a strange man but also his dog in tow."

Hazel chuckled. She was wearing her thick fair hair in a loose ponytail, which together with the jeans and oversized shirt gave her a casual look, in marked contrast to the police uniform she'd been wearing when they first met. He thought she was also more relaxed than she had been. She'd had a rough time. It had ended with her shooting someone dead. You don't put that behind you with a stiff drink and an early night. But Ash thought she was finding her balance again.

25

He was relieved. He'd felt guilty for what he'd involved her in. It hadn't been his fault, but that hadn't stopped him from feeling guilty. Guilty was his default position.

"He's used to it. Not strange men so much," she added hastily, "but friends staying over. When you live miles from anywhere and there's no last bus for people to catch, you're used to making up a spare bed on the sofa. I think the record was seven twenty-year-old undergraduates. There were bodies everywhere — on the kitchen table, in the bath, and two of them slept in the greenhouse."

A bend in the drive brought the building Ash had glimpsed from the gate lodge into full view. The beauty of it made him catch his breath. Hazel, covertly watching for his reaction, gave a faint, satisfied smile.

It wasn't what most people mean by a stately home. It was too small, too — if it isn't an absurd way to describe a house with nine bedrooms — homely. It would be more helpful to think of it as a manor house, a two-story, plus attics, stone building, the severity of its classical Georgian lines softened by Virginia creeper. The stones glowed with two hundred sunny summers, the sixteen-pane windows sparkled because none of the glass squares lined up precisely with any of its neighbors, and at the top of a modest fan of stone steps one of the heavy double doors stood open because a man in washing-up gloves was polishing the brass knocker.

Hazel shouted, "Hi, Pete!" and Lord Byrfield shaded his eyes with one yellow hand and waved.

"Hi, Hazel. Come to help?"

"You think I don't have brass work at home I could polish?" she said, grinning as they met. "If the urge took me. Pete, I want you to meet a friend of mine. Gabriel Ash, Peregrine Byrfield. And this is Patience."

The earl and the lurcher regarded one another solemnly for a moment. "Delighted, I'm sure," said Byrfield, and Patience waved her tail.

Ash saw a man taller than himself, and narrower, and maybe ten years younger; unremarkable-looking, with fair hair and blue-gray eyes and a rather weak chin. A man you could have ridden the 8:10 to Paddington with every weekday for a year and not recognized if you'd seen him in the supermarket on a Saturday. But he did have a nice smile. "Gabriel, hm?"

Ash nodded long-sufferingly. "Peregrine?"

"I know." Byrfield sighed. "Still, I suppose there are worse things to be called after than

27

either an angle or a hawk. I'd hate to be called after a nut."

Hazel thumped his arm hard enough to make him wince.

Byrfield left the brasses half polished and took them inside.

As with most houses, big and small, life at Byrfield revolved around the kitchen. There was a collection of leather armchairs and an overstuffed sofa arranged around a low oak table, an oak dresser black with age, and a television on a chest in a corner. Hazel flung herself into one of the armchairs as if she'd been coming here all her life. Ash took the sofa, and hoped Byrfield wouldn't notice that Patience had jumped up beside him, so that they were now sitting side by side like a married couple.

"Dad says you're digging again."

Byrfield brought the coffee over. You could tell he was aristocracy by the plainness of the biscuits. "David Sperrin's working on the far side of the lake. You remember David? His mother's the artist, she lives at Wool Row. He left for university while you were still a child, but he's been back at intervals."

"I remember. He did history at Reading."

"Archaeology," said Byrfield, nodding so the correction seemed more like an elaboration. "Then he worked abroad for several

28

years. I caught up with him last time he was home and asked him to come and do a survey for me."

"Anything interesting turned up?"

Byrfield gave a self-deprecating grin. "It's *all* interesting. You know how I feel about this place. If you mean Saxon gold or Roman mosaics, then no, nothing like that. The footings of some walls we didn't know about. Some medieval pottery. Oh — and this." He was rummaging in a drawer of the dresser, unfolded a cotton-wool parcel in front of her.

"What is it?"

"It's Romano-British — third, fourth century. It's bronze, probably the handle of a tankard. But look — it's a horse."

Ash peered closer, too. "It's the Uffington White Horse."

Hazel looked at him in surprise, Byrfield in approval. "Exactly. David thinks whoever made it must have been to Uffington."

"It's a long way from here."

"Where's Uffington?" asked Hazel.

"Oxfordshire, I think," said Ash. "A hundred and fifty miles? It's a long way on foot."

Byrfield shrugged. "People got around more than you'd think two thousand years ago. After all, the Romans came from Rome. Some of the artifacts we find came from

29

farther afield. It would have taken a lot longer than a budget airline — well, a bit longer than a budget airline — but sailing ships only need wind, and horses can go long distances on not much more than grass. If you could plan for journeys lasting years rather than hours or days, you could travel until you met something you couldn't cross. The Atlantic Ocean, for instance. The Himalayas. The Sahara. Lots of people died doing it. But others got through, or at least completed one stage of the journey. Artifacts are durable. If needs be, they can lie half buried in the sand until the next caravan comes along to carry them another hundred miles."

"Pete!" said Hazel, mischievous with delight. "You're a romantic!"

He looked bashful. "No, I'm a farmer. But I do find this stuff fascinating. Listen, stay for dinner. We'll prime David with half a bottle of burgundy and he'll talk till the cows come home. The places he's been, the things he's dug up." Suddenly his face clouded. "I'm sorry. Just because I love this stuff doesn't mean everyone has to listen. There are probably better topics of conversation for a sophisticated dinner party."

"Sophisticated?" echoed Hazel. "Us? I haven't even brought a posh frock." She looked down at herself critically. "I've got this shirt and another one just like it."

"You'll still be overdressed for my dinner table." Byrfield chuckled, relieved. "David leaves his overalls on the boot room radiator, and I try to remember to kick my wellies off, but that's about it. My mother refuses to eat with us. She has a tray in her room. Short of some major disaster like the maid's day off, she still does the whole changing-for-dinner thing. Then she eats alone in her sitting room."

"How the other half lives," remarked Hazel, the note of wonder in her voice only slightly tempered by the desire not to appear rude.

"I *am* the other half," said Pete Byrfield grimly, "and *I* think it's bizarre."

CHAPTER 3

Except as a paying visitor, Ash had never been in a country house. He had no idea what to expect. Five years ago, at the height of his career, he'd spent generously on good cars, on family holidays, on their London home. It had never occurred to him to employ a maid. At Byrfield, he discovered by trying to listen without appearing nosy, there was even in these straitened days a respectable staff — in addition to Lady Byrfield's maid and Fred Best, who was the handyman, there were a cook-housekeeper, a gardener, a groom, and a boy. Ash didn't know that boy was an official position, so when Byrfield made a passing reference to "my boy," Ash thought he was being made privy to a personal confidence, and felt that it was too much information much too soon.

Hazel seemed to read his mind, or at least the faint, dark lowering of his brow, and gave a secret grin. "Derek's the hall boy," she explained when Byrfield's attention was elsewhere. "That's his title — he does all the heavy stuff that isn't somebody else's job."

Ash felt himself coloring. "I thought . . ."

"I know," said Hazel. "But he's engaged to one of the farmers' daughters, so I don't think he's that way inclined. Actually, I don't think Pete is, either."

Ash felt awkward and stupid and out of his depth. At least Hazel knew how the system worked. She had more in common with the earl of Byrfield, who was her father's employer, than Ash had. It was the difference between old money and new money. The rich man in his castle and the poor man at his gate at least share the same world. Byrfield and his boy were probably equally puzzled by people like Ash — men in suits who appeared to run everything without ever making anything.

Across the table, David Sperrin barked a gruff laugh. He was a small, dark man a few years older than Byrfield, with a deep musical voice that nevertheless told of long hours in wet holes. There was a rattle in his chest when he laughed. "I think your ability to provide Byrfield with an heir is being questioned, Pete."

Byrfield looked up from carving the lamb,

apparently without rancor. "Yes? There's time yet. The Byrfields have always been better at breeding cattle and horses than sons — it took the aged parents three goes and twelve years to produce me. But we always seem to manage eventually. I expect I'll get the hang of it sooner or later."

And that, thought Ash with quiet admiration, is what generations of good breeding buys you. Grace.

The Bests had, so far as anyone knew, no trace of blue blood anywhere in their veins — nothing but commoner back to the ark. Perhaps that was where Hazel got her fierce sense of loyalty. She turned on the archaeologist as if he'd kicked her spaniel. "How about you, then, David? Made Diana a granny yet, have you?"

Sperrin flashed her a wolfish grin, all teeth and no humor. "My mother doesn't really do children. She wishes she'd drowned me at birth."

Wonderfully inoffensive, Byrfield murmured, "Don't we all?" and the tension left the air in pretend scowls and genuine laughter.

Ash steered the conversation onto safer ground. "How's the dig coming? Anything unexpected?"

"It isn't a dig yet," explained Sperrin, "just

34

a survey. I'm sticking ranging rods into interesting-looking humps to see if any of them are worth excavating."

"I thought that was done with radar these days."

"Geo-phys." Sperrin nodded. "It is, when you've got it. If you haven't, it's amazing what you can learn by poking things with a stick."

"David thinks I'm a cheapskate for not buying him everything in the toy shop," said Byrfield cheerfully. "He doesn't understand that I'm not a government department. This is my hobby. I'm not going to impoverish the estate pursuing it."

"We could be missing things," warned Sperrin. "Important things."

"They're not going anywhere," said Byrfield with equanimity. "If I don't find them, my descendants will. Maybe *your* descendants will do the spadework."

Sperrin acknowledged himself beaten with a gruff chuckle. "Pete thinks the feudal system is still alive and well and living in Burford. That because he's expected to follow in his father's footsteps, the same goes for everyone."

"My father was a soldier and I'm a police officer," volunteered Hazel. "It's not that different."

Ash found curious eyes on him. "My father was a tax inspector. I worked for the government, too."

"David?"

Sperrin grinned with the sheer pleasure of discomfiting people. "My father's a gypsy. He tarmacs drives. Maybe that's where I got my skill with a spade."

"So it's not just the landowning gentry who follow the well-worn path," observed Byrfield with quiet triumph. "You're all every bit as bound by your family history as I am. You're just more reluctant to admit it."

Gabriel Ash looked down at the white dog curled at his feet. Patience met his eyes with a steady golden gaze. *If anybody's interested,* she said, *my ancestors were all dogs, too.*

From the absence of startled gasps around the table, Ash assumed that no one else had heard her.

Later, the remains of the meal replaced by an enormous, somewhat battered coffeepot, Sperrin turned to Hazel. "Will you still be here tomorrow?"

"Sure. We're driving back on Sunday. Why?"

"We're planning to take the top off a

funny hump by the icehouse. I think it's probably a cist — a burial mound. If you've nothing better to do, you're welcome to watch."

Hazel raised inquiring eyebrows at Ash. "Sounds like fun."

It wasn't the word he'd have chosen, but you don't have to be a ghoul to be intrigued by the graves of people who lived thousands of years ago. "A cist — that's like a dolmen, is it?"

"Pretty much. Usually stone slabs rather than boulders, but the idea's the same — to create a void under the earth where your chief or whoever can rest undisturbed until they invent archaeologists."

"What'll be inside?"

"Hard to say till we open it," said Sperrin, taking more coffee. "Right now it's just a hump in the grass with something solid inside it. It could even be a boulder that's got covered with earth over the years. But it seems very regular — almost square. I think someone made it."

"When?"

"Well, that's certainly the right question. If we find bones, or grave goods, or if — please God! — the stones are decorated, we can make a fair stab at dating it. But you can't date plain stone. You can look at the base layer and see what it was built on, but the lake has probably inundated the site at intervals, and that confuses the picture. Educated guess? Neolithic. But it could be later."

"And Neolithic is . . . ?" There were lots of things Hazel knew, and lots she didn't, and she had no qualms about asking when she came up against one of the latter.

"New Stone Age. Maybe five thousand years ago. Maybe more."

In a time when a new car is old in eight years, and a new computer in three, five thousand years is an impressive span. Two hundred generations. The time of Stonehenge and the pyramids, when the cutting edge of cutting-edge technology was a stone. When you shaped the kind of stone you wanted by hitting it with another stone, and mostly what you did with it then was hit some more stones. That's why it's called the Stone Age. When someone got the bizarre idea — and you can imagine how his wife looked at him — that by heating some of those funny-colored stones in a really hot fire you could produce a metal knife, or a spearhead, or a needle, it was a leap in technology comparable with nothing since. The wheel was inspired by a log rolling down a hill; the steam engine was developed from the kettle; the jet aircraft was designed by people — clever people — putting together successive increments of engineering discovery. But whoever first thought there was something to be gained by burning rocks?

"Count me in," said Hazel. "What time should we come over?"

"Actually," suggested Byrfield, "I wondered if Ash fancied staying here tonight. Unless Fred's extended my gate lodge without telling me."

Hazel had been resigned to sleeping on the sofa. But she hadn't expected to enjoy it, and if Byrfield was offering one of his guest rooms, she wasn't going to refuse. It would also be nice to have a little time alone with her father. "All right with you, Gabriel?"

"Yes, of course," said Ash. "If we're not putting you out?"

"Not a bit," said Byrfield graciously. "I'll send Derek down for your bag." But when Ash was once more talking tumuli with David Sperrin, Byrfield murmured to Hazel, "We?"

She rolled her eyes. "Him and the dog. Get used to it."

Around ten o'clock, still early enough to

have supper with her father, Hazel excused herself. Sperrin volunteered to walk her to the gate lodge. It was a kind thought — an unexpectedly kind thought — and Hazel refrained from pointing out that (a) she'd been walking up and down this drive, alone and with company, in the daylight and in the dark, since she was a child, and (b) she was a police officer. If there *was* anyone lurking in the bushes, she could entirely ruin their evening.

She said none of this because she didn't think David Sperrin was a man to whom gallantry came easily. So she thanked him for the offer, and let him carry the torch, and tried not to notice when he tripped on rough ground and steadied himself against her.

When he'd recovered his poise, Sperrin said, in a half-jocular sort of way that suggested this was better than asking the question outright, "So what is it between you and dog boy?"

Hazel kept a rein on her patience. "He's a friend. A good friend, but nothing more. All right? And don't call him that. At least not in his hearing."

Hazel could hear the cocky grin in his voice. "Why? Do you think he could take me?"

40

"I doubt it," she said frankly. "But I'm pretty sure his dog could."

As the lights of the gate lodge came into view around the sweep of the drive, she steered the conversation back toward something simpler than her relationship with Ash. "What happens if you *do* unearth a burial tomorrow?"

"Well, *if* is the critical word. Mostly what you find inside oddly-shaped mounds is oddly-shaped boulders. But if it is a cist, then there are some hoops to jump through. People to inform, approvals to seek, big boys' toys to whistle up. All the stuff we haven't got here. The days are long gone when archaeology was a kind of educational hobby for vicars and their daughters.

"There's only so much of it, you see," Sperrin continued seriously. "You can't have people blundering around, confusing or even destroying important sites. All excavation is destruction — the only way you can justify it is by recording meticulously everything you see, everything you find. I couldn't do that on my own, even with Pete helping. You hope that if you find something significant, you'll be involved in the excavation, or at least recorded in connection with it. But the important thing is that you've contributed to the sum of knowledge. In the end, that may be all the reward you get."

She looked at him, a dark profile against the white wall of the lodge, in surprise. Talking about his own subject, the combative wit and sharp-honed cynicism that sprinkled his general conversation disappeared. Perhaps he felt sufficiently confident of his abilities in his own field not to need them.

"It was a good choice, then?" said Hazel. "Archaeology. I seem to remember people around here being a bit surprised that was what you wanted to study."

"I imagine half the people around here had to look the word up in a dictionary," said Sperrin drily. "The other half don't own a dictionary." The cynic was back.

Hazel shrugged. "This is farming country. There are only so many ways you can spell *sheep.*"

"I've never regretted it," he said, answering her question. "It's endlessly interesting. Even the small details are interesting. And there's always the chance of finding something no one has seen for thousands of years. Or something that makes sense of things we've been seeing but not understanding. Plus, I don't need to wear a suit."

Hazel laughed out loud. "That was the deciding factor, was it?"

In the backwash of the torch she saw him

42

smile. "Not exactly. But . . . It's like this. Once you wear a suit, the die is cast. Until then, you still have the luxury of wondering what you'll do when you grow up."

They were almost at the gate lodge. Fred had left a lamp burning in the porch. Hazel said, "How long will you be working at Byrfield? Diana must like having you home."

Sperrin shook his dark head. "I'm not staying at home. There's more room at the big house."

Hazel was surprised. She was pretty sure that Diana Sperrin's cottage was bigger than her father's. She had room there for her studio.

Her silence seemed to put Sperrin on the defensive. "I stick my head in from time to time. She's busy, too. And we never were what you'd call a close family."

There were only the two of them. Diana had raised her son alone while her husband indulged his wanderlust. Hazel wondered if Sperrin's gypsy father had finally returned home, but didn't know how to ask without risking offense. "Is she still painting?" Diana Sperrin was a moderately successful artist. She had exhibited in London, and Hazel had read newspaper articles on her work.

"Lord, yes," said David fervently. "Nothing short of death will stop her. Even then

43

she may manage a quick sketch of the afterlife on the inside of her coffin lid."

"That must be where you get it from," Hazel said with a chuckle. "Your creative side."

He seemed genuinely puzzled. "I'm an archaeologist. A scientist."

"You're saying you aren't moved by the beauty of the things you find as much as by the information they give you?"

He hesitated, as if considering that for the first time. "They *are* beautiful . . ." he admitted.

"You see?" said Hazel triumphantly. "The artist speaks!"

". . . And so is knowledge."

They regarded each other levelly in the scant light of the torch. Then, almost simultaneously, they smiled.

"I'll see you in the morning," said Hazel.

CHAPTER 4

Saturday-morning breakfast at Byrfield was a slightly odd affair. As three single men of education and intelligence, with barely ten years between the eldest and the youngest, they should have had more in common than they seemed able to find. Of course, Ash wasn't single by choice — he was a married man in every way but the one that counted most. Only Sperrin appeared to be single by inclination. Byrfield seemed to be single mainly through lack of initiative. They compared notes on their experiences of university — archaeology at Reading for Sperrin, agricultural college for Byrfield, PPE at Oxford for Ash — and still found nothing in common.

With a hint of desperation Byrfield asked the archaeologist if he liked dogs, and Sperrin looked at him in astonishment and said, "Good God, no." Under the table Patience rubbed sweetly against him, coating his trouser legs with hair.

They finished eating in silence.

Sperrin had gathered some tools in the courtyard. He distributed the load among them. Byrfield got a spade and a crowbar, Ash a bundle of ranging rods, and Sperrin took the rest: a camera, a nest of buckets filled with sponges, cotton wool, Bubble Wrap and plastic bags of assorted sizes, a large bottle of water, a small bottle of glycerin, some wooden wedges, a sledge-hammer, and a GPS position finder. When he saw the smaller man about to tip over backward, Byrfield took some of the heavier items and shared them with Ash. Thus encumbered they set off down the path.

Hazel, leaving the gate lodge at the same time, cut across the meadow and reached the edge of the lake while the men were still laboring through the stable yard. Without hurrying, she made her way around the rushy margin until she came to the stone igloo of the icehouse and the interesting hump Sperrin wanted to examine. She knew it was the right hump because he'd left one of his stripy rods sticking out of it.

It was years since she'd been here last, but it was no more effort than she remembered to scramble up the curved wall of the icehouse, and the view was as rewarding.

She made herself comfortable, sitting cross-legged on the cool stones, and waited for the men to join her.

The dog saw her first, bounded through the sedgy meadow, and joined her on her eminence, curled elegantly, enjoying the June sun on her white flank. Byrfield waved his spade.

Hazel had entirely caught her breath before the men arrived, and she watched in tolerant amusement as they panted up the last bank. Of the three, Byrfield was probably the fittest — a farmer with a title is still a farmer, and it's a physical job — and Ash the least fit. Not just because he was ten years older than Pete but because he'd spent four of them all but housebound. It was his therapist who talked him into getting a dog, so at least he was out in the fresh air. The indoor pallor that had marked his skin when Hazel first knew him was already less noticeable.

"Well?" she demanded when she thought she'd been patient enough. "Are we going to open this mound or what? I've decided it's a Saxon hoard, incidentally — gold jewelry, armor, weapons, all that. I want my name as cofinder on the plaque at the British Museum."

Ash was regarding the grassy hummock

47

doubtfully. "Isn't it a bit small for a ship burial? Unless rather lowlier Saxon chiefs got buried in a dinghy."

Sperrin took the spade and thrust it at an angle into the turf. "It isn't a Saxon hoard," he said, timing his sentences between efforts. "It isn't a hoard of any kind. I've told you what it is. It's either a Neolithic cist" — the steel blade rang dully on stone under twenty centimeters of grass and earth — "or a bloody great rock. And this," he added, turning the spade to start removing the turfs, "is where we find out which."

It was easier than Hazel had expected. She hadn't much interest in gardening, but she'd planted the odd shrub from time to time and knew that the ground was like iron if you wanted to dig more than a hand's span into it. The surface of the buried stone, impenetrable to roots, unmoved by the weight of the overburden, must have created a natural weakness, because one after another the turfs peeled away to an identical thickness. Peering into the growing hole, Hazel saw only mud, but as the archaeologist labored, both energetically and with care, she saw a muddy surface appearing.

Byrfield leaned over the hole, too. "Dressed stone rather than a boulder" was his diagnosis. "I think you've got your cist, David."

Only Ash wasn't jockeying for a better view. He was watching his dog, aware of the tension of her slim, strong body, the way she'd pinned her long ears flat against her neck.

"Jesus, I don't know," swore Sperrin in breathless puzzlement. "It's queer bloody stone. It's not like stone at all, it's more like . . ."

He dropped the spade and groped in his kit for the water bottle and a sponge. On his knees, he reached into the hole and washed the mud away from a portion of the surface. Then he rocked back on his heels, confounded. "More like paving slabs," he finished lamely.

"Paving slabs!" exclaimed Byrfield. "Why would anybody bury some paving slabs?"

In the silence that followed everyone heard the low, distant machinery rumble that was Patience growling in her throat. Ash said softly, "Because you can get them anywhere, without anyone asking why."

Hazel looked at him uncomprehendingly, her brows knit. "Gabriel? What do you think it is?"

He considered for a moment. "I think it's a burial," he said then.

49

Sperrin was shaking his dark head impatiently. "Don't be stupid. They didn't have garden centers in Neolithic times! If they're paving slabs, it's modern. It's a joke — a hoax."

"Here?" Byrfield looked around him, taking in the absolute peacefulness of the lakeside scene. "Why bother? We might never have found it."

"Then whoever did it," said Sperrin angrily, stabbing at the slabs with the crowbar, seeking a purchase, "had a funny sense of humor." He straightened up, glaring at Byrfield. "I don't suppose it was you?"

Pete Byrfield was visibly astonished. "Me? You think I made a pretend burial and then paid you to come and dig it up? You think I've nothing better to do with my time and money?"

"It isn't a pretend burial," said Ash. His voice was hollow.

In a flood of understanding Hazel realized what he was saying. What he suspected. "Listen," she said sharply, "I think we should leave this for now — get someone out to have a look at it before we go any further. . . ."

She might as well have talked to the stones. Sperrin jabbed again at the surface he'd uncovered, and this time he got the

50

crowbar into a gap and threw his weight against it. As something inside the mound shifted, Byrfield added the edge of the spade and between them, sweating and gasping, they managed to lift one slab halfway onto another. A faint earthy smell, earthier than the mud, came out of the void at their feet.

Sperrin reached behind him again, this time for the torch. He and Byrfield, and Hazel, leaned forward.

The dog, still softly growling, backed away.

Slowly, Hazel straightened up. "Okay," she said carefully, "so now we know what it is. It's a crime scene. Throw a coat over it. Don't try to put the slab back, we don't want to risk it falling in. I'll call the police."

CHAPTER 5

In the carefully constructed grave, made of paving slabs and once lined with blankets, was the body of a child — a boy of eight or ten years. It had been in the ground long enough to be entirely skeletonized, making it difficult to judge the sex on initial inspection, but there were things in the little tomb — David Sperrin would have called them grave goods — that made it more than an educated guess. Boys' toys: a wooden train, a pair of cheap plastic binoculars, a yellow digger, a battered Frisbee. And though at first glance the clothes could have belonged equally to a boy or a girl, when Hazel leaned closer, she saw that both the jeans and the denim jacket fastened left over right.

One might not have been significant, an item passed down from an older sibling; two were suggestive. DNA would prove the matter conclusively, but Hazel had no doubt that she was looking at the remains of a little boy, laid to rest by someone who loved him with as much care and dignity as could be managed without benefit of clergy or churchyard. It was a crime scene because it's illegal to bury members of your family in the woods without telling anyone. The discovery launched a murder investigation because no one could think why anyone should bury in such a way a child who had died of natural or accidental causes.

The senior investigating officer from the local division was a tired-looking middle-aged man whose Wellingtons had started to leak halfway across the water meadow. "Detective Inspector Edwin Norris," he said, one slightly rheumy eye settling on Hazel. "You're Constable Best?"

She nodded. "My father works on the estate."

He went around the others, establishing who was who, why each of them was there. "Who opened the grave?"

"I did," said Sperrin.

"Why?"

The archaeologist shrugged. "It's my job."

"Digging up children's graves?"

"Finding unexplained lumps in the landscape and explaining them."

"I'll be interested," rumbled Norris, "to hear your explanation of this."

"Not exactly my period," said Sperrin airily. He seemed entirely untroubled by the discovery. Of course, thought Hazel, he's used to digging up human remains.

"Which is?" asked Norris.

"Well before plastic toys," said Sperrin.

"Did any of you touch anything inside the grave?"

Hazel shook her head. "We looked in. When we saw what it was, everyone backed off and I called you."

"Good." The inspector turned ponderously to Pete Byrfield. "This land is yours, sir?"

Byrfield nodded, then turned and pointed. "My house is over there."

"Where's the nearest public access?"

"The gate lodge." Byrfield turned a quadrant, pointed again. "About half a mile."

As he went through the routine questionnaire, DI Norris recognized that it didn't apply terribly well to the current circumstances. "How long have you lived here?"

"All my life."

"It belonged to your parents?"

"It belonged to my ancestors."

"Since when?"

Byrfield looked slightly embarrassed. "After Bosworth."

"Who was he, and when did he leave?"

David Sperrin made little attempt to disguise a smirk.

"The Battle of Bosworth Field," explained Byrfield. "August twenty-second, 1485. When the first Tudor defeated the last Plantagenet, there was a major reallocation of national resources. The first Lord Byrfield had done something useful for Henry Tudor and this was his reward. The land, that is. The current house is the third one on the site."

Norris looked across at the grave, now covered by a forensics tent, and back at Pete. "So we can safely say that, whenever that child was buried, your family were living here."

"Yes."

"Who would have had access to it?"

Byrfield gave a helpless shrug. "I can tell you who was living in the house if you can give me a date. But all sorts of people use the land, with and without permission. It's not like it's our garden — it's rough grazing and woodland, we've never objected to local people coming here. You try to discourage poaching, but you can't stop that, either, the best you can do is keep it manageable.

"There are four farms on the estate, so the families there and anyone working for them might pass through here. The local children play around the lake. Stockmen drive cattle across from one holding to another. Anyone mislaying a beast might come here looking for it. I'm sorry, Inspector, I can't give you a list of people with a good reason to be here. People don't *need* a good reason to be here."

Norris breathed heavily at him. "Then can you tell me when you first noticed this mound?"

Byrfield did no better with that. "I never noticed it at all," he admitted. "The whole area's covered in lumps and bumps. David singled it out when he was field walking — surveying the land for possible archaeology. But that was less than a month ago, and you can tell from the turfs that it's not been disturbed for years."

Norris turned back to Sperrin. "What made you open this mound rather than any of the others?"

The archaeologist shrugged. "Instinct? Experience? It looked a bit more regular than some of them, it's slightly separated from a lot of them, and when I stuck a ranging rod into the earth, I met stone. I didn't *know* it was anything. I thought it was worth a look." He grinned wolfishly. "You can't say I was wrong."

Norris squinted at him. "Sir — you are aware that we're talking about the death of a child? I'm not sure your tone is altogether appropriate."

Sperrin remained unconcerned. "Whatever happened here, it happened decades ago. Possibly before I was alive. Possibly before *you* were alive. It hasn't been a tragedy for a very long time. Now it's just a puzzle."

The inspector continued to look at him just long enough to register his disapproval. Then he turned his gaze to Hazel. "Thank you for your help, Constable. We'll get formal statements off everyone, but as Mr. Sperrin" — he pronounced the name carefully, the way you might handle something sticky — "points out, this isn't a recent event, there's no reason to connect it to any of you people. Even Lord Byrfield" — his lips formed a letter *M* before he remembered and corrected himself — "was probably a babe in arms when this happened. Not much point asking what you remember."

Byrfield was looking thoughtful. "You could talk to my mother."

Norris was taken aback, as if he thought earls arrived in the world in a different manner from normal folk. "She still lives here?"

Byrfield gave a slightly strained smile. "Oh yes. She has an apartment in the house. I'll take you, if you like."

The inspector considered. "Maybe later. No point troubling her until I know what questions to ask. Right now I don't have even an approximate date of death. When I've had a preliminary report from Forensics, then I'm sure it would be helpful to talk to her. Er — I'm assuming she's still — er . . ."

"In full possession of her faculties? Believe it," said Pete Byrfield fervently.

After a moment Hazel touched his arm gently. "Come on, let's leave them to it. There's nothing we can do here except get in the way."

He blinked, then gave her a grateful grin. As they walked back up the water meadow he said wistfully, "Isn't it funny how the world changes? An hour ago, all I had to worry about was whether or not I'd got a Neolithic tomb on my land. Now it turns out that for most of my life there's been a small child buried within sight of my house and nobody knew. I played down here when I was a boy. I don't doubt I scrambled over that mound along with all the others. It makes you feel a bit . . . well, funny."

"I think it's rather nice," said Hazel. "That

58

even after he was dead, he still had other kids coming around to play."

Byrfield smiled. He'd forgotten — or rather, not forgotten, just not thought about it recently — that she'd always had the ability to make him smile. They hadn't been close friends when they were growing up — four years is a big age difference in your teens — but she'd always been somewhere on his radar, in the same way he'd always been somewhere on hers. He'd gone away to agricultural college, then she'd gone away to university, and it's doubtful if either had given the other more than a passing thought in all the years since. But a link remained, and the link was Byrfield itself. Only in the most literal sense did Byrfield belong to Pete. In every other way Pete belonged to Byrfield, and so did the daughter of his handyman. Land has a grip like iron.

"I'm glad you were here," said Byrfield. A thought occurred to him. "Does this mean you'll be staying?"

Hazel hadn't thought about it. She thought about it now. "We probably should, if only for a few days. Until Detective Inspector Norris says he's finished with us. It's not as if either Gabriel or I has anything to rush back to."

"Good," said Byrfield quietly.

CHAPTER 6

In fact, Ash had an appointment with his therapist on Tuesday, which he now doubted he'd be back in Norbold in time to keep. He excused himself as the party returned to the house and called her from the privacy of his room.

He wasn't ashamed of having a therapist. Hazel knew anyway, and he suspected the others wouldn't be surprised. But he was a private man. He avoided doing any personal business in public.

Laura Fry, after changing the bookings in her diary, showed an almost indelicate interest in the discovery by the lake. After Ash had told her all he knew, she was still asking for more details. "And are you all right?" she kept asking.

Ash, who hadn't until then considered the possibility that he might not be, thought she was seeking an excuse to come and join in a real-life game of Cluedo. "Absolutely fine," he said firmly.

"If you need to talk, call me."

"I will."

"Anytime."

"Thank you. I will."

He was heading back down when a door opened behind him and a woman said icily — he could almost hear the crackle of frost — "We don't let the dogs upstairs."

His first instinct was to apologize. For four years, almost the only intercourse Gabriel Ash had had with the world beyond his front door had been in the form of apologies. It had been his fallback position, as if by preemptively apologizing for anything and everything he'd ever done, including getting born, he could avoid engaging with other people.

But in the last few months things had begun to change. At Laura Fry's suggestion he'd acquired the dog. Owning a dog had made him go out, and he'd crossed the paths of a lot of people who bore him no ill will. The apologies had started to feel misplaced. Then he'd met Hazel Best, and life had immediately become more complicated but also more rewarding. He hadn't always been a shambling excuse for a man, and his heart held to the faint, stubborn hope that he wouldn't always be one. He bit back the apology unspoken and turned to face his accuser.

"I'm Gabriel Ash, and this is Patience. We're staying here."

"Yes, I know." She was a woman of about sixty, not tall but noticeably slim, with short, geometric ash-blond hair. The color may have come out of a bottle, but the cut was clearly, expensively, the real thing. Her arched, pencil-thin eyebrows and berry red lipstick were as flawless as a doll's. She was wearing a pale linen jacket, a silk blouse, a tailored skirt, and pearl earrings. "We have no shortage of guest rooms. Nor, indeed, of sheds."

Ash supposed he was talking with Byrfield's mother. But the countess hadn't introduced herself, and he saw no reason to guess. "We'll try to stay out of your way. But neither of us will be sleeping in the shed."

At the sound of voices, Pete Byrfield appeared at the foot of the stairs. He looked worried. More than that, he looked as if worried was *his* fallback position, at least when dealing with his mother. "There's coffee and sandwiches in the kitchen, Ash, if you're hungry. Mother, I need to talk to you. Something rather awful has happened."

"I know," said the countess, still looking

at Ash. "Dogs. In the bedrooms."

"Oh, for heaven's sake!" Byrfield was climbing the stairs two at a time. "Patience isn't a *dog,* she's a *guest.* If she wants a long hot soak in Lady Anne's marble bath, followed by a mani— a pedicure and a tea tray in the orangery, that's exactly what she'll get while it is in my power to provide it. Now, can we go to your room while I tell you what's going on?"

Halfway down the curving staircase, Patience said smugly, I like that young man.

Edwin Norris began his career when the best chance of dating an illicit burial was if the murderer had wrapped the murder weapon in a copy of that morning's newspaper and tossed it into the grave. It never failed to amaze him how accurate modern forensic science could be. The downside was how long you had to wait to be amazed. Medical examiners used to at least throw you a bone — "Hard to be sure, but death probably occurred between midnight and six on Friday morning" — to chew on until the autopsy was complete. These days about all they were willing to vouchsafe until the full results came back was that the victim was indeed dead.

A little boy, around ten years old, buried

in a makeshift but carefully furnished grave on the Byrfield estate. Buried with toys and nicely dressed, laid out in what you might otherwise describe as a comfortable position. However he'd ended up dead and whoever was responsible, the person who had buried him had cared about him.

Norris had seen little graves like this before. Secret graves, usually quite tiny, for infants whose mothers had told no one of their pregnancy and meant to tell no one of their loss, but whose whole hearts went into the ground along with their child.

But the Byrfield boy had been ten years old. His hadn't been a brief life known only to his mother — he must have had schoolfriends, teachers, neighbors, people who knew about him and missed him when he vanished. His birth must have been registered, and people must have asked questions when he disappeared. When Forensics finally came back with a time of death — to the nearest year would do — he could begin trawling through the records for missing children. Not just from this area. There was no knowing how far the child had traveled to his final rest in the peace of the Byrfield woods.

Norris was still pondering along these lines when his scenes of crime officer came in. As a mark of the years they'd worked together, he tapped on the detective inspector's door after he'd opened it.

SOCOs always used to be policemen. Now they weren't. But Kevin Green was one when Norris first knew him, so he sidestepped the whole staff-versus-agency issue and went on calling him Sergeant. "Any news for me, Sergeant?"

He was expecting the answer no. When Green nodded, his eyebrows climbed. "Oh? What?"

"Something . . . not very nice," rumbled SOCO.

"As distinct from a ten-year-old child in a makeshift grave, you mean."

SOCO sniffed. "You saw what I saw. You were thinking the same things. That someone had put that child to bed. That maybe they hadn't done things properly but it was the best they could do in the circumstances. That they cared about him."

Norris concurred. "So?"

"So why, if people cared so much about him, did he die of a shotgun blast to the face?"

Though lacking the same facts, Hazel was pondering the same contradiction. "Whoever made that tomb loved him. But they couldn't keep him alive, and they felt they couldn't report his death. Why not?"

"Something to hide or someone to protect," said Ash immediately. Criminology had been part of what he'd been good at.

"You mean either one of his parents killed him in a fit of anger and then buried him in a state of remorse, or one of his parents killed him and the other buried him and kept the secret."

"I suppose so. Anyone could have killed him, but then why would his parents keep quiet about it? It had to be a family affair. Nothing else makes sense."

"It still doesn't make sense." Hazel was talking about it mainly because the alternative was sitting quietly and thinking about it. "Whoever loved him enough to bury him like that should have wanted justice for him. Even if it was their other half who killed him. You don't go on loving someone who killed your child."

"We don't know yet what happened to him," Ash reminded her. "It may have been an accident, but the circumstances were such that they were afraid they wouldn't be believed. It may have been a momentary act of violence, or even carelessness. It doesn't take much to end a child's life. The one responsible may have been grief-stricken the moment it was too late. And the other one, who'd already lost their child, now faced losing their partner as well.

"Maybe, in that situation, you could imagine keeping quiet. Telling the neighbors your son had gone to stay with his grandparents, and later telling them he was doing so well there he was going to stay. Telling his school the same story. It might be challenged, but the odds are it wouldn't be. In these days of pick-and-mix families, children are a bit of a movable feast." There was a wistfulness in his tone that, of those present, only Hazel understood.

"Or, of course," said David Sperrin, a man who may have had finer feelings but didn't give them much exercise, "some perv may have grabbed him, had his bit of fun, and buried him there when he was finished. Byrfield isn't exactly Area Fifty-One — it's not difficult to get in and out unobserved."

Pete Byrfield regarded him with disapproval bordering on dislike. "Thanks for that, David. I was just about coming to terms with the idea of a family tragedy. Now, every time I see someone crossing the estate I'm going to wonder what unspeakable mischief they've been up to."

Sperrin shrugged, untroubled.

Hazel shook her head with conviction.

67

"This wasn't the work of a pedophile. The murder, if it was murder, might have been, but not the burial. By the time a pedophile gets around to burying his victim, he isn't concerned with making him comfortable, only with disposing of the evidence. No way would he build a DIY mausoleum out of paving slabs. He might have wrapped the body in a blanket, he'd have brought a spade to get it underground, and the minute that was done he'd have been away.

"Pedophiles might think — some of them — that they love their victims, but they don't really. They're playing at it, like playing with dolls. And what do you do with a broken doll? You throw it away. A man like that wouldn't have risked discovery to create what we saw."

Byrfield nodded, a little comforted. But not much. "But doesn't that mean it was someone local? You don't drive a hundred miles with a dead body *and* a dozen paving slabs in your car! It must have been someone with an excuse to be down there with a Land Rover or a tractor or something."

Hazel thought about it and nodded. She'd have liked to tell him no, that it was probably a stranger, but the situation was upsetting enough without confusing one another with lies. "A hole in the ground and a blanket, that could be anybody. The slabs make it look like someone who knows the estate. And is probably therefore known on the estate."

"Or *was* known here, years ago," said Sperrin. "That's not a recent grave. Forensics will get closer, but it has to be twenty years old and could be a lot older. Whoever was responsible is probably long gone, and quite possibly dead by now anyway."

"I hope so," murmured Byrfield.

"You might as well think so," said Sperrin cheerfully. "We're never likely to learn the truth now."

CHAPTER 7

When Ash took Patience for a walk, Hazel went after them, jogging to catch up. She fell into step beside her friend.

"Are you all right?"

The same question that had tasked his therapist. "Yes, of course."

"Don't say it if it isn't true. This has been a difficult day for everybody. For you, it must have been awful."

He made a gesture with one hand. "No different for me."

"Of course it's different for you," Hazel said sharply. "This isn't personal for us the way it is for you. We can imagine what it's like to lose a child. You know."

"Yes," Ash said softly.

"If you want to leave here, we can go now."

"I think Pete wants you to stay."

"Yes?" She considered that, then shook her head. "It doesn't matter. He might think he needs his hand held, but he doesn't really."

"And I do." It was half a question, half a statement.

"You've more reason. Anyway," she added briskly, "Pete's got his mum for moral support. She can hold his hand."

Ash remembered the encounter on the landing. "Only if he scrubs it first," he muttered, and Hazel laughed. Ash grinned, a little shame-faced. "I'm fine. Really. I think we should stay, at least for a day or two. We shouldn't leave Pete to deal with this on his own while he's still in shock. I don't think either his mother or Sperrin is likely to be much help to him."

Hazel agreed. "What did you make of our countess, then?" Ash thought from the sly tone of her voice she was hoping for an indiscretion.

"Isn't she a dowager countess? Since her husband's dead?"

"No, she's the countess until Pete marries. Then she becomes the dowager, to avoid confusion."

Ash didn't want to give offense. He knew Hazel had connections with these people that could not be explained in practical modern terms. And, so far as he could see, she counted the earl a genuine friend. But she had asked. "She doesn't seem an easy woman to like."

Hazel wasn't offended. "That's because she isn't. She and the old earl were like chalk and cheese. He loved Byrfield, loved everything and everyone about it. She's always thought of it as a rather big piece of jewelry, something to flash and make the other countesses jealous."

"It makes you wonder what they saw in each other."

Hazel stared at him, wondering — not for the first time — how an intelligent man could be so dense. "She saw a title and a historic house. He saw enough money to help him keep them together."

Ash couldn't help feeling a little shocked. And yet, that was the reality — that something like Byrfield was always going to need more income than it was capable of generating. An heiress every few generations was probably as vital to its survival as the phone number of a good woodworm operative. He shrugged helplessly. "I suppose, if they were both satisfied with the arrangement . . ."

"They both did what was required of them, anyway. They preserved Byrfield, and they produced an heir. Eventually."

"What was he like?" asked Ash. "Pete's dad. The . . . somethingth earl?"

"Twenty-seventh," said Hazel with a smile. "Pete's the twenty-eighth. He was very like Pete. Not to look at — he was short and tubby — but in personality. He was a very kind man. He put a value on people, and if he could help them, he did. Like David Sperrin. The old earl helped him get to university. He was a good man, and a good earl. No one around here has a bad word to say about him."

Ash glanced back, but they'd walked far enough from the house not to be overheard. "But people aren't as fond of the countess?"

"Let's just say she never courted popularity," said Hazel. "People whose families had farmed the estate for generations objected to the way she behaved as if she owned the place." She caught his expression and laughed. "Yes, I know — technically speaking, she did. But her father was a supermarket magnate, and there's nothing that the ancient poor like less than the new rich. So the tenant farmers and their laborers gathered in the saloon bar of the Spotted Pig in Burford to scowl into their beer and ask one another, 'Whom do her think she is? Her's nobbut a grocer's daughter.' "

Ash laughed out loud. "Funnily enough, Patience" — Hazel's curious eyebrow warned him just in time that he'd strayed onto shaky ground, and he edited as he went along — "looked as if she was thinking much the same."

The Spotted Pig in Burford village was the center of social life on and around the estate. The oak bar, so blackened by generations of cigarette smoke that it was probably carcinogenic in its own right, rumbled with the conversation of the locals, punctuated by the click of snooker balls in the adjoining room and the thud and occasional "Ow!" of a darts match. The landlord was also a surprisingly good cook, and the six-table restaurant did a thriving trade even midweek. On a Saturday night, Ash was lucky to get a cancellation.

When he invited Hazel and her father out for supper, he wasn't sure they'd want to go. It hadn't been the sort of day to warrant celebrating. But if he and Hazel spent the evening at Byrfield, they'd go on doing what they'd been doing all day — staring at the same few faces, struggling to make conversation, trying not to dwell on what they'd found and succeeding hardly if at all.

Rather to Ash's surprise, Hazel thought the Spotted Pig an excellent idea. "It'll cheer us up."

"Should I ask Pete and David?"

She shook her head decisively. "They can cheer each other up."

Alfred Best wasn't entirely sure what to make of his daughter's friendship with this man. She told him, and he believed *she* believed it was true, that friendship was all it was. That Ash was not only still legally married but also still in love with his wife, and that wouldn't change if they found proof tomorrow that she'd been dead for four years. And he didn't blame Ash for the difficulties Hazel had found herself in, or even the dangers she'd faced, though he knew she would have met with none of it if she'd never met Ash. He understood that Ash was a victim of events as much as his daughter was.

None of which would have got in the way of a thorough dislike if Gabriel Ash had been the sort of man you *could* dislike. Fred Best was *ready* to dislike him. He thought Hazel would have been better off if they'd never met, if she'd been on the day shift the night Ash was mugged in the park, if someone else had stumbled on the mechanism by which crime in Norbold was kept at record-breaking lows. But Best was also a realist. That wasn't what had happened. Given the circumstances, Hazel had done what she had to, done what honor demanded, and done it with courage; and actually, so had Ash. Perhaps there was nothing in their friendship to regret.

So he accepted Ash's invitation as he had accepted the man into his home, with good grace for the sake of his daughter.

Poking around in her old wardrobe, Hazel had managed to find a dress that still fit — she was both slimmer and more muscular than in her teaching days — which together with a locket from her mother's jewelry box made acceptable eating-out attire. Ash put his suit on and looked as if he was making an effort, even though it only fit where it touched. Fred Best brought out his regimental tie. Thus caparisoned, and leaving Patience to guard the gate lodge from the comfort of the sofa, they walked the half mile into Burford.

There wasn't a cook among them, but they were all capable of appreciating good cooking, and good cooking was what they got — good food well prepared and plenty of it. Away from Byrfield, Ash felt himself relaxing. "What a day."

By now Fred Best knew as much about the discovery as those who'd been at the lake. In fact, he may have known more. "How did young Davy take it?"

Hazel frowned. "David Sperrin? About

how you'd expect — as if it was a bit of a lark. As if it was a scientific conundrum he'd come across, not somebody's ten-year-old son."

Ash was watching the older man carefully. "Mr. Best — why Sperrin? Why do you ask about him rather than Byrfield?"

Best hesitated. His gaze traveled between them, settling on Hazel. "Surely you know? You must."

"Know what?"

And when he did the math, there was no reason she should know. It had happened not only before the Bests came to Byrfield but before Hazel was born. It was common knowledge in the village, but perhaps not among the children, and she hadn't been much more than a child when she left here. "About Davy's brother. Diana Sperrin's elder son."

Hazel was staring at him as if she thought he was making it up. "*What* elder son? There were only ever the two of them — Diana and David. After he left for Reading, there was only her."

"In your time," agreed Best. "But she had two sons. The older one was taken back to Ireland by his father thirty years ago. At least that's what everyone thought. What Diana believed."

Hazel stared at her father. Ash, too polite to do the same, was making connections in his head. "You think that's who we found? David Sperrin's brother?"

"I've no idea," said Fred Best immediately. "But it was the first thing that came into my head when I heard what you'd found, and it seems I'm not the only one. There's a fair bit of gossip going around the village. People who lived here at the time, before we came to Byrfield, are scratching their memories for what they actually know as distinct from what they've been told and what's always been assumed.

"And what everyone seems agreed on is that although Diana has always believed that her boy was taken to Ireland by his father, there's no actual evidence of that. He'd be a man of forty now. You'd think that some-where in the last twenty-odd years he'd have popped over to see his mother. But if he did, nobody else saw him. And now people are thinking that maybe there's a good reason for that."

"They think . . ." Hazel heard her voice soaring and started again, more discreetly. "They think Diana's husband abducted his own son, then killed him and buried him at Byrfield?"

Best shrugged. "Something like that. Apparently he took the child from Diana's house in the middle of the night, when everyone was asleep. It was assumed that he'd taken him back to Ireland. The police tried to find him, but they didn't get far. Again, maybe that's why."

"But why would he kill the child? Why take him if he didn't want him?"

"Who knows? Maybe something went wrong. Or maybe it isn't the Sperrin child at all," said Fred Best. "I'm just saying, that's the word around the village." He looked across the table at Ash. "This is a small community. A lot of the people here — a lot of the people in this pub — were here when it happened. They remember the child being taken. It might have been thirty years ago, but a stolen child is a stolen child. Nobody forgets in a hurry. Half an hour after you opened that grave by the lake, Burford had pretty well decided who was in it."

"What happened?" asked Hazel quietly. "Or what's supposed to have happened?"

"I only know what I was told," Best said again. "This was ten years before we came here. But everyone tells you the same thing. The family lived in that same cottage Diana's in now. Her husband, Saul, was an Irish traveler — sometimes he was around, sometimes he wasn't. They had two sons,

James and David, about five years apart. Diana was the breadwinner — she sold enough paintings to keep them fed and clothed, without much help from her husband. Then one day he came back from his travels, collected the older boy, and vanished again."

"And she never got him back?" whispered Hazel, horrified.

Best shook his head. "No one knew where they'd gone. It was assumed that Saul had gone back to Ireland, and our police asked the Gardaí to watch out for him. But either the Gardaí didn't look very hard or he hid out among people who kept his secret, or maybe he never went back to Ireland at all. Anyway, he never showed his face in Burford again."

"Oh hell." Hazel puffed her cheeks out. There was a certain schoolgirl element to her repertoire of gestures. Of course, she'd gone straight from studying to teaching to law enforcement. She'd seen things and done things most people wouldn't, and wouldn't want to, in a lifetime. But she'd always worked within the kind of structure that limits personal expression, and sometimes hers seemed limited to that of a fourteen-year-old hockey player. "Do you suppose David knows?"

"If he doesn't," said Ash in a low voice, "he will soon. We should warn him what people are saying. Before he hears it on the street."

"You don't think we should leave it to DI Norris?" To Hazel it seemed a matter of professional courtesy.

Inevitably, Ash saw it from the family's point of view. "It could be a week before Inspector Norris knows anything more. And it's not just David — there's his mother to think of. We shouldn't let her hear the rumors tomorrow in the grocer's."

A shade reluctantly, Hazel nodded. "All right. Have a word with him when you get back to Byrfield. He can go see his mum tonight, before the gossip reaches her some other way."

Best agreed. It was the only humane way to proceed. But, unlike his daughter and her friend, he'd lived in this tiny community for twenty years. He knew how fast the bush telegraph worked. "She may already have heard."

"All the more reason David should go and see her." Ash was paying the bill before the coffee was even poured. "Come on — we should get back."

CHAPTER 8

It was immediately obvious to Ash that what was common gossip in the Spotted Pig came as lightning from a clear sky to David Sperrin. He had not considered, even momentarily, whether the sad little grave he'd opened might have anything to say to him personally rather than as an archaeologist. For long seconds after Ash broached the subject he continued to look careless and sardonic, an expression he used as a kind of shorthand for superiority. Only when Ash failed to respond to this lazy substitute for charm did some understanding of what he was being told start to percolate through into his eyes.

Predictably, his initial reaction was that he was being lied to. "You're crazy," he said flatly. The hooded amusement in his gaze had given way to a dangerous spark.

Ash had picked a moment when Pete Byrfield was otherwise occupied, updating the estate books at the kitchen table. Even so, across the room the man raised his head just slightly, and Ash thought, Yes — Hazel's told you about me.

To Sperrin he said calmly, "Possibly, although my therapist says not. David, I'm not saying this to upset you. I'm saying it because I heard talk in the pub and thought you ought to know. To prepare your mother for what she might hear when she goes out tomorrow."

Following as fast on understanding as the tender follows a steam train came anger. Sperrin's voice had a hard, rough edge. "What did you hear? That my dad abandoned us and took my brother back to Ireland? So every family is not a happy family — so what? It's all a very long time ago."

"That grave has been there a very long time," murmured Ash. "And people have been doing their sums, and thinking back, and maybe they've put two and two together and come up with seven, but being wrong won't stop it from being hurtful if the first your mother hears of this is a nosy neighbor pressing her for information. Don't you think you should have a word with her? Tonight?"

At least Sperrin glanced at his watch. "It's gone eleven. She'll be asleep."

"You could wake her."

"I could get my ears boxed!"

"She needs to know."

Sperrin was looking at him as if he didn't know quite what to make of Ash. As if he'd made a judgment when they first met but now Ash had jumped out of his pigeonhole and was roaming around unrestrained and Sperrin wasn't sure what he was going to do or where he was going to settle. This was something Ash was familiar with. Disconcerting people. Alarming them, even. He didn't do it deliberately. He didn't usually know he was doing it until he noticed that characteristic expression in their eyes, wide and still and slightly glazed.

It was in Sperrin's eyes now, and David Sperrin wasn't a man who was easily alarmed. He cleared his throat, as if he might thereby clear his mind, too, and made one last attempt at laying the subject to rest. "That wasn't my brother's body we found."

"You hear from him?"

"My mother does. He's fine. He lives in Ireland."

"Good," said Ash, and meant it. He felt a sense of relief that, even if it was still somebody's child who'd been moldering beside the lake for thirty years, at least it was no one whose name was known, who was remembered around here. It was no less sad, but it was less personal. "Then it's just a question of warning your mother about the talk in the village."

David Sperrin was not a big man. But you didn't notice until he tried to look bigger. "When I see her, I'll tell her about your . . . *concern.*" He invested the word with a wealth of scorn.

Ash nodded. He said nothing more, because he knew that if he told Sperrin to go immediately, he would refuse and nothing would persuade him then. But he was pleased to note that when Pete Byrfield made a last batch of coffee on the kitchen range, there were three mugs but only two of them to drink it.

The cottage where David Sperrin had grown up was at the Byrfield end of a terrace of farm laborers' dwellings built by the estate in the mid-nineteenth century. They were all the same when they were built — kitchen and parlor downstairs, two bedrooms upstairs, outhouse in the backyard — but in the twentieth century they had been modernized and extended in as many different configurations as there were cottages, which was six. All now had internal plumbing and even central heating. One had a whole extra floor of bedrooms — a head stockman in the 1930s had bred almost as prolifically as his best bull — while another had acquired a tiny but beautifully designed conservatory, and Diana Sperrin's had her studio tacked on the side.

No lights were burning in the studio as he turned in at the gate and under the shelter of the little wooden porch. Diana's bedroom was at the back of the house. It was possible she was still awake, reading or sketching in the big oak bed he'd been born in. He gave the wrought-iron knocker a single sharp rap and called through the letter box.

"Mum — it's David. Come down and let me in."

He didn't have a key anymore. She'd made an excuse to get it back after he left home and never provided him with another.

After a few moments he heard movement inside. The narrow stairs creaked whenever someone went up or down. An irritable voice demanded, "Whatever do you want at this time of night?"

"I need to talk to you. Let me in."

For a long moment he thought she was going to refuse, that he was going to be left on her doorstep and have to return to Byrfield, his mission unaccomplished. Finally he was saved that humiliation by the sound of the iron key turning in the lock.

Diana Sperrin stood in the doorway, a coat over her nightclothes, her strong, intelligent face set in angry lines and framed by a froth of gray hair. "Good grief, David! Couldn't you stagger another mile and wake Pete Byrfield?"

"I've just come from there," he said, hanging on to his patience in a way he did for no one else, "and I'm not drunk. Something's happened that I need to tell you about."

"And it won't wait till morning?" She still hadn't let him in, barring the door with her strong, thick body.

"No, it won't." He advanced into the open doorway until, grudgingly, she stood back to admit him.

"I suppose you want coffee."

It was such a small thing, and if she'd been asleep, she could be forgiven for resenting the disturbance. But she could just have put the kettle on without making him feel it was too much trouble. They didn't talk much these days, and one reason was this: that she never failed to remind him how it had felt growing up with a mother who didn't like him.

He answered in kind. "It wouldn't hurt."

In fact, she could hardly have been asleep — the water in the kettle was still hot, and it boiled again in seconds. She filled a mug for David but not for herself, stood over him, waiting with ill-disguised impatience. "Well? What is it that's so urgent?"

Walking over here, he'd wondered how to broach the subject. In the event it proved easier than he'd imagined: already irritated with her, he no longer felt much of an urge to spare her feelings. "I was digging up at Byrfield this morning. I found a body. A child's body. There's talk in the village that it might be Jamie."

That kicked the annoyance out of her face. He watched the color drain after it, leaving her white and slack-jawed, and he felt ashamed. Not even so much for hurting her, but because this was the kind of relationship they had. Ashamed that, although for most of his life he'd had only one parent, and for most of his life she'd been raising only one child, he still hadn't been able to make her love him.

He would have died slowly over hot coals rather than admit that to anyone, including her.

He'd managed to surprise her. She hadn't left the house all day, knew nothing of the discovery that had set the village to speculation. But she was a strong woman, and with a deep breath she took her feelings in an iron grip and forced them behind her. Her voice was rough. "What are you *talking* about, David? Of course it isn't Jamie. Jamie's in Ireland — you know that."

"I know that," echoed Sperrin in a low growl. "I didn't say *I* thought it was Jamie. I said people in the village are saying it might be, and I thought you'd want to know. So it wouldn't come as a shock."

"Unlike being dragged from my bed in the middle of the night in order to be told nonsense, you mean." She might have given him points for meaning well. But she'd never given him an inch, and that wouldn't change now.

He had no idea what he'd done to deserve her dislike, or whether she was just entirely unsuited to the maternal state. Perhaps Saul Sperrin had known that when he took his elder son away. More than once, growing up, David had wished he'd taken his younger son, too. He'd probably be a tarmac contractor now instead of an archaeologist, but maybe he'd be a happier man.

Defeated by her hostility, as he always eventually was, he put down his cup and let himself out the way he'd come in. "I'm sorry I disturbed you. I thought it was for the best."

"Thought?" she said. And: *"You?"* She

could invest two words with more contempt than anyone he had ever known.

CHAPTER 9

If anything, Sunday breakfast was even more strained than Saturday's. Sperrin didn't look at Ash, and Ash — not wanting to provoke an argument — kept his eyes on his kipper. It fell to Pete Byrfield — as host, as Sperrin's current employer and longtime friend — to break the dogged silence.

"You saw your mum, then, David?"

Sperrin nodded tersely.

"Had she heard about what we found?"

"No."

"A good job you went over, then."

"Why?" Sperrin looked at Ash pugnaciously. "It's nothing to do with her."

Byrfield sighed long-sufferingly. "Ash was only concerned that she might be upset. That someone might say something to her in the village and she might be upset."

Sperrin swiveled in his chair to give Byrfield the benefit of his searchlight gaze. "You've met my mother, have you? She doesn't get upset. She gets angry. If anyone in Burford got smart with her, she'd rip their ears off." He didn't add, though he might as well have done, Instead of mine.

Byrfield shrugged. "I still think it was best. If there's talk in the village, sooner or later the police will hear it and they'll want to talk to her. Better if it doesn't come out of the blue."

"So she can think up a plausible story, you mean?" Sperrin's tone walked the knife edge of objectionable. "Instead of admitting that she murdered my brother, buried him beside your lake, and told people he'd been taken to Ireland?"

But Byrfield had known him a very long time and, in spite of his prickliness, liked the man. "Nobody's thinking any such thing," he said wearily.

Hazel chose that moment to come in and so missed the start of the conversation. That may have been why she said what she did. Or she may just have been tiring of Sperrin's bad manners. "When did you last see your brother?" In the fraught silence that followed, she poured herself coffee from the pot.

Sperrin stared at her as if he couldn't believe her impertinence. But in the end he had to either answer or refuse to, and he wouldn't give her the satisfaction of a refusal. "I haven't *seen* my brother since I was a child. But my mother gets a card from him every Christmas and every birthday. That's how I know he's in Ireland, not under the mud down by the mere."

Hazel nodded, apparently accepting the answer at face value. "You've never wanted to go and look him up? It's a sad thing when families lose touch."

"I don't know where he *is*," snarled Sperrin. "They're travelers, yes? They travel. That's why they're called travelers. The clue's in the name, really."

At which point Byrfield judged that if he didn't change the subject, they were going to witness the top of an archaeologist's head blow off and steam come out. "Okay. Well, we can't do any more digging until we get the all clear from Inspector Norris. Agriculture beckons — anybody want to help me move some cows?"

Predictably, Hazel volunteered, and Sperrin grunted, "In a parallel universe," and disappeared into the library. Ash caught his dog's eye and raised an inquiring eyebrow, but Patience simply turned around and settled deeper into the sofa. Ash was only grateful that Byrfield used the kitchen, with its well-worn leather chairs, as a casual

don't-worry-about-your-boots sort of snug
for his guests. He was horribly afraid that if
they'd been offered the priceless antiques in
the drawing room, Patience would still have
appropriated the sofa with the thickest cush-
ions.

"We'll give it a miss, if you don't mind,"
he said, as if the decision had been his.

As a result, when a car drove into the
courtyard behind the kitchen, Ash was the
one who saw it, recognized Detective Inspector Norris, and went out to greet him.
"I'm afraid Lord Byrfield isn't here. He's
out doing something with his cows. Hazel's
with him — I have her mobile number,
somewhere. . . ." He was patting pockets
more in hope than expectation.

But it wasn't Pete the inspector had come
to see. "Did Mr. Sperrin go with them?"

"No. He may be in the library. It's this
way . . . I think. . . ."

Detective Inspector Norris, who was
famed for his observational powers, noticed
how the big, dark, shambling man hesitated
in the hallway but the white dog, stretching
unhurriedly as it climbed off the sofa, pad-
ded past him and up the stairs. At the top
they all turned left, and the first door they
came to was open. Inside was a world of
books.

"Shall I leave you?" asked Ash.

"Not on my account." The archaeologist glowered. Taking that as the closest Sperrin was likely to come to asking for moral support, Ash lowered himself onto one of the leather benches lining the walls and busied himself with stroking his dog's ears.

"I've just come from your house," said Norris. "I couldn't get a reply."

"It's not my house, it's my mother's. She's probably out."

"Her car is there."

Sperrin shrugged. "She may have walked to the shop. Or she's painting. She wouldn't notice nuclear war breaking out if she's painting."

"I need to speak to her. Will you let me in?"

"I don't have a key." The policeman said nothing that could be interpreted as surprise, but Sperrin somehow felt the need to explain. "Why would I? I haven't lived there for fifteen years. While I'm working here, I stay at Byrfield."

"Fair enough," said Norris, although he looked a little puzzled at the man's vehemence. "Maybe you can help me anyway. We've got a bit more information on the body you found. Not the full autopsy results, but a couple of things to help narrow the search. The age and sex of the child, the age of the burial — give or take a few years — and a couple of other things. So the next thing we do is compare those facts with records for the period — see what children were reported missing in this area at around that time."

"And you came up with my brother, James," said Sperrin shortly. "Well done. Except he didn't go missing — he was taken to Ireland by our father. He and my mother had split up, it all got a bit acrimonious, sometime later he came back and took Jamie, leaving my mother chasing his car down the road in her bare feet."

"You remember this, do you, sir?"

Sperrin elevated an eyebrow at him. "Since I was five years old at the time, my recollection is a bit sketchy. I know what my mother told me. I know losing Jamie blighted her life. She expected you to bring him back. She went on expecting it for years, but you never did."

"So if you were five," said Norris, doing sums, "this was . . . ?"

"Thirty years ago, give or take."

"And your brother would have been . . ."

"Ten. Inspector, none of this is relevant to your investigation. I know where Jamie is — he's in Ireland."

"You have an address for him?"

It was a rerun of the conversation over breakfast. Ash found himself tensing in anticipation of Sperrin's loss of temper.

"No, I don't have an address for him! They're travelers — they could be anywhere. They could be in England. If you're that desperate to talk to him, ask the Gardaí to find him."

"We asked them once before. They didn't manage to find him then. Or your father."

"Inspector, were you ever in rural Ireland in the 1980s? The Guards didn't have the facilities that the quietest two-man part-time police station in England had. At the start of the Troubles, the authorities in Northern Ireland were furious that they weren't getting better cooperation from the police across the border. Then they found out that half the time they couldn't get hold of one another when they needed to. There wasn't full radio coverage — there weren't even enough radios. There were parts of the wild west of Ireland at that time where policing was practically a Third World operation."

Norris was watching him thoughtfully. "How do you know that, Mr. Sperrin?"

Sperrin gave a sudden fierce grin and glanced around at all the books. "I read,

Inspector."

The policeman flicked an amiable smile. "You're quite right, of course. People like your father are always hard to keep tabs on, even now. The officers looking for James thirty years ago were actually reassured by the fact that they couldn't find Saul, either. If they'd found him and he didn't have your brother, that would have been bad. As it was, he'd simply vanished off the radar. Every line of inquiry hit a brick wall. And there's no wall as solid as that thrown up by one gypsy protecting another."

This time the smile was apologetic. "But the upshot of all this is, we can't actually prove that the body in that grave *isn't* your brother's."

Sperrin returned the smile coldly. "Of course you can, Inspector, and both of us . . ." He glanced at Ash by the door. "In fact, all three of us know it. DNA. And I'd lay good money that you've already taken samples from the grave, and now you want a sample from either me or my mother. And you thought" — his head came up haughtily; for a small man he seemed to spend a lot of time looking down his nose at people — "that it would be easier if the suggestion came from me."

Inspector Norris chuckled. "Well, you've

98

got me bang to rights there." Ash had never heard anyone say "bang to rights" before. "I ask, and it sounds like I'm asking you to disprove a suspicion; you volunteer, and it feels like you're helping us to advance the investigation. Either way, of course, it's in your interests that we know for sure it isn't James in that grave and we need to pursue our inquiries elsewhere. For what it's worth, it'll also put a stop to the gossip in the village. It can't be very pleasant for your mother."

Sperrin sighed theatrically. "Inspector, if it's any help, you're welcome to a sample of my bodily fluids. It'll only confirm what I'm telling you — that James is alive and well, and sending a card every Christmas from whatever part of the British Isles he happens to be in."

Norris took the offer at face value and made no comment on the manner in which it was made. "Thank you. I'll arrange it. I appreciate your cooperation."

"Why wouldn't I cooperate?" Sperrin glowered.

Norris was on his way out of the library door when Ash reminded him of what he'd said. "That a couple of things emerged from the preliminary examination of the body. Can you tell us what?"

The detective seemed to consider this for a moment. Whether his decision was aided by the fact that the two men had been present at the opening of the grave, or whether he knew something of Ash's background, his expression — carefully, professionally blank — did not betray. "All right, yes, there was something. This child, this little boy, died violently. Well, that's not too much of a surprise — you don't bury people under the rhododendrons because they've had a heart attack or fallen off a wall. All the same, it's still — thank God — a rare occurrence when a small child is shot dead."

He paused there to watch the effect of his words on his audience. But it wasn't much help. The one who turned white was Ash, who'd had no connection with this area until very recently. Sperrin hardly reacted at all.

Norris continued. "But even before that he wasn't" — he searched for the socially acceptable term, couldn't remember it, settled for what people said in everyday life — "normal. The DNA will confirm it, but our medical examiner thinks he had Down syndrome."

David Sperrin gave a gruff, almost triumphant little snort. "That settles it. There was nothing wrong with my brother, James. Ask my mother. James was frigging perfect."

It was an easy task that Byrfield could have managed alone. It's always easy moving cows to fresh grass — you open the gate of the new field and stand back. There's usually one young heifer that thinks it would be really funny to run the opposite way and hide behind the slurry tank, but on the whole cows are ruled by their stomachs — all four of them.

So there was less running around and swearing than there would have been moving bullocks, and more ambling down a green lane with a switch to keep the animals walking. Which is what Pete Byrfield had hoped for when he'd issued the invitation. He'd also hoped Hazel would be the one to take it up.

It had rather surprised him, how glad he'd been to see her. Their paths didn't cross very often these days — she'd been busy building her career, he'd been busy building his herd. And they'd never been an item. But they'd been friends for so long there was perhaps more shared history than if they had been. When Alfred Best mentioned his daughter's impending visit, Byrfield had found himself grinning, and planning what he could show her and what they could talk about, and only afterward wondered why. He concluded that he must have missed her more than he realized. He wondered if he could persuade her to stay a little longer. He'd hoped David Sperrin's survey might do the trick. You know what they say: Be careful what you wish for. . . .

Hazel was glad to see him, too. Of course, Hazel was usually glad to see people; it was the kind of person she was — open, gregarious, empathic. It was what had made her good at her job — at both her jobs. It probably didn't mean very much that she'd taken the chance to walk down this lane with him, shooing cows and dodging the inevitable results. But it might have done.

Then, too, both of them were glad to get out of the house for a while, away from the sadness that had inevitably descended. The discovery at the lake had left them all in a kind of limbo, unable to get on with their lives until a resolution of some sort hove into sight.

Out in the sunshine, Hazel felt her mood lightening with every step. "It seems a while since we did this last, Pete."

He waved an airy hand. "I try to show a girl a good time. You can only have so many nightclubs, casinos, and skiing holidays before boredom sets in. But shifting cows never grows old."

Hazel laughed out loud. "On a morning like this, with the hedges full of honeysuckle and bees, who'd want to be anywhere else?" She skipped over a fresh cowpat. "You wouldn't, would you?"

He shook his head with certainty. "Never for a minute. I mightn't have had much choice about the life I was going to lead, but I've never wished for another one. I love this place. I love the house, and the land, and all the people on the land. I love the whole idea of getting land to feed you. It just seems so *right*."

Hazel regarded him affectionately. "I'm glad you're happy. That you're not doing this because it's expected of you, and you'd rather be — oh, I don't know — lead dancer with the Bolshoi Ballet."

Byrfield looked down ruefully at his wellies. "Have you *seen* my feet? We aristocrats are supposed to be delicate, effete little things. But you wouldn't get feet like that on a Shire horse."

Hazel chuckled. "A bit of common blood must have crept in somewhere." Then, more soberly, she said, "Can I ask you something personal?"

He had no idea what to expect. He nodded anyway. "Sure."

103

"Does it ever trouble you? Having all this? Being the master of all you survey?"

"You mean," he appended astutely, "when I haven't worked for it."

"I know you work," she said quickly. "I know you work hard. All the same, most people work hard. But nobody could expect to have something like this without inheriting it."

"Or, of course, being a rock star or a footballer," said Byrfield, just tartly enough that he must have been tired of the question. "But isn't that pretty much the point? If you want there to be places like Byrfield — hedges, honeysuckle, house and all — there have to be people like me. Like the Byrfield family.

"Somewhere like Byrfield isn't the creation of one lifetime. One man couldn't carry the burden. It needs to go hand in hand with a family, so someone is ready to pick up the reins when the last coachman falls off the box. I don't know if it's fair. I think it's the only way for a country to preserve this kind of heritage. If you sold off all the grand houses in England, and paid off all the mortgages, and settled the tax liability, and divided what was left among the entire population, people would get a book of stamps each. And it would have cost them an important part of their history."

Hazel looked at him and saw the commitment shining in his eyes, and her smile was warm. "You're right. This is worth preserving, even if it takes a little inequality to do it. I inherited my mother's jewelry and a half share in a small rental property in Basingstoke, you inherited Byrfield and its title. There might be a difference in scale, but it's the same principle."

"The title *does* bother me, sometimes," admitted Byrfield. "I can be worthy of the estate by working it well, and using it to give other people employment. The title's different. It says I'm different to other people for no better reason than that a distant ancestor, hundreds of years ago, was better, or braver, or maybe just sneakier than the people around him. And it goes on saying that, however little I contribute to the family's prestige. All that's required of me is to produce a son before I die, and if I can manage that challenging task, the title goes on.

"And if I can't, the title will go elsewhere and take Byrfield with it. It's ridiculous, when you think about it. In theory, my mother could be walking the streets if I don't do my duty by her! And some second cousin whose real talent lies in making violins or translating Sanskrit could be the next earl, with all of this to manage."

"Who is the next in line, anyway?" asked Hazel. She wondered if he'd even know.

The promptness of his answer told her, more than anything he'd said, that the future of Byrfield was never more than a thought from his mind. "My father's younger brother's second son, Rodney. The older son died in a car crash when he was twenty."

"And does cousin Rodney want to be earl?"

"Not as far as I know. Doesn't come into it — you don't get a choice. You can't pass a title on to a good home, as if it was an unwanted puppy. You can get rid of it — drown it, effectively — if you feel strongly enough, but it's quite an undertaking, and your descendants can't get it back if they feel differently."

"What about daughters?" asked Hazel mischievously. "Viv would have made a good earl."

"There *are* titles that can travel down the distaff line," Byrfield acknowledged, a shade loftily, as if it was a little infra dig, "but ours isn't one of them. Even if I hadn't come along, the only way my sister could be

Countess Byrfield would be if she married cousin Rodney. Which used to happen quite a bit, of course. It explains why the children of the nobility tend to have teeth like a row of gravestones but no chins."

Hazel laughed again and linked her arm companionably through his.

They followed the plodding cows in silence for a minute. Then Byrfield said, with some reticence, "Can *I* ask something personal?"

"Always," said Hazel. She meant it, but before Byrfield had time to take up the invitation, she'd already jumped in with the answer. "Ah — me and Gabriel. Yes?"

"Well — yes," admitted Byrfield.

"David wanted to know the same thing."

"Did he indeed?" If Hazel saw him glower, she thought nothing of it. "What did you tell him?"

"The truth. That we're friends — nothing more, nothing less. He's married. At least . . ." And then she had no option but to fill in some of the details. "He doesn't know if his wife is still alive," she finished. "He works on the assumption that she might be. I don't think he's ever going to know for sure."

"He could —" Byrfield stopped there, aware that he risked impertinence.

"Have her declared dead? Yes, he could, eventually," said Hazel. "But you see, that's not what he wants. All that keeps him going is the remote possibility that she might be alive somewhere. Or if not Cathy, then his sons. If he knew for sure they were gone . . ." She shrugged unhappily.

"What?"

"He says he'd find the people responsible and kill them, or die trying."

It's just a cliché when someone says it on a TV show. It's different when it's for real, and it's someone you know. Despite the warmth of the sun, Byrfield felt chills running under his skin. "He doesn't seem the violent type."

"He isn't," Hazel said fervently. "In spite of which, I think he means every word."

CHAPTER 10

DNA samples are taken by swabbing the inside of the cheek. It requires a few moments and no privacy. Hazel, this early in her career, had already seen it done too often to find it interesting, but Pete Byrfield watched intently.

By the time the technician arrived to map David Sperrin's entire family history from a few cells of mucous membrane, the cows had been moved and the cowherds had returned. Sperrin had brought them up-to-date with every appearance of satisfaction, as if he thought the conversation with DI Norris had proved something.

Perhaps Byrfield thought so, too. As the day wore on, Hazel noticed him becoming more and more quiet, looking more and more troubled, until — anxious about him — she cornered him on the stairs and asked plainly what the problem was.

"Problem?" he echoed, prevaricating weakly.

"Pete, you look like you lost a twenty-pound note and found a euro! What's happened? Did David tell you something he didn't tell us?"

"No, of course not. It's just . . ." The words dwindled and died.

Hazel took a lot more putting off than that. "Yes? What?"

Byrfield swallowed. "David seems pretty sure that wasn't his brother we found."

"Yes, he does. Well, people try to believe what suits them. Unless you've some reason to think he's wrong?"

"No — no," he said quickly. He looked around, although there was no one else within sight or earshot. "But if it wasn't Jamie Sperrin, who was it?"

Hazel didn't understand his concern. "If it wasn't Jamie, it probably wasn't anyone you'd know. No other local children went missing about that time, did they? So he was brought here. Not a nice thought, I know, but better than the alternative. Norris will have to go back to the PNC — national records — and see what he can turn up around that time. Assuming David's test proves what he thinks it will."

"I'm afraid it will," mumbled Byrfield.

She couldn't ignore that. Even without a police officer's instincts she would have known that wasn't just careless speaking — something coming out other than how he meant. Hazel took a deep breath. "Now, what exactly do you mean by that?"

He'd said it precisely because he needed to talk, to her or to someone. He just didn't know how to start. He'd been dwelling on a notion for hours now, and far from laying it to rest, he'd invested it with more and more credibility the longer he'd worried at it. By now it had assumed the proportions of a mountain ready to fall on him.

The first step was to get out of this house that he loved and that burdened him. They walked out into the empty courtyard. Then Byrfield said tentatively, "This all happened about thirty years ago."

"Apparently."

"I'm thirty years old."

"Yes?" And then, because he seemed to be waiting for something, she said, "I'm twenty-six."

Byrfield shut his eyes for a moment and tried to compose himself, to put his thoughts — his fears — into some sort of coherent sequence. Then he started again.

"My parents were married" — he did the sums — "forty-two years ago. My sister Viv is thirty-six. Two years later they had Posy. Finally, to sighs of relief all around, they produced a son."

"Okay," said Hazel, still waiting.

Byrfield raised his haunted gaze to her face. "Suppose I wasn't the first son? Suppose their first child was also a son?"

Now he'd lost her. "You think Vivienne was born a boy?" She supposed it wasn't entirely impossible — stranger things make the front of the Sunday tabloids. . . .

"No, of course not." His tone was impatient, but in the hollows of his eyes was the despair that he was going to have to spell it out — that she couldn't guess what was troubling him. "Hazel, you've known us long enough — known Byrfield long enough — to know how families like ours operate. The title's like an hereditary disease, passed down the male line until the line runs out. Girls don't inherit. Viv doesn't resent that — it's been a fundamental part of her life, of her understanding of how the world works, since she was a tiny child.

"But what if the firstborn son can't do the job, either? Because there's something wrong with him — something he was born with, something that's never going to change, something that means he'll never be able to run a place like Byrfield or produce a suitable heir in his turn? What would a family like mine — parents like mine — do then?"

Hazel didn't know, either. "It must happen sometimes. I suppose someone else runs the family business during his lifetime and the title moves on when he dies without issue."

"Yes," agreed Byrfield. "The immediate line ends there. Which any titled family is going to see as a disaster, personally and financially. Don't underestimate what it meant to my parents to produce a viable male heir. Particularly, perhaps, to my mother. If she'd outlived my father and not had sons, she'd have lost Byrfield. If she'd outlived her only son and he'd died without children, she'd have lost Byrfield."

Mentally, Hazel held that up against what she knew of the countess. "She wouldn't have been a happy bunny."

Despite his deep anxiety, the understatement made Byrfield choke on a laugh. "No, she wouldn't. You know my mother: Can you see her taking it lying down? Accepting it as the luck of the draw and putting a brave face on it?"

Hazel could not.

Byrfield went on. These were hard things for him to say, but getting them said was helping him to deal with them. "Even thirty years ago, it would have been obvious pretty well immediately if their first son was born with Down syndrome. The implications would have been pretty obvious, too. That a time might come when they'd wish he'd never been born at all."

Hazel was shocked. But it didn't stop her thinking. "But surely any son is better than no son?"

Byrfield nodded. "That's the other side of the coin. If they have another son, it's better if he's the heir. But if they don't, at least they can hold everything together for one more generation. That was the dilemma."

"You think . . . what? That they kept his birth a secret? Until they knew if they could have another child?"

"Not another child — another son. They gave it another shot, and came up with Viv. Then they had Posy. And then finally — *finally* — they had me." He swallowed. "So what would they do then?"

Hazel stared at him. "What do *you* think they did then?"

"I don't know. But what I'm afraid of — Hazel, what I'm mortally afraid of — is that they waited for a dark night and got rid of the spare they'd been keeping in the attic."

Hazel paled. Her voice seemed to come

from a very long way away. "Pete, that's crazy talk! You think you had an older brother, and your parents *killed* him — put him down like culling a defective puppy — when a better candidate for the title came along? You *can't* think that! You can't believe that of your own family."

Byrfield put both hands to his face, spoke through the gap between them. His voice was thin and he picked his words carefully. "I wouldn't believe it of *your* family. I wouldn't believe it of most people's families. But the more I think about it, the more I believe it *is* something my family could do. In the interests of the title and the estate. Thinking they were doing the right thing."

"To murder a helpless child? Their own child?" Her tone was outraged.

"You have to try to see it through their eyes," he said, pleading in his voice. "The world looks different if you're a Byrfield. You aren't just an individual with an individual's rights and responsibilities. You're the guardian of six hundred years of history. Byrfields come and go, but Byrfield has been going for nearly six centuries and should last as long again if everyone does his duty. Marries when he's required to, marries money if it's running short, and produces a male heir before time's winged chariot runs him down."

He lowered his hands, flicked her a tiny, fragile smile. "When you were a little kid, what were your mum and dad's expectations? That you'd work hard at school? That you'd be a loving child, a kind friend, and an honest member of society? Byrfields don't give a toss about any of that. From as far back as I can remember, the only thing that was required of me was that I'd father a son. That's it. It's not a lot to expect, is it? Most people manage it without even being asked. But you see, when it's *all* that's asked of you, it starts to assume more importance than it should.

"My parents had two terrific daughters, and they were desperately disappointed in both of them. They were inordinately proud of me. As if they'd bred a prizewinning bull. But what if I hadn't lived up to expectations? What if it had been clear from the start that I wouldn't? Would they have taken the view that the Byrfield title was more important than any single incumbent? I think they might have done. I think, if they believed they could get away with it, they might have quietly smothered me and made me a comfortable little grave down by the lake, and kept trying."

"You're serious? You think you had an

older brother?"

"Hazel, I don't know," he cried in anguish. "But if that's what happened — if their first child was a son but he was disabled — God help me, I am terribly afraid that could be how they dealt with the situation. Because they thought it was their duty to protect Byrfield. The title, the house, and the land."

He shuddered. "People think we own the land, but we don't. It owns us. It gets its claws into us and won't let go until we're dead. People think it's just marrying our cousins that makes us crazy, but I don't. I think it's the land. We love it too much — me as much as anyone. We love it, and it uses us. It looks soft and green and gentle, but that's just the velvet glove. Underneath it's rock-hard, and it doesn't care who it hurts. It grabs us in its iron fist, and it never lets us go."

Hazel had known Pete Byrfield most of her life. He'd been a slightly supercilious fourteen-year-old on a quad when she was an enthusiastic ten-year-old exercising his sisters' outgrown ponies. Later they'd grown to a friendship that was casual but deep, enduring. She hoped, and with some confidence expected, that they'd still be friends in their dotage, corresponding in increasingly shaky hands from their respective nursing homes.

She knew when he was scared. He was scared now.

So she didn't tell him to stop being a drama queen, that such things didn't happen in the twenty-first century — or even late in the twentieth. In the world he was born into, which he knew better than she, perhaps they did. That didn't mean he *wasn't* jumping to a terrible, unwarranted conclusion. It did mean that she had to take his concerns seriously, and help him if she could.

"They couldn't have kept their first child a secret," she said gently. "People would have known it was on the way. Even in ordinary families, you tell people before it becomes blindingly obvious. In your family it would have been a cause for particular celebration. They couldn't just shut him away in the attic like Mrs. Rochester!"

"She had a miscarriage," mumbled Byrfield.

Hazel froze. "What?"

"My mother's first pregnancy ended in a miscarriage. At least, that's what they told people. That she was pregnant, that she lost it during a holiday abroad. But Hazel" — his eyes were tortured — "what if she didn't lose it at all? What if they kept him for ten years, out of sight, as an insurance against Byrfield going to cousin Rodney? And then got rid of him when it looked as if they weren't going to need him after all?"

The shock of that — that he thought that might have happened, in his own family; that he might have been the beneficiary of it — struck her like a blow. Nevertheless she gripped his forearms with her two strong hands, making him look at her. "Pete, listen to me. I'm not going to tell you it isn't possible. I think it's highly unlikely, but it really doesn't matter what I think, or even what you think, because you can find out for sure."

"I can't ask my mother!" There was a shrill note of panic in his voice.

"You *could* ask your mother," Hazel retorted. "What's more, you *should* ask your mother. Whether there's any truth in it or not, she ought to know what's on your mind. But if you really can't face talking to her, or wouldn't believe what she told you, get yourself DNA-tested."

"Ask Inspector Norris to test me as well as David? He'd want to know why! In fact, he'd guess why. Because I've reason to think I might be related to that poor dead child. I can't do that to my family, even if . . ." He stopped and swallowed. "I'm sorry, Hazel,

119

maybe I should, but I can't."

"You don't have to involve the police, at least not at this stage. Go to a commercial lab. It's a standard procedure these days, the staff will assume it's a paternity issue."

Byrfield was drawn to the idea. But already he could anticipate problems. "They'd need the child's DNA to compare it with. How would I get that?"

"You couldn't," Hazel conceded. She gave it some more thought. "Okay, how about this? Get the test done, and send the results to Norris under my name. I'll explain that it's purely to rule something out, and that if there's no correlation between the two results, I'll be respecting the subject's wish to remain anonymous. If, God forbid, there *is* a correlation, then we'll have to be honest with him. This is a murder inquiry, we can't withhold evidence that would help him solve it."

She regarded her friend with compassion, taking in the haggard face and haunted eyes. "Are you ready for that, Pete? Because once we start this we have to see it through. If you're right, you can support your mother but you can't protect her. Not from this."

Byrfield nodded jerkily. "I understand. I suppose, if . . . if that's what it shows . . . I wouldn't want to protect her."

"We're talking as if your mother is the only one who could be implicated," Hazel realized. "But if you had an older brother who was kept a secret for ten years and then killed, your father had to be involved as well. She may claim it was his doing."

Byrfield flinched as if she'd slapped him. "You knew my father. Which of them would you feel inclined to blame?"

Hazel didn't have to think long. "Fair enough. So, is that what you're going to do?"

It was almost as if he'd committed himself by talking about it. While it was just a worm eating away in his brain he had the option of doing nothing about it. But he'd chosen to share his fears — with a police officer, of all people — and even if Hazel wouldn't have bullied him into doing something he didn't want to, his own conscience would. It wasn't just a sick thought anymore. He'd acknowledged it was a possibility, and now he owed it to the child buried by his lake — whoever he might turn out to be — to find the truth.

And, of course, the same sample that could turn his whole family upside down could equally well set his mind at rest. If it did, he swore to himself he would never complain about the weather or the suicidal tendencies of sheep or the fact that his expensive new bull was a card-carrying member of Gay Pride ever again.

He set his jaw. As a member of the aristocracy it wasn't his best feature, but he did what he could. "Yes," he said. "As soon as I can arrange it."

"Will you tell David what you're doing?"

"No."

"Or your mother?"

"Good God, no!" Byrfield sounded horrified. "I'm not telling anyone, unless I have to. If the results mean that I have to."

Hazel nodded. "It's your decision."

"But you don't think it's the right one."

"Pete," she said patiently, "it's none of my business. Only that you're my friend, and I want you to walk away from this with your soul intact. Do what you're comfortable with. Do what you can face doing. But there's a risk that events may take the decision out of your hands. If that happens, it may become harder, not easier, to talk to your mother. I wouldn't like to think you missed your last best chance."

His gaze dipped. "You think I'm being pathetic."

Hazel shook her head. "I think you've had a shock. I think you're trying to deal with it without hurting anybody's feelings. I just

122

think this is too important for hurt feelings to be an issue. You need to be honest with your mother. I'd like to think she'd be honest with you in return."

"You'd think so, wouldn't you?" he said wistfully. "I know you're right. It's just . . . I haven't got your moral courage. I know what you did in Norbold. You did what was right, what needed doing, even though it put your life in danger. I'm not that brave."

"Pete." She reached out and took his hand. She was surprised to find he was actually trembling. "You may have to be. If this thing goes pear-shaped, it'll be your job to hold the family together. To look after your sisters, and Byrfield. You'll need to be brave then, and strong. But you know, don't you, you can count on your friends."

He managed a shame-faced little smile. "I'm glad you're here."

CHAPTER 11

Countess Byrfield, returning late from a charity lunch in Cambridge, passed the strange dog on the stairs up to her apartments. Each turned her head to watch the other as the countess continued climbing and the lurcher headed toward the kitchen. The countess was thinking, In better days than these the gamekeeper would have shot a mongrel like that. Who knows what Patience was thinking?

At least her own rooms remained a haven of peace from her son's ridiculous friends: the one who was always covered in mud, the impertinent one with the dog, and the one who if memory served — and it always did — was actually the handyman's brat! Alice Byrfield closed her door behind her with an audible sigh of relief. At least in here the world still operated according to the rules that had obtained for most of her life. At least in here things knew their place.

At least here she had the privacy to consider how these new developments might affect her. How much, if at all, she should admit to knowing. She was alone — her maid didn't come in on Sundays: how very different things were when she was a girl! So slowly, thinking all the time, she took off her jacket and hung it up, and took off her earrings and put them away, and pressed the button on the electric kettle, which was as close to domestic work as Alice Byrfield ever got.

With the cup of Earl Grey thus provided, she sat down in her wing chair in the bay window, with its matchless view across the park toward the lake and the fields of Home Farm, and thought about the little hummock in the grass and whether the discovery of its contents had the power to disturb the life she had created here.

Finding herself at a loose end after tea, Hazel gravitated — as she had in spare moments through much of her childhood — toward the stables. The brick-built boxes were empty, but curious heads lifted from grazing in the paddocks beyond. She recognized Viv's old hunter, twenty-five years old but still game for a day out if the opportunity presented; the old earl's favorite broodmare, barren now, which Pete Byrfield occasionally threw a saddle on; even one of the old ponies Hazel had ridden. A quick calculation told her their combined ages must now be something over seventy. Don Jackson, the local knacker, who for years had looked forward to getting a call about them, had just about given up, suspecting that the three horses would dance at his funeral.

A footstep on the cobbles behind her warned Hazel she had company, and she turned, to find Lady Vivienne Byrfield — unmarried despite her mother's best efforts, highly successful as Something in the City — bearing down on her like a Corvette at full revolutions. She hadn't been a pretty girl and she wasn't a handsome woman, but she radiated a mixture of self-confidence, genuine competence, and a totally unsentimental kindness that made people like her anyway.

"Hazel!" she boomed as she strode across the stable yard. She always managed to give the impression of being a much bigger woman than she was. Her brother had monopolized whatever tall genes dangled from the family tree: Viv was on the short side of medium height and the broad side of medium build. "Taking Starlight for a spin?"

Hazel gave a rueful grin. "I'd need something a bit bigger these days. The last year I Pony Clubbed him, I had to pick my feet up over the jumps."

"Take Leary, then."

Even from half a field away, even at twenty-five, Cavalier was a bigger, stronger horse than Hazel had any ambitions to ride. "Thanks for the offer, but — would you believe it? — I left my parachute at home."

Viv grinned. "He's a bit keen, that's all. You'd enjoy him."

"No," said Hazel carefully, "Mill Reef was a bit keen. Desert Orchid was a bit keen. Arkle was a positive slug by comparison. Maybe I'll get Pete to saddle Blossom for me sometime."

"That old thing!" snorted Viv, tossing her dark brown hair as a horse tosses its mane. "Couldn't jump out of your way. Couldn't fight its way out of a wet paper bag."

"My point entirely." Hazel smiled.

Viv Byrfield gave in with a good grace. "I'm really here to see Pip. Just wanted to say hello to the old chap on my way in."

As they walked toward the house, Hazel reflected on the paradox of the English nobility — or one of them — which was that someone like Lord Byrfield could trace every relative, every forefather (and -mother), every dotty aunt, disappointed cousin, and strategically married sister back to the Battle of Bosworth and still be not quite secure in his own identity. She decided it was something to do with the names. Guardians of the lineage gave their children names like Peregrine because they'd look good on the pedigree, not because they'd wear well on the child. They didn't even use them themselves — his mother called the current earl Pippin, his sisters called him Pip, friends called him Pete. No wonder he was never entirely sure who he was.

"I got this weird phone call from him a couple of hours ago," confided Viv. "I don't suppose you know what it's about?"

Hazel played for time. "What did he say?"

"Just that something had happened and he needed me down here, ASAP. My first thought was Mother, but he said she's all right. He said he was all right, too, though I'm not sure I believed him."

There were things Byrfield had said to Hazel that Hazel couldn't possibly pass on, not even to his sister. But there were other things that were a matter of public record, and if Viv knew about the grave they'd found, it might make it a little easier for

Pete to open the conversation that was to come. Though God only knew how he was going to end it.

So she explained about the archaeological survey, the grassy mound between the woods and the lake, and what it turned out to be hiding. "So now Byrfield's in the middle of a police investigation. My friend and I just happened to be visiting my dad at the time. I imagine Pete's looking to you for moral support."

Viv broke her mannish stride just long enough to give Hazel what used to be called an old-fashioned look. "Really? When you're here?"

Hazel shrugged that off without much thought. "Of course I want to help, any way I can. But when things get unpleasant, there's nothing quite like family."

"That's true," agreed Vivienne. "There's certainly nothing quite like mine."

Ash, who seemed to have slipped into the role filled in earlier times by the butler, met them at the door. Hazel was introducing them, and about to ask where Byrfield was, when the answer preceded the question. Despite the immense solidity of the building, raised voices were making their way through the heavy doors and down the wide staircase. It was hard to make out words, impossible to follow the conversation, but when Hazel identified one as Byrfield's — she'd never heard him shout before — she knew at once both who the other was and what the subject of the argument must be.

She glanced at Viv. "Do you think you should go up?"

Viv was already on her way, taking the broad steps two at a time. "Probably not," she cast back over her shoulder, "but I will anyway."

Even without the voices to guide her, she'd have headed directly to her mother's rooms. In this house, disputes had almost always revolved around Alice. She tapped — no, rapped — on the door as she went in, but the absence of an invitation did not deter or even delay her. With no children of her own, Vivienne Byrfield had always felt keenly protective of her younger brother.

Before the door shut, Hazel heard the words "And now we've got the Last Tycoon sticking his oar in!" — delivered not, as they might have been, in good-natured exasperation or even irony, but with a hard-edged deliberation designed to hurt. Then the thick timber lodged against its equally substantial jamb, and the rest of the exchange was muffled to mere rumbling.

Viv Byrfield clenched her jaw on all the

sharp, angry, telling retorts trying to fight their way out, knowing that another argument with her mother about her own way of life could only distract from whatever business her brother had here. That had to be serious, because nothing avoidable would have made him confront the countess, or stay if he found himself confronted. There had been a time when she'd envied Pip his inheritance, resenting the absurd rule of primogeniture that gave the title and the estate to the younger child when she knew that she herself would have done a better job. She didn't envy him anymore. If his inheritance included sharing the house with their mother till death should part them, he could keep it.

She said, tight-lipped, "Would one of you care to explain this . . . *performance*?"

Alice swiveled, her haughty gaze coming around like the beam of a lighthouse. "Since this is my *home,*" she declared imperiously, "I think I'm the one entitled to an explanation."

Viv tried her brother. "Pip?"

He passed a hand across his mouth as if to stop himself from screaming. Then he turned to face her. "You've heard about the child?" Viv nodded wordlessly. "They can't be precise, but he's probably been there about thirty years. You'd have been five or six when he died. Viv — have you any recollection, from when you were small, of another child in this house? An older child?"

When she realized what he was asking, her eyes flew wide. She tried hard to remember. "I don't think so. I remember the cousins coming and sometimes staying. There were parties here — children's parties. But that's not what you mean, is it? You mean another child who lived here. Our . . . brother?" While she was still reeling from the implications of that, she thought she spotted the flaw in his reasoning and relief flooded in. "But Pip — if we had an older brother, he'd be the earl, not you."

"If he'd lived," said Byrfield in a low voice.

"Well yes, if he'd lived. What I'm saying is, if they had a son before me, they'd have been over the moon. Everyone would have known about it. There'd have been announcements in the London papers, for heaven's sake! And almost certainly no more children."

"He wasn't . . . normal," mumbled Byrfield. "The medical examiner thinks he had Down syndrome. A son, but not a very satisfactory heir. I want to know if . . ." And there he ran out of words.

"If?" demanded Alice harshly.

Byrfield's sister pressed him, gently, as well. "Pip? What is it? What is it you're thinking?"

There was no alternative. He had to say it. He had to say it, and risk his mother's fury and his sister's disbelief. He had to say it if the sky should fall. "I want to know if they had a disabled son and kept quiet about him in the hope of producing something better. I want to know if they got rid of him when I came along."

The silence that followed was like an animal in the room with them, huge and dark and dangerous, the stench of its breath burning the air. They were transfixed by the certain knowledge that if any of them spoke again or moved, it would strike.

Predictably, it was Alice who broke the spell. For something over forty years she'd been confident in the knowledge that the most dangerous animal in any room was probably her, and even an accusation of murder wasn't going to intimidate her for long. "You" — she spun the word out while she looked for something substantial enough to follow it — "pup! How *dare* you say that to me? I am your *mother*. You owe everything to me. I will have your respect."

Byrfield's voice came from somewhere in

the toes of his boots. "Then tell me I'm wrong."

"Wrong?" Her voice rang with soaring contempt. "You're not just wrong, you're insane! If we were trying to improve the Byrfield stock, whatever makes you think we'd have settled for *you*?"

Byrfield flinched as if she'd slapped him. Viv shouldered between them as if she, too, anticipated violence. "Stop this, both of you! Are you mad? Pip, you can't really think . . . ?" But it was clear from his face that nothing he'd said had been thoughtless, or casual, or merely for effect. He looked as if he'd dragged the words up from inside his bones and they'd left bleeding, open wounds. Viv turned a quadrant. "Mother? Is this making *any* sense to you?"

Alice fixed her with a cold glare. "You have to ask? Ask *him* what evidence he has. Or if it's just another opportunity to hurt me. I know none of you can ever resist the chance."

"That is *so* unfair," whined Byrfield, and Viv nodded fierce agreement.

"Don't let's open the book on who hurt who most, Mother," she said tersely, "it really doesn't show you in your best light."

"I haven't had a civil word from any of you since the day your father died!"

"Pip has shown you every courtesy! Which is a great deal more than you ever showed him, or any of us!" She turned back to her brother. "I wouldn't put it past her. But is it even feasible? If they had a child before me, even if he wasn't perfect, it would be a matter of public record. I don't see how they could have kept him secret for ten years."

"The miscarriage," mumbled Byrfield wretchedly.

"What?" Alice's voice climbed to a crescendo of furious disbelief.

Viv was watching her brother intently. "Mother's first pregnancy ended in a miscarriage. I know."

"Abroad. Italy, wasn't it?"

"On a yacht in the Adriatic, so I was told." She glanced at her mother for confirmation, but the countess just stared bitterly over her shoulder. Viv shrugged and carried on. "A last chance for a holiday before parenthood hit them. But how does that help?"

Byrfield looked utterly miserable. "What if she didn't lose the baby? What if he was born alive but" — he, too, glanced at his mother — "unsatisfactory? There was time for them to decide what to do. What to tell people. If they said she'd miscarried, people would sympathize and wish her better luck next time. And there was no reason to suppose their next two children would be girls."

Lady Vivienne Byrfield had built a successful career on two things: dropping the title, which suggested to the business world that she might be better at opening factories than buying and selling them, and seeing the whole picture — the broad outline *and* the fine detail. She could look at a proposal and see, almost instantly, if it was a goer and where the problems would lie. That's what she was doing now. "If they were prepared to kill their first child, why would they go to the trouble of smuggling him back into England — back to Byrfield? God knows, a yacht in the Adriatic was a pretty good place to dispose of an unwanted baby!"

"But they needed to be sure they could do better." Pete Byrfield could hardly believe he was saying these things out loud. But he had to if they were going to be dealt with. And he was damned if he was going to back down now and never know, one way or the other. "If they had another son, they could afford to dispose of Mark One. But if they had only daughters, then it was important to have a male child — any male child — to keep the estate in the immediate family for as long as possible. If Dad died first, Mother would be able to stay here if she could produce — like a rabbit from a hat — a legitimate heir. For as long as *he* lived, she was secure."

Viv said nothing, trying very hard to see where his reasoning had broken down. But all she could see were minor procedural difficulties, hardly an obstacle to a determined woman like her mother.

Alice Byrfield said, with all the hauteur of which she was capable, "There is no truth in any of this. Not in any of it."

They were the words her son longed to hear. It was their tragedy that he couldn't believe them. Biting back tears, he said, "There is a way to be sure."

"Yes, there is," agreed the countess. "You can believe what I'm telling you."

"But you'd tell us the same thing whether it was true or not," said Viv, with devastating accuracy. "What way?"

"DNA testing."

They thought Alice had been angry before. Now it was as if someone had found her fuse and lit it. Her voice rocketed; her face was incandescent with rage. "Peregrine Byrfield, you will do no such thing! If you speak of it again, I will disown you. I will leave here and I will never see you again."

"Mother . . ." By now he'd given up all attempts to contain the tears.

Viv was a much tougher proposition. "And the downside of that is . . . ?" She had a sharp intellect and a sharp tongue. Sometimes she was quick enough to think of the smart retort and too slow to realize it would be better left unsaid.

There were no tears in Alice's repertoire. But all her weapons were honed sharp. "Thank God your father didn't live to see this! He'd never have believed you could treat me this way. After everything I've done for you — everything we both did. We lived our entire lives in a way we wouldn't have chosen so that you could live yours exactly how you want. I never expected gratitude, not from either of you. But I didn't expect to be accused of murder!

"If you go on with this, you'll bring the family down. Don't you understand that? You're not some small-town solicitor with doubts about his wife's fidelity. You're the twenty-eighth earl of Byrfield. You carry six hundred years of history on your shoulders, and the hopes of all the future generations. But if you get yourself tested, everyone will assume it's because you've fathered a bastard. Now, I know you well enough to know that's unlikely, but not everyone has my advantages. You turn up at some grubby little laboratory, and from that moment on the integrity of the Byrfield line will be in question. It wouldn't be worth it if there was something much more important at stake than the identity of some child who died three decades ago!"

"Some child? Or our brother? Mother, please," begged Byrfield, "if you know the answer, tell us. It's going to come out now, whether you want it to or not. For pity's sake, don't let us hear it from a policeman!"

"*What's* going to come out?" demanded Alice. "I'm not keeping anything from you! This . . . *fantasy* of yours is just that. Something you made up. Maybe it's your own guilty conscience tormenting you. Because you haven't been a resounding success as master of Byrfield, have you? There's really only one thing that's required of you, and thus far you've been a great disappointment!"

"I think Pip's shown remarkable foresight," Viv shot back. "He's clearly decided that if this is what the Byrfield family is reduced to, it's probably time it was allowed to die out. Anyway, you've made one thing patently obvious. Since we can't trust a word you say, DNA is the only way to resolve this. If Pip doesn't want to do it, I will."

Byrfield was more touched than he could

say. "Viv . . ."

She laid her hand on his arm. "Let me do this," she said quietly. "I've nothing to lose."

He cast her a grateful smile. "No, it's my responsibility. It sort of goes with the title. But I could use some moral support, if you felt like going with me."

"It's a date, little brother." She squeezed his hand. "You do know I'm proud of you, don't you?"

CHAPTER 12

Detective Inspector Norris was not a happy man.

He was old enough, just, to remember when detectives raced to the scene of a crime because such forensic evidence as they could collect would become harder to read with every hour that passed. Fingerprints and blood spots were about all the help you got with the typical inquiry. The job of finding out who did what to whom was down primarily to the man asking the questions. And he was in a hurry, too, because a lot of the people he wanted to question were just leaving on foreign holidays, and the rest were reminding other people how they'd spent the relevant hours with them, their gray-haired old mothers and if at all possible their parish priests. Speed was the essence of good police work.

Now he seemed to spend most of those vital early hours, and often enough days, waiting for lab results to come back. Of course it was helpful, immensely helpful, to be able to prove beyond reasonable doubt who was present at the scene of an incident. All the pesky little fibers that flew up from a carpet when you stamped on someone's head were as good as a witness. Better, because they couldn't be intimidated. But it all took time. Edwin Norris couldn't get his head around the fact that important work was being done, work that could convict the criminals, when he wasn't doing it.

Take the Byrfield business, for instance. Not even DI Norris could claim that time was of the essence when whatever happened had happened decades ago. But that sad little grave had gone unnoticed for all those years. Now it had been found, people who had thought themselves safe for a quarter of a century could be dusting off their suitcases and passports right now. He wanted to be rounding up anyone who might know any-thing — anyone, say, who was both alive and within twenty miles of Byrfield in the 1980s — and interrogating them under the full glare of an eco-friendly long-life ten-watt bulb. He wanted to be asking the good folk of Burford if they remembered a Down syndrome child living in or visiting the vil-lage thirty years ago.

And he couldn't, because he had to wait for the lab results. Asking the right person the wrong questions was worse than asking the wrong person the right questions. It told him you weren't as clever as he was afraid you might be. It showed him your hand without requiring him to show you his. And it breached the first rule of successful detecting, which is always know the answer to a question before you ask it.

Norris knew all this. He knew that when the results came in, he could have an identity for the dead boy, a cause of death, and a time window in which that death had occurred, and he wouldn't have risked asking an innocent question of the one person in the district who was not an innocent person. The lab results would be objective, more reliable than people's memories, and more detailed. They might identify the child for him; or if they couldn't, they ought to be able to pinpoint the part of the country he came from, or if he'd moved around, what areas he'd moved through and even approximately when. The minerals laid down in his growing bones would be a log of his brief life. When they compared that log with the known history of the small company of children reported missing around that time, it should be possible to zero in on a probable identity and confirm it by DNA-testing the surviving relatives.

Then he'd have to wait for the results to come back from the lab.

He had not, of course, been entirely idle. He'd made contact with his opposite number in Dublin to inquire whether Saul Sperrin had come up on the Gardaí's radar recently, or if they could place him at a definite location at any time in the last thirty years. He'd been through to the Police National Computer, to run the sparse early facts known about the Byrfield child against prepubescent boys reported missing anywhere in the UK in the relevant period. He'd set up an incident room and was putting together a murder board — a device almost as complex and stylized as the London Underground map — made up of colored felt-tip time lines, evidential photographs, and snippets of information as they came in, printed out on labels like luggage labels and pinned to a nexus where they seemed to make sense. Pinned, not glued, so they could be moved as more information, conflicting or confirming, came in and changed or strengthened the picture.

He was told, by detectives of a younger generation, that a lot of this could be done more quickly on a computer screen. But to

Norris a murder board was more than just a way of illustrating the state of play. It was an extension of his own brain. In his more fanciful moments he felt it might keep working after he'd gone home, that one morning he'd come in and it would present him with the answer. It would then be promoted over him.

Monday morning was still taking shape when one of his DCs stuck his head around the inspector's door. "Miss Best's here, sir."

"Constable Best," Norris corrected him thoughtfully.

The detective constable looked surprised. "Really?"

"Apparently."

"Shall I show her in?"

"I think you'd better," Norris said. "The last senior officer who annoyed her ended up on a slab."

When Hazel had called him, Norris had been sufficiently intrigued to make inquiries about her background. What he learned startled him but seemed to have little relevance to the present case. The girl had grown up on the Byrfield estate; that was all. Her father still worked there. She'd been there when the dead boy was found but not when he went into the ground. She probably hadn't been alive then. Norris agreed to see her mainly out of curiosity as to what she wanted to say.

Hazel had done a lot of police interviews in her short career, not all of them from the right side of the table. She was no longer intimidated by the mere procedure. It didn't matter what you were asked, only how you answered. To a larger extent than was widely recognized, the interviewee was in control of the session. If you kept calm, listened to the questions, answered concisely, and didn't feel the need to fill every silence, you wouldn't be tricked into saying anything more or other than you wanted to. This applied equally whether you were telling the truth or not.

So she greeted DI Norris politely and took the chair he indicated, then took a moment to compose herself before starting to explain the purpose of her visit.

Norris heard her out almost without interruption. He, too, had learned the power of silence, and it was hard to judge if he was surprised, or suspicious, or happy to consider an offer that might advance his inquiry but could do it no harm if it didn't.

He made notes as she talked, went back to check them when she'd finished. More silence as he struggled to read his shorthand. Hazel waited.

Finally the DI looked up and smiled. "Let me see if I have this straight. You're going to provide me with a DNA profile. It isn't your profile. It's the profile of a friend of yours who'd like to remain anonymous unless the results make that impossible by proving a relationship to the dead boy. Am I right so far?"

Hazel indicated that he was.

"Your friend, I presume, has concerns that he's anxious to allay. He —"

"Or she," interjected Hazel, deadpan.

"— Or, as you say, she thinks he —"

"Or she."

"— May be related to this child and wants to know for sure. He or she hopes that a comparison of the two profiles will prove otherwise so he, she, or it can sleep nights again." He sniffed. "Of course, far from allaying these fears, the lab work may confirm them. Your friend must be aware of this, and so must have decided that even bad news would be better than not knowing and always wondering. Still on track?"

Hazel risked a little smile. "On track and on time." She'd once dated a steam railway enthusiast.

"This friend of yours is aware that if the results yield any pertinent information there can be no further question of anonymity?

They'll become part of the case whether they like it or not."

"We discussed this. It's a chance they're willing to take." Like Norris, she opted for the ungrammatical rather than the endlessly pedantic.

"I see." The DI made another note. "And what do I get out of all this?"

Hazel blinked. She'd been ready for questions, but not that one. "Sorry, sir?"

"Well, your friend gets to know for sure about something that's troubling him. Some possible blot on his family escutcheon that he hopes I'll be able to remove. But what do I get? A potential witness, someone who might know something about a crime — and not just any crime but murder, the murder of a vulnerable little boy — doesn't want to talk to me about it. Doesn't want to tell me what he knows, or at least suspects. Doesn't want me to know what grounds he may have for those suspicions. Doesn't even want me knowing who he is. Where I come from, *Constable* Best" — he emphasized the word just enough to remind her both that she was still a police officer and that she wasn't a very senior one — "we call that obstruction."

Hazel shook her head insistently. "That isn't at all my friend's intention. You get the same thing out of it that they do. Certainty. If there's no connection, you won't need to know who provided the sample because it will have ruled them out of the inquiry. But if it comes back positive, then what you have is someone ready to tell you everything they know. Which may not be much, but at least you'll be barking up the right family tree. You stand to lose nothing, sir, and you could avoid a great deal of wasted time and effort."

Norris, still thinking, squinted at her. "And what do you get out of it?"

Hazel beamed. "The warm glow of knowing I've helped a friend *and* the police."

"If — *if* — I agree, how does it work?"

Hazel knew then that she'd succeeded. Whether, in the long run, that would be a good thing, only time would tell. "My friend will have the laboratory send you a copy of the profile, under my name. You'll compare it with the DNA taken from the boy. Then you'll call me. If they don't match, I'll set my friend's mind at rest and you'll keep looking for the boy's real family. But if it shows my friend and the dead boy are related, I'll bring him, or her" — she remembered just in time — "in and you can ask all the questions you need to."

"Your friend has agreed to this?"

"Absolutely. They need to know. If the boy *was* part of their family, they'll want to know how he died and who killed him."

"They may not want *me* to know how he died and who killed him."

"If that's the way this goes, they won't have a choice. They understand that."

"Understanding it now, and still understanding it when their family tragedy is about to go public, are two different things."

"I have their word."

"And that's enough, is it?" He waited with lifted eyebrow, but Hazel made no response. "Well, since I'm prepared to take your word, I can hardly criticize you for taking your friend's. But I want you to be very clear about where your priorities lie, Constable. My investigation takes precedence over your friendship. The moment you involved me in this, it stopped being a private concern and became a police matter. Even if you weren't a serving officer, you would owe me the truth if it turns out that you have access to it."

"Yes, sir."

"Yes sir," he echoed woodenly. "Easy enough to say. But divided loyalties are about the most difficult test a police officer has to face."

"Oh, I know that, sir." Hazel's tone was

heartfelt.

"Yes, you do, don't you?" he said softly. DI Norris reached a decision. "It's not exactly by the book, but I can see that I stand to gain more than I stand to lose. All right, set it up. We'll compare the profiles. If we learn nothing helpful, no one who doesn't already know should learn it was ever done."

"Yes, sir. Thank you, sir." She headed for his door, a lightness in her step from the sense of a difficult job well done.

"Miss Best?"

Hazel paused in the doorway and looked back. "Sir?"

"You can tell Lord Byrfield I've no idea who this friend of yours is."

CHAPTER 13

Some sense of Norris's mounting frustration must have found its way to the forensic science laboratory, because the results he was waiting for started coming back on the Wednesday.

Edwin Norris remembered when forensic results were delivered in person because the white-coated boffins who produced them didn't trust the down-at-heel coppers who'd ordered them to understand what they meant. Now everyone in a police station, including the tea lady, was expected to be able to read a DNA profile, and the results came by fax.

The detective inspector spent half an hour studying the papers in front of him, making sure that he understood them, making sure that his reading was confirmed by the accompanying report. This wasn't something you wanted to get wrong. He was about to tell a woman that the son she'd believed to be safe with his father in Ireland, who'd sent her Christmas cards and birthday cards as regular as clockwork, had been quietly moldering under a grassy mound within a mile of her home for thirty years, until his own brother dug him up. Norris didn't want to have to go back to her tomorrow to say, "Well, actually, we may have got that wrong. . . ."

But there was no room for doubt. The profile extracted from the sad remains in the little grave matched exactly the swab provided by David Sperrin. Same mother, same father. The grave was that of Jamie Sperrin, and Edwin Norris had the unenviable task of telling Diana.

He wanted David there, too, to support his mother. Her world was about to be blown apart. The fact that it had been built on a false premise would be precious little comfort. So he drove first to Byrfield. When the twenty-eighth earl answered the door, Norris had to remember not to wink at him. The deal had required discretion unless something turned up that left him no discretion to use. Well, that wasn't going to be a problem now.

"I'm looking for Mr. Sperrin," he said, his special policeman's expression that was noncommittal to the point of stony cranked into place.

They were in the library. There seemed to be some sort of a game going on. It involved the books that lined the walls to above head height, and occupied the two men who were scanning the spines intently, but not Hazel, who was sitting in a chair half turned away from them, leafing through a magazine and looking bored. Even the white dog seemed more interested in the game, gazing up at the shelves as if they had some meaning for her. But the dog was just looking where her owner was looking.

The other thing that DI Norris's well-honed observational skills told him was that David Sperrin had expected to win and was, in fact, losing. There was a flush on his face, and an exasperated grin, as if losing was something that happened to other people and any moment now this paradox would resolve itself and events play out as they were meant to. Norris let his view expand to take in Gabriel Ash's face. Ash was enjoying the game, too. He enjoyed winning, even if he didn't wear his emotions as plainly as Sperrin did. And the role reversal that so startled Sperrin was no surprise at all to Ash. He might look like someone you'd meet at the allotments, Norris realized, but he thought like someone you'd meet in a chess tournament.

The DI cleared his throat. "Mr. Sperrin, could I have a word?"

"Sure." A cynic might have thought he was glad to be called away before Ash's impending victory became a matter of record. What a cynic, or even a policeman, would not have thought was that David Sperrin was in any way troubled by the detective's visit. "What can I do for you?"

"I'm heading down for a word with your mother," said Norris quietly. "It might be helpful if you were there, too."

"Me?" Sperrin raised dark eyebrows. "I will if you want, but I wouldn't recommend it. My mother and I in the same room isn't a recipe for calm and productive discussion."

"She might need someone to stay with her."

"*My* mother?" hooted Sperrin. "You have met her, have you?"

And then, finding every eye in the room on him, and with Hazel coming quietly from her chair to stand beside him, the thing DI Norris wasn't saying — or wasn't saying yet, was preparing him for — got through to David Sperrin. The color drained from his face as if an artery had been cut. "No," he said, and his voice was hollow. "That isn't possible. You've made a mistake. Someone's made a mistake." And then he swayed, and hands reached for him and steered him to one of the leather benches.

Byrfield went to get him a glass of water, thought better of it, and came back with a shot of whiskey. He gave Norris a defensive look. "He's not going to be driving, is he?"

The peat-scented spirit, or perhaps the time it took to drink it, got Sperrin over the shock and back to his default position, which was to argue. "You *are* wrong," he insisted. "We hear from him two or three times a year. We always have done. Who's been sending the Christmas cards if it isn't Jamie?"

Norris didn't want to speculate. Hazel, who wasn't here in a professional capacity, saw no reason not to help him to the obvious conclusion. "It might have been your father. To reassure Diana that Jamie was safe."

"For thirty years?"

"I suppose, once the expectation was formed, it was easier to keep meeting it than to stop and risk her wondering why. It might have brought up the whole business of the abduction again. Easier just to keep sending the cards."

Sperrin swiveled back toward the DI.

"You're sure? I mean, you're absolutely sure?"

Norris nodded. "The DNA doesn't leave any room for doubt."

The younger man swallowed. "You said he was shot?"

"That's right, sir." There was no need to go into any more detail than that, not yet.

Sperrin took another bite out of the whiskey. But even as he did so, he was thinking. "But was it murder? Could it have been an accident? I mean, kids — country kids — get hold of loaded shotguns all the time. Usually someone grabs them back quickly enough, but . . . *Could* it have been an accident?" He sounded desperate for a crumb of hope.

All Norris's instincts were on high alert. "What makes you think it was a shotgun?"

"Because that's what people prop up in their kitchens in places like this! Not Uzis, not AK-47s, not Peacemaker Colts, but shotguns. Of course it's stupid. But it happens."

"Was there a shotgun in your kitchen when you were a child?"

"Our house? Never." Sperrin seemed certain. "My mother wouldn't have guns anywhere near her. Not even toy ones. She didn't think they were a suitable thing for children to play with."

"What about your father?"

"I don't remember him, Inspector. I was too small when he left. But it would be my mother's view that counted."

Norris sighed. "Well, however it happened, it *was* a shotgun injury. It would have been immediately fatal. As to whether it was an accident or murder, we're going to have to ask someone who was there when it happened. It *could* have been an accident. But finding him in an unmarked grave thirty years later makes it a suspicious death — one that needs investigating until we're sure exactly who did what."

Sperrin was breathing carefully, as if he might lose the knack if he didn't concentrate. "You're going to tell my mother? Now?"

The policeman nodded. "That's why I want you there. It'll come as a shock."

"Oh yes," said Sperrin unsteadily. "The thing is, I really wasn't joking. My presence won't make it any easier for my mother, it'll only irritate her. She decided that about thirty years ago, too." He looked around him in a kind of quiet desperation until his gaze found Hazel. "I don't suppose you'd . . ."

She didn't even have to think. "Of course

I will. I'll stay with her as long as she wants me to, and help her with whatever needs doing." She looked across at Ash. "Let my dad know where I am."

Diana Sperrin was in her studio, working furiously. This was evident from the length of time it took her to answer DI Norris's knock at her door, and the amount of paint spattered about her person when she did. Not just her smock, which was designed for the job, but her hands, her arms, her face, and her wild gray frizz of hair were decorated with blobs and trails in a dozen different colors, some of them nameless.

She must have thought it was David again. She flung the door wide and demanded, *"What?"* in a tone of the utmost annoyance.

Finding a policeman on her doorstep pulled her up short. She did a sort of double take. Then she recognized Hazel, and the machinery of her mind spun and whirred, trying out theories as to what could have brought those two to her door together.

Hazel saw the moment when she hit the right one. Something like a shock wave passed through the older woman's face, and her paint-spattered arms dropped to her sides. Her voice was a low moan. "No . . ."

Hazel had done this before. Every police

officer had. She'd worked hard at finding the balance between breaking it gently and prolonging the agony, and she thought she was quite good at it. People said it got easier with time, but it hadn't yet. "I'm sorry, Diana," she said quietly. "It isn't good news."

Inside, Edwin Norris found himself relegated to the kitchen to make tea. He had the seniority, and he also had the information, but until the news had sunk in, what Diana Sperrin needed most was comfort, and Hazel could sit with her and hold her hand without it feeling inappropriate.

He wandered around the tiny kitchen looking for things, but that was all right — he was in no hurry. By the time he'd set the tray — none of the cups matched because all the ones that did had brushes steeping in them — and brewed the tea, the brute facts of the situation were getting through to Diana, pushing some blood back into her face and some strength into her slumped body. She hadn't just lost her son: she'd lost him thirty years ago, only it had taken till now for the news to get here. Perhaps, thought Norris, pouring her tea, a part of her had always known. Perhaps she'd striven to keep the faith when she'd actually known, at a bone-deep, womb-deep level, that if James had been alive he'd have called her, or come to see her, or *something* at some time in the last twenty years. Of course, even after he was a grown man he'd still have been disabled. But she might have expected to hear something from him or about him. Something more than a signature scrawled on a Christmas card. When she didn't, surely some deep internal instinct must have offered an explanation.

Hazel was saying, "DI Norris has already told David. He was upset, of course. We thought it would be better if I came to sit with you for a bit. But if you want him, we can call. He'll be here in a few minutes."

Diana straightened in her chair — ramrod straight. "I don't need David. I don't need anyone." She managed a tiny flicker of a smile in Hazel's direction. "Thank you for coming, but I'll be all right now." She looked at Norris. "Is there anything I need to do? Undertakers . . . anything?"

Norris shook his head. "Not right now. I'll take care of him for the moment. You and I will need to chat again, but it doesn't need to be now. All you need to do for now is look after yourself. You really shouldn't be alone."

"I'll be fine," she retorted, a hint of the old testiness coming back as the shock subsided. "I suppose . . ." She blinked a sudden mistiness out of her eyes. "I suppose you're sure? I mean, after thirty years . . . ?"

The policeman nodded somberly. "David gave us a swab for DNA."

"And, of course, they have the same genetics." Diana was nodding slowly, hypnotically. Then she barked a little laugh. "They weren't very alike, my two sons, but of course they shared that."

Despite Norris's concern, and Hazel's willingness, Diana really didn't want anyone to stay with her. She wanted to be alone. She had always dealt with things best on her own, and this was no exception. She saw them to the door.

"I'll come and see you again in a couple of days," said the detective inspector. He gave her his card. "If you want to talk to me before that, or if you want anything, call me. And I think Miss Best is staying at the big house for a few more days?" An elevated eyebrow asked the question, and Hazel confirmed with a nod.

"I know we let you down before," said Norris quietly. "When James went missing. Efforts *were* made, both here and in Ireland, to find your husband, but I suppose no one appreciated what it was they were seeking him *for*. Now we do. If it's humanly possible, we'll find Saul now and we'll find out what happened."

"Yes," said Diana Sperrin distantly. "Good."

Walking back to his car, Norris said to Hazel, "Whatever she says, you might keep an eye on her. She might think she's over the shock already, but I don't think it's hit her yet."

Hazel thought he was probably right. "If she wants some details, how much should I tell her?"

"Anything you know and think would help her. After thirty years of wondering, some facts may be all we can give her."

Hazel was surprised. "You mean, until you find Saul."

"Until then, yes," agreed Norris. He looked at her sidelong. "I meant what I said — we'll pull the stops out. But it won't be easy, and it won't be quick. And it's possible we won't get any further this time than we did before."

"I don't think I should tell her *that*!"

"No." Norris sighed. "But she may very well guess."

CHAPTER 14

Unless you counted the dog, Hazel and Ash were alone in the dining room that evening. Sperrin didn't appear at all. Byrfield appeared briefly, worried and apologetic, and filled a tray to take upstairs. "I have some fences to mend with my mother."

Patience looked up sweetly. Anything to keep the old dear from wandering off, she said; and Ash, embarrassed because he always forgot other people couldn't hear her, shushed urgently, and Hazel exchanged a long-suffering look for Byrfield's puzzled one because neither of them knew why.

For a minute longer, like aristocracy in a play, they sat at either end of the long table. Then Hazel moved her meal up to Ash's end and they ate for a while in silence, both occupied with their own thoughts.

Hazel was picking over her own contribution to the Byrfield family's falling-out. She'd advised Pete to talk to his mother;

he'd taken her advice, and this was the outcome. That didn't make it bad advice, necessarily; but it did make Hazel wonder if she should be a little more circumspect about giving advice generally.

Finally, looking up with a rueful smile, Hazel said, "I'm sorry about all this. When I talked you into coming to visit my father, I never guessed we'd still be here six days later. Was there anything you were rushing back for?"

Even as she said it, she realized how silly it was. There was only one matter in Gabriel Ash's life that was of any consequence at all, and there had been no news about his family since the day four years earlier that he'd got in from work and found them gone. Since Patience was with them, he had nothing to return to, much less to hurry for. There was probably no one else in England as amenable to being hijacked from his usual routine and kept almost under house arrest in a comfortable country mansion.

"Nothing," he reassured her. "I wanted to see Stephen Graves and I've done that. He mentioned a couple of other people I could talk to, and I can do that from here if we're going to be at Byrfield much longer. Not because there's any urgency, just for something to do. Graves didn't hold out much hope that any of them could help, and I don't, either. You just feel" — he shrugged self-deprecatingly — "you have to explore every avenue. Then you don't ask yourself later if you missed something, gave up too soon."

"Gabriel," Hazel said softly, "you've been at this for four years. Whatever you do next, you've left it too late to give up too soon."

When he'd deciphered the syntax, he gave her a painful little smile. "It's all right, you know. I'm really not holding my breath. I'm not going to fall apart again if I can't work up a viable lead. It's just that I've nothing better to do."

That wasn't entirely honest, and both of them knew it. For the rest of his life, or as long as he had the mental and physical strength, Ash was going to do anything he could, anything that occurred to him, to find out what became of his family. To track down the people responsible. But, realistically, he was aware that the chances of a breakthrough, of any kind of success, had diminished by now to almost nothing. They'd been at their best when he was living as a hermit on Orkney, desperate to convince the kidnappers he posed them no threat. If any hope survived that time, probably it vanished when he made a very public scene in the heart of London. It would be a miracle now if he picked up a trail leading anywhere. But that's the thing about miracles: You can never quite dismiss the possibility.

"Actually," said Hazel, wondering if it was impertinent but deciding to say it anyway, "there *is* something you should be doing."

Trusting her, he failed to see the trap. "What?"

"You should be building a life for yourself."

Ash continued regarding her over the corner of the massive table for a long time. She met his gaze and held it steady. She wasn't going to apologize and change the subject. Maybe she had no right to tell him this, but someone needed to.

Finally he said, "I had the life I wanted."

"Yes," said Hazel. "And now you don't. Gabriel, I don't want you to stop missing your wife and sons. I don't want you to stop looking for them. But I want you to have a life as well. The search can be the most important thing that you do without being the only thing that you do. I don't want you to invest so much of yourself in it that there's nothing left over."

She meant *if you fail,* and Ash knew she

167

meant that. He took a moment to marshal his thoughts. Then he said quietly, "You didn't know me a year ago. In a way I wish you had. Not because that's how I like to be remembered. And not because I think you could do with a shaking, although sometimes I do think that. But because then you'd know what a difference you've made to me. You, and Patience.

"I know that . . . how I am . . . exasperates you sometimes. It exasperates me. But I remember how I was a year ago, and I don't think you have any idea. I *have* a life now. It may not be what I hoped for when I was at Oxford, but it's worthwhile and even rewarding in a modest way, and when I think back to how I was before I knew you, I can't believe how far I've come. It's like I spent three years trying to drag my face out of the gutter, and now I'm walking on the pavement with the normal people — and you want to know why I'm not riding a skateboard!"

Hazel had been determined not to apologize for caring about him. But he'd shamed her into it. "Gabriel, I'm sorry. I didn't mean to belittle the progress you've made. I mean well, you know, even if it doesn't always seem like it. What is it they say about good intentions?"

"That the road to hell is paved with them," said Ash. "They don't know what they're talking about. Intention is the only difference between an accident and murder. Good intentions is about all we *can* promise one another. None of us knows how things will work out — all we can do is try to do what we think is right.

"I know you're on my side. I know, and I don't think you do, that if I'd never met you and someone else had taken Patience home from the animal shelter, I would still be facedown in the dirt. I wish I could explain to you how much richer my life is for having you in it."

Warm with pleasure, on impulse she reached out and laid her hand over his wrist. Ash replied with his solemn, studious-child smile. Under the table she felt the soft rhythmic thump of the dog's tail against her ankle. "If I need slapping down sometimes," she said, "feel free to slap."

"If I need a poke with a sharp stick," said Ash, "poke away."

From under the table Patience murmured hopefully, And if I need a nice bit of fried liver sometimes . . .

Hazel helped herself to fruit from the sideboard. She looked up at the ceiling. "I wonder how that's going."

Ash winced. "Not easily. I can't see the countess throwing an arm around him and telling him it was a mistake anyone could make."

"She never was an easy woman to get on with."

"And by and large, people — unlike wine — don't improve with age."

The meal having been done as much justice as two people could do it, Hazel headed for the kitchen door. "Say good night to Pete for me, will you?"

Ash glanced at the shot-silk evening sky. "Can we walk with you? Patience likes a stroll before bedtime."

At first they walked in a companionable silence. But Ash was still pondering the enigma of the Byrfield family dynamic. "Pete's mother might not be the sweetest-natured woman in the world," he said, worrying at it like a troublesome tooth, "but it's a big step from being sharp with the staff to murdering your own child. What has she ever done to make Pete think she was capable of that?"

Hazel hadn't told him about Byrfield's fears, which had been shared with her as a confidence. She stopped, thunderstruck, and stared at him in the deepening twilight.

"What . . . why . . . what makes you think
. . . ?"

Ash blinked at her. "I haven't passed the
last six days in a drug-induced coma! When
David was so certain it couldn't be *his*
brother he'd dug up, and Norris said the
child was disabled, Pete started to worry.
Really worry. He called his sister up from
London, and had a stand-up argument with
his mother. Bits of which percolated through
shut doors and plastered ceilings. There
might be other explanations, but that
seemed the likeliest one. Are you saying I
got it wrong?"

"Well — no," admitted Hazel. "But it was
supposed to be a secret. I wouldn't want
Pete thinking I'd been gossiping about it."

"Of course not." It was one of the things
he was good at: keeping his own counsel.
And another was this: putting together snippets of overheard conversations and significant exchanges of looks, and the things
people were about to say and then didn't,
and arriving at a conclusion that might have
occurred to almost no one else. Sometimes
he *was* wrong, but not often. Being right
was the basis of both his careers, first as an
insurance investigator, then as a security
analyst. It was hard to keep secrets from
him, even now.

Especially when it meant keeping them from Patience as well.

Hazel, recovering her composure, decided there was nothing to be lost now by answering his question. "I've never heard that she's done anything dreadful. But then, I didn't grow up in her house. Pete would have a better idea what she's capable of than I would."

"People seem to remember his father more fondly. You said he helped David get to university?"

She nodded. "It was the sort of thing he'd do from time to time — identify a need and step in. He didn't have to. But he recognized that David had the brains to do well, and maybe needed to get away from Burford, but wouldn't have made it on his own."

"Diana couldn't help?"

"Diana's talented, but I don't think she makes a lot of money from her painting."

Again, Ash seemed to hear what she hadn't said. "Do you suppose she'd have helped him if she could?"

Hazel had her mouth open to say "Of course she would," then shut it again and thought. "I don't know. That's another family that doesn't enjoy the easiest relationship."

"David's convinced his mother doesn't

like him. I wonder if he knows why."

"Apart from him being a loudmouthed smart-arse, you mean?" In the dusk they smiled at each other. Hazel went on thoughtfully. "I suppose losing her elder son — I know she thought he was safe with his father, but she'd still lost him — was bound to affect how she related to the one she had left. She might have smothered him, kept him close for fear of losing him, too. Maybe what she did instead was put a distance between them so that if Saul came back for David, she wouldn't be hurt as much. And once she started telling herself that losing her younger child would be less of a wrench, the rest followed. She convinced herself that Jamie was the precious one, the perfect one. David was an also-ran."

"He didn't know that his brother was disabled," murmured Ash.

"I suppose he was too young to have noticed. And Diana may have edited her memory of him — really does remember him as perfect. Which is a lot easier to do with someone you've lost than someone you see every day."

They'd nearly reached the gate lodge. A battered horse box rumbled past the end of the drive.

"I wonder what happened," Hazel mused.

"Saul Sperrin hardly went to the trouble of coming back here to murder his elder son. And then there's that grave — that took time, and trouble, and love. He must have wanted Jamie with him. But something went wrong. Perhaps the child panicked, started yelling for his mother, and Saul tried to hush him and managed to suffocate him. Something like that?"

"It's possible," agreed Ash. "Jamie might have been his son, but he was breaking the law by abducting him. It would have been important to get away without causing a disturbance."

"It's the cards that break my heart," admitted Hazel. "Thirty years' worth of Christmas and birthday cards that he shopped for and sent, all the time knowing Jamie was buried a short walk from his mother's house."

"I suppose the search for a man who'd taken his own child back to his own country was never going to be as intense as a murder hunt. While Diana thought Jamie was safe, Saul was safe, too. At least" — he paused as another trailer rattled past — "safer than he would have been with the police forces of two countries hunting for him."

"Well, they'll be hunting for him now."

"Do you suppose they'll find him?"

"It's not easy to disappear for good," said Hazel. "So many things these days mean having to prove who you are — financial transactions, traveling, getting a child into school — and a flag comes up on a computer to say you're being sought. It was easier thirty years ago."

"Yes. But that applies more to people like us — the settled community." Ash said it with hardly a trace of irony. "Travelers are still hard to keep tabs on. It's the nature of their life — it suits them, and you have to conclude it suits the authorities, too. If Saul Sperrin hadn't been a gypsy, he'd have been found years ago. But for someone wanting to assume a new identity, the traveling community is a good place to do it, and thirty years should be time enough."

Though Hazel nodded, her attention was elsewhere. She was looking up the Burford road with a puzzled expression. "Isn't it a bit late for people to be going to a horse show?"

"Er — I suppose." Her ability to ride two trains of thought at the same time always unsettled Ash slightly.

"And here comes another," said Hazel, stepping back to let the trailer pass and then craning on tiptoe. "And . . . yes, it's another black-and-white one."

Ash frowned. "The trailer?" He'd have put a fair bit of money behind his judgment that it was, although in need of painting, brown.

"The occupant of the trailer. In the three trailers that have passed us there were a total of five horses, and three of them were black and white. What does that tell you?" She looked at him expectantly.

Ash was slowly smiling. "Not a horse show — a fair. A gypsy horse fair. They're going to park up somewhere overnight and trade tomorrow."

"Exactly." Hazel sounded like a schoolteacher who's finally got one of her dimmer pupils to recognize the difference between *there* and *their*. "Now, if those trailers are passing every couple of minutes, it seems likely that the fairground isn't too far from here. Come on, the car's right here — let's follow."

"Now?" Ash had always been someone who planned ahead. Hazel's impetuosity startled and often alarmed him.

"Of course now." She had the gate lodge door open and was shouting to her father. "Why not — do you turn back into a pumpkin at midnight?"

"I just feel we ought to think this through."

"I have," she assured him. "I think those trailers are going to meet up with a whole lot of other trailers, and about half the people towing them are going to be related, one way or another, to Saul Sperrin. If they don't know where he is, or even if he's still alive, no one will."

"You're probably right," conceded Ash. "But Saul Sperrin is now a murder suspect. Looking for him is the job of the police."

"I *am* the police."

He took in her determined expression and refrained from pointing out that she was a fairly recent component of the police and was currently on sick leave. "I mean Detective Inspector Norris won't thank us for interfering in his investigation. If there are people at the fair who know where Sperrin is, he'll want to be the one asking them."

"But he isn't here," she explained, unnecessarily, "and we are. If we don't follow these trailers, they'll disappear into the countryside and Norris won't know where to begin looking for them. Plus, even if he finds them, if the police show up at that fair tomorrow, no one will admit to knowing anything. Tonight, in the dark, with people arriving from all over England, with people unloading ponies and unhitching caravans, and everybody tired and wanting something to eat, it'll be chaos. There'll be lots of strange faces about. Anybody could wander around asking a few questions, as long as he doesn't seem too pushy and doesn't look like a policeman. Neither of us looks like a policeman. You look like a gypsy at the best of times. And Patience is the perfect dog for the job. No one who sees us walking our lurcher will challenge our right to be there."

Ash was horribly afraid that she was right. Afraid, because he knew that what she was proposing was dangerous. He knew he couldn't talk sense into her when Hazel was in this mood. He looked down at his shoes. All he could do was refuse to go, and if he did that, she would go alone. "I should let Pete know. . . ."

"We'll phone him. You know — that little gismo I made you buy, that you're supposed to carry with you but which, in fact, leaves home even less often than you do? It's really clever. You tell it some numbers, and then you can talk to somebody even farther away than the end of the street. Get in."

Hazel was already starting the engine. Ash let Patience onto the backseat and climbed in the front. "All right, so we're going to a gypsy horse fair and we're going to ask if anyone knows where Saul Sperrin is. Even if we ask someone who knows, do you really think he's going to tell us?"

"Probably not," she said ironically, "if I

say he's wanted for murder! I'm not stupid, Gabriel. I've no intentions of starting a fight. I'll just say" — she slowed down, thinking it through as the words came — "I need to talk to him about a horse. I'll say someone died and left him a horse, but if I can't find him, it'll go to someone else. The gypsy hasn't been born who'd pass up the chance of a gift horse. Rather than let that happen, someone will remember where Saul Sperrin hangs out these days and how to get in touch with him."

Ash was unconvinced. "He was Saul Sperrin thirty years ago. He may have been someone else for most of the time since."

"He may have been someone else as far as the authorities are concerned. My bet is, among people who've known *his* people back to Finn MacCool, he's *still* Saul Sperrin. Or at least they'll know who I mean. Maybe we'll get lucky and he'll be here. But if not, maybe someone will let him know he's due a horse and he'll come looking for me."

"Hazel — are you sure you *want* him looking for you? This is a man who may well have killed his own ten-year-old son. Maybe it was an accident, but even so it's the kind of accident that happens more to people who're quicker with their fists than their

179

brains. And he's had thirty years to get over whatever guilt he felt, to get used to the idea that he got away with it. If some stranger starts asking questions about him, the prospect of a gift horse may not be enough to stop him wanting to shut you up."

"Then aren't I lucky to have someone to protect me?"

Ash felt himself flush. "Hazel, you know I'm not much good in a fight. I'll do my best, but you really don't want me to be the only thing standing between you and physical injury."

There was a moment's silence. Then she said cheerfully, "It won't come to that. I'll be careful."

As they drove down the road, Ash heard a modest voice from the backseat saying, Actually, I think she meant me.

CHAPTER 15

They drove for fifteen minutes into the night. Twice, unsure which way to turn, Hazel pulled over and waited until another horse box came trundling along. Both times a pied rump was visible over the tailboard, and when she had let it get far enough ahead to avoid suspicion, she pulled out and followed. The second time she kept the tail-lights in view until suddenly they glowed extra red and the tow car began pulling off into a field on the right. All across the field were the lights of other vehicles, cars and lorries, caravans ancient and modern, and the flickering light of campfires. It was a scene that touched something primitive in Hazel's heart, and she could not have said whether it was a good thing or a bad thing — yearning, or fear.

Ash had his mouth open to say, "You're not going in, are you?" when she did.

They were, he felt sure, about to be challenged, when Hazel did one of those very clever things that kept surprising him. She was a lot younger than him, most people would not have accused her of sophistication, and everyone who met her — unless already in handcuffs — marked her down as a pleasant girl, a kind girl, a nice girl, rather than a smart girl. Being pleasant and kind and nice can be an effective disguise. Ash had known her long enough now to realize she was a lot smarter than most people gave her credit for.

So as they approached the knot of men by the gate, men keeping a casual but still keen eye on who was arriving, she lifted one hand off the steering wheel to wave to them — and then lifted it higher still and waved energetically to some imaginary friend in the crowd farther up the field. Nodding vigorously that she was on her way, and with a last friendly wave to the men at the gate, she drove steadily through the press of bodies, human and equine, and the randomly parked vehicles toward a vacant spot near the far hedge. And nobody, Ash realized, nobody at all was watching them. Hazel had performed her fitting-in magic again. Somehow, nobody ever looked at her and saw a stranger. Even here, where almost every head was dark and every skin tanned, her fair hair and rosy, freckled face did not mark her as different.

And somehow, because of that, and because in this place of friends and families people let their guard down without even knowing they were doing it, she was able to talk to the travelers as easily as she passed among them. Ash, bemused, moved in her wake and offered no contribution beyond his own vaguely Romany looks; and he marveled at how these private, suspicious people who had never seen her before took her on trust, and chatted away without realizing they were being questioned, and offered her and her companion mugs of strong tea from the supper fires.

Patience, too, was attracting admirers. Several of the children, yawning with tiredness, paused to stroke her, and one of the men offered to buy her. Ash gave a troubled, apologetic shrug. "I'm sorry, I couldn't . . ."

"Okay," came the amiable reply, but Ash felt eyes following him afterward in a way that they had not before.

When they were alone, Hazel hissed, "Try to keep your mouth shut. The moment you speak, it's like a great big neon INTERLOPER sign flashing over your head."

Ash knew it. What he didn't understand was why the same sign didn't light up when

Hazel spoke. She didn't sound like a gypsy any more than she looked like one, and yet she could chatter away for half an hour without raising either hackles or suspicions. "It's probably getting time we left."

Hazel nodded. "I've one more guy to talk to. He's down by the gate. We'll take the car."

Ash allowed himself a tiny sigh of relief. At least, if they had the car with them, they could make a run for it if they were rumbled. "This guy — does he know where Sperrin is?"

"Maybe," murmured Hazel. "No one else seems to. But they all reckon if anybody's going to know, it'll be Swanleigh."

"Swanleigh?"

Hazel gave a graceful shrug. "That's his name."

They found Swanleigh, as directed, by the gate. He was a big man in his fifties; something about the way other men were orbiting around him, going where he pointed and laughing when he made a joke, suggested he was one of the movers and shakers in the camp. Hazel wound her window right down and leaned her elbow on it. "Are you Swanleigh?"

He looked her up and down, took in the dark man beside her and the white lurcher on the backseat, and did a sort of facial shrug. "Who's asking?"

Hazel left the car running and got out. "My name's Hazel Best. Everyone's telling me you're the man I should be talking to."

One thick eyebrow lifted quizzically. "About the fair, is it?"

"No. But it is about a horse. It's not my horse — it belongs to Saul Sperrin, except he doesn't know it yet. Is he here, do you know? Or is he coming?"

The big man's head tilted over to one side in a manner he clearly believed made him look cunning. "A horse now, is it?"

"A horse and a half." Hazel laughed. "Damn great black-and-white thing with more hair than a seventies rock group, and it's eating me out of house and home!"

"And this is Saul's horse?"

"It belonged to a neighbor of mine. She was traveler folk. When she died, I said I'd look after it until the solicitors could contact Saul to collect it. But they say they can't find him. And I can't keep it for much longer — I need the stable. I'm going to have to sell it and give the money to the solicitors to dole out among the other heirs."

"Don't be doing that!" exclaimed Swanleigh, horrified, as if she'd suggested barbecuing the animal. "I'm sure we can find

185

your man for you. Saul Sperrin, you say?"

Hazel nodded. "You know him?"

"Oh yes, yes," agreed the big man. "Now, I haven't seen him for a little while, but I've a good idea where to find him. You could always —"

She interrupted his hopeful suggestion. "You're not expecting him at the fair tomorrow, then?"

The man shrugged. "Anything's possible. Anyone can turn up at a horse fair. Now, this big colored horse of his — where do you have it?"

Hazel gestured in the direction of Byrfield. "He has family in the area. At least he had."

"We could pick the horse up. You know — for him. . . ."

She shook her head apologetically. "He'll need to collect it himself. The solicitors need him to sign for it. You don't know how I could get hold of him?"

"Saul Sperrin," Swanleigh said again, thoughtfully. "Where was it I saw him last, now? Ireland, I think."

Hazel nodded. "His people were from Ireland."

"Yes, that'd be right."

"Recently?"

"Oh, not very long at all. I'm sure we can

get word to him. Who do you say he should call?"

"Strictly speaking, the solicitors." She gave the name of a firm in Norbold, which would, she felt sure, forgive her the liberty. "But ideally I'd have liked to get together with him, arrange for him to pick the thing up. I could leave you my number." She scribbled it on a piece of paper.

Swanleigh folded it carefully and put it in his pocket. "I'll have him get back to you. Soon as I can get him word."

"Thanks," said Hazel. "Have a good fair."

"Always!" said Swanleigh, beaming.

"How do you *do* that?" whispered Ash, still half holding his breath as Hazel drove unhurriedly away.

"Do what?" she asked innocently. "Lie?"

Ash shook his head. "I know about lying. I've met a lot of liars. It wasn't the lie that swung it. It was the way you . . ." He couldn't find the right words.

"What?" asked Hazel. She was genuinely interested. She welcomed a compliment as well as the next person, but she was still learning her trade, and she valued the assessment of someone who'd been in the security business a lot longer than she had.

"You *belong,*" said Ash carefully. "You

generate an aura of belonging. People trust you because they think you're one of them. Even when you're nothing like them, somehow you talk to them for half a minute and they file you as *us* rather than *them*. You can't teach technique like that. It's more than a skill — it's a kind of magic."

Hazel felt herself blushing, all the more because she knew it was not flattery, but an honest opinion. He was always honest. She wriggled her shoulders self-deprecatingly. "I just find it easy to get on with people. My mother was the same — she couldn't stand in a bus queue without getting all the information on everybody's children. Nobody thought she was nosy. They just recognized that she was interested in them, and on the whole people like that. Most people would rather be friendly than aggressive. Give them a chance and most people will be helpful rather than obstructive."

That hadn't been Ash's experience of the world. He envied her that it had been hers. "You must miss her," he said quietly. "Your mother."

"Yes, of course," she replied frankly. "For a long time I missed her every day. Now, I suppose I think about her less but get more pleasure from it when I do. I've reached the point where it's the good things I remember rather than the terrible sadness of losing her."

"You were very young."

Hazel nodded. "Sixteen isn't a child anymore, but it's a time when you've nowhere near as much confidence as you want people to think you have, when you can really use someone in your corner who knows you well enough to understand that. My dad was brilliant — always was, still is. But it was different. I missed *her*. And I missed having someone to be soft and silly with. To talk about my day, not in terms of objectives achieved but who said what to who and who's frankly *deluded* if they think they can wear green. You can't talk like that with a man. No offense intended, but sometimes you just need another woman."

When he said nothing more, Hazel thought he'd lost interest, and she frowned at the dark road ahead, kicking herself for getting too personal, sharing too much. But hell, he'd *asked*. . . . Then the gleam of oncoming headlights — another horse box heading for the fair — picked up the glitter of tears on his cheeks, and Hazel felt a surge of remorse beneath her breasts.

"Oh dear God, Gabriel, I'm sorry," she stammered. "I'm telling you this stuff? You know."

He nodded, and blew his nose, and rubbed away the tears he hoped she hadn't noticed with the back of his hand. "It's all right," he lied. "It's just . . . it still hits me sometimes. That when I get home they won't be there. Do you want to hear something awful? Sometimes I wish I knew that they were dead. If I knew for sure that my family were dead, I think I could do a better job of grieving for them."

She let go one side of the wheel long enough to squeeze his hand. "There's no such thing as doing it better. Or worse. It's not something we do — it's something we are. We are in mourning. It's a process we go through. Everyone has to find their own way, but it's not something you can get right or wrong. All you can do is come out the other end."

It was four years since a woman had held his hand, even briefly, except to restrain him. There was something startling about it, as if he'd forgotten the sensation. It reminded him how he'd felt the first time Patience licked his hand — how surprised, and how comforted.

Hazel saw him smile in the light from the dashboard and, puzzled but reassured, let go of his hand. After another mile she said hesitantly, "I never mean to hurt you. But I know I do sometimes. Forgive me."

He looked straight ahead. "There's nothing to forgive. You — and Patience — brought me out of a dark place. I think, without you, my life would have been pretty well over. Don't worry about my . . . heightened sensitivities. I'll get better at handling them. If it isn't too much to ask" — a faint grin lifted one corner of his mouth — "just treat me as normal."

Hazel grinned, too. "The moment I work out what that is, I will."

But normal was busy with other people that night. Another mile and she felt the atmosphere in the car change as Ash stiffened, adjusted the wing mirror, watched it steadily. Without turning in his seat, he said, "We're being followed."

Hazel was aware of the car behind them. It had been sitting a hundred meters back for a few minutes now. She'd thought nothing of it. "What makes you think so?"

"It's gone midnight on a remote country road. Everyone else is heading for the fair."

"Except us," she said reasonably.

"My point exactly."

She flashed him a quick sideways look. "Sperrin?"

"Maybe."

She began checking the road ahead for

somewhere to pull in. "We should stop."

Ash's hand caught hers as she reached for the indicator. "No. We shouldn't."

She frowned. "But this is what we came for. To find Saul Sperrin. Well, he's taken the bait."

"He doesn't want to talk to us."

Hazel didn't understand. "How do you know?"

"If he wanted to talk to us," said Ash, still watching the mirror, "he'd be on your bumper, flashing his headlights, not cruising far enough back that we mightn't notice him. He doesn't want to talk to us. He wants to see where we go."

"There's a difference?" But of course there was, and she saw it, too, just a little more slowly. "You mean, he might have something in mind other than conversation. But why? If he believed what I told Swanleigh, he thinks he's getting a horse. If he didn't believe it, or didn't care, why follow us at all?"

"Because he knows something that Swanleigh didn't. That thirty years ago he killed a child. For years and years he must have believed he'd got away with it. But he never forgot that if the police ever found Jamie and then found him, he was going down for murder. A man would be infinitely cautious in a situation like that. Anything strange or unexpected, anything that didn't quite add up, that's the first thing he'd think of. He wants to see where we're going before he commits himself."

By now Hazel's thinking was keeping pace with Ash's. "So we'd better not head for Byrfield. That's bound to set the alarm bells ringing. And I told Swanleigh I had this horse at my place, so it needs to be a stable or a farm or something. If we head for the nearest town with a police station, he'll be gone."

"Call Norris," Ash advised. "Tell him what's happening — that Sperrin's following us and we need to know where to take him so the police can have a welcoming committee waiting."

There they hit a problem. Hazel had DI Norris's number on her phone. But Hazel was driving, and Ash still hadn't mastered his own phone, which was of the simple, big-button variety designed for senile grannies. The chances of him negotiating his way through Hazel's bells-and-whistles model was slightly lower than Patience winning Crufts. But Hazel had seen the consequences too often to use the phone while she was driving.

"Okay," she said. "You drive and I'll call

Norris. It'll be interesting to see what Sperrin does when I pull over."

It took another minute to find a suitable spot. But then the car behind did the only thing it could without confirming their suspicions: It kept traveling, overtook them while they were switching places in a gateway, and drove on steadily until its lights disappeared around the next bend.

"He won't go far," predicted Ash. "He'll be waiting up the next farm lane, with his lights off. Give him five minutes and he'll be on our tail again."

Ash still owned a car. It was locked in the garage behind his mother's house in Norbold. He could have counted on his fingers the number of times he'd driven it since returning to the town where he was born. But he'd been a good driver once, and even in the dark he quickly familiarized himself with Hazel's hatchback. Cars differ one from another less than phones do.

Norris had given her his mobile number, so it was answered not by a police radio-room operator but by a tired, grumpy, and slightly disorientated detective inspector who'd finally gone to bed half an hour before and had just managed to get off to sleep. *"What?"* he demanded angrily.

Hazel told him twice who she was, and

gave him time to absorb the information. She heard his responses become more focused as his brain switched into work mode. Then she told him where she was and what she'd done. "I think it must be Sperrin following us. I can't think who else it would be. Can you suggest somewhere we can meet you — well, not *you*," she added hurriedly, "but a squad car — enough bodies to sit on him if he tries to run?"

Norris didn't have what he needed in front of him — a map, a record of where the area cars were tonight. "Give me five minutes and I'll call you back. Head north when you get a chance — he won't follow you to Byrfield for a whole herd of horses. I'll call you back with a sat-nav reference." Then he was gone, without a word of farewell, much less thanks.

"You're welcome, sir," Hazel said pointedly to the dead phone.

"Shall I keep driving?" asked Ash.

"Yes. He's calling me back. Take your time, though. The longer he has to get ready, the better."

Ash nodded. He found to his surprise that he was rather enjoying himself. He still found Hazel's lightning-fast, intuition-guided decision-making process a little alarming, but he was learning to trust the answers she came up with. She wasn't always right, but then the methodical, textbook approach didn't always work, either. She was right more often than she was wrong. Ash was coming to understand that this was only partly due to good luck. Even when she was thinking quickly she was thinking clearly. And she was guided by a natural goodwill that meant that, though her decisions were occasionally question-able, her motives were always sound and the outcomes often better than could rea-sonably be expected.

And it felt good to be doing something again. For four years he hadn't done much of anything at all. The only movement in his life had come from the winds of chance buf-feting him. Now, with Hazel, he felt as if he was achieving something again. Nothing dramatic — he wasn't trying to persuade himself of that — but here and there he felt to be contributing a little know-how, a little intellectual spadework, that made him feel more alive than he had for years and might ultimately help someone.

Baby steps, Laura Fry had said. He had to measure his progress in baby steps. Well, yes. For a long time any progress had seemed impossible. Baby steps had seemed the most he might manage. Now he was beginning to feel that one day — not now, maybe not even soon, but one day — he might be capable of walking, of living, of operating like a fully-fledged adult man again. In one way, it was a scary prospect. In another, it couldn't come too soon.

He said, "You know, when this is over —"

The flash of lights killed the sentence in his mouth. Not from behind — from the side. Sperrin had waited up a farm lane for them, and now he was coming at them hard and fast. Not following at a distance, shadowing them discreetly, hoping to remain unnoticed until he knew more about them. They heard the roar of his engine as he drove straight at them, a couple of tons of steel accelerating hard from safe conveyance to lethal weapon.

Momentarily his lights blinded them, filling their car. Ash swerved desperately — he might have been out of practice, but the instinct for self-preservation is the last one that you lose — then the other car's grille hit them square in the side and kept coming, the engine note climbing, their own tires squealing a manic protest as sheer momentum forced them sideways across the road. Getting no response from the wheel, Ash just had time to reach back and grab Patience's collar — he'd bought her a seat belt, but she'd refused to wear it — and to see Hazel's mouth wide in indignant astonishment; then the nearside wheels hit the verge, plowed through a foot of soft earth, and disappeared into a deep ditch, tipping the car on its side.

CHAPTER 16

It's easy getting into and out of cars. Most of us do it every day, and think so little of it that we can chat to our companions, talk on the phone, or finish our homework — or at least hone an excuse for *not* finishing our homework — at the same time. But that's because everything is designed to make it easy. The car doors hang perpendicular. The seats are at the right height. Everything is familiar.

Now try turning everything eighty degrees. The doors are no longer perpendicular, their weight carried by strong columns: One can hardly open before it runs into the ground; the other is almost too heavy to lift. The occupants are lying half suspended, possibly half strangled, in their seat belts, certainly stunned, probably concussed or injured. Even the car's instruments are now in the wrong places, the hand brake and gearshift where you're accustomed to finding the floor, the door and window buttons up around your right ear somewhere. Add to that the sudden ingress of cold, muddy water and it's little wonder that people who survive an impact can find it impossible to escape their vehicle afterward and drown in half a meter of ditch water.

Given time — to extricate himself from his seat belt, to drag his feet out from among the pedals and brace them against the dashboard, to make sure he wasn't doing this while standing on Hazel's face — Ash could probably have opened the driver's door. He wasn't, physically, the man he'd been four years ago, but he was well built, and in an emergency he could probably have found the strength necessary. But there was no time. He couldn't see much except a long view up a ditch, brilliantly lit by his own headlights, but he heard the bang of the other car's door as someone got out and the beat of urgent footsteps. People who've deliberately pushed you into a ditch don't come to see if you're all right: they come to finish you off. When a shadow crossed the side window above his head, and a bit of that shadow was long, thin, and straight, Ash wasn't a bit surprised.

He must have been afraid. He must have been. But all he was conscious of was anger.

Not for himself — he hadn't that much to live for, hadn't had for a while — but for Hazel Best, who was twenty-six years old and had people who loved her and should live long enough to be a good police officer, a loving mother, and a doting grandma.

It made no difference to the weight of the door. It was too great to throw up with one hand and scramble out faster than Saul Sperrin could fire a shotgun. About all Ash could do in the time he had left was fumble for the button to open the windows. In a parade-ground roar quite unlike his normal speaking voice, he rapped, "Turn around. Now. Before either of us sees your face."

There was a gasp beside him. "Gabriel . . ."

Hazel wasn't worrying about the shotgun. She hadn't time to. It was taking all her energy to keep her face out of the muddy water pouring through her open window.

Ash hadn't thought of that. He threw off his seat belt and screwed his body around, holding her head with one hand, groping under the water for the catch that would free her with the other. But maybe that was wrong; maybe he should concentrate on getting the window shut. The water was still flooding in. If he couldn't free her soon, she was going to drown in his arms.

"Help me!" he yelled, his voice running up shrill, so distraught that he failed to see the inherent improbability of the man who'd run them into this ditch, who was pointing a shotgun at them, now abandoning his murderous agenda in order to help Ash save his friend. "You have to help me. She's going to die!"

"Yes." It was all that Sperrin said. The only word Ash heard him speak from beginning to end, shocking in its very conciseness. He paused a fraction in his desperate fumbling, as if his brain couldn't quite process what it had heard. Then, knowing with absolute certainty that he would get no help from that source, Ash turned his back on the gun, wiped it from his mind, and turned all his attention to Hazel and her plight.

She'd been stunned by the impact, confused to find herself suddenly hanging sideways, with dark water pouring in around her, but she'd never lost consciousness and she, too, was trying desperately to free herself. Her hands slapping frantically for the seat belt release obstructed Ash's attempts to thumb it. He needed her to sit still and do nothing for five seconds; that was all, but it was a lot to ask when those five seconds must have seemed to her like all the rest of her life that she could count on. He toyed briefly — very briefly — with the idea of decking her, decided that she'd probably deck him back and if she knocked him out, they'd both die. Instead he hissed, "Constable — *freeze!*"

And the authority in his voice was such that even in her current predicament she couldn't fail to understand and obey. Her whole body went rigid. Ash's right hand found the seat belt catch and his left hand pulled her out of the rising water and onto his hip. Where a more cynical soul than either of them might have noticed that she formed a pretty effective shield.

But she didn't stay there long. The driver's side window was wide open in front of her nose. With the access of energy only the urge to survive can supply, she clawed and grappled her way across him and up through the window frame. A flash of white in the corner of her right eye told her the third occupant of the car was also jumping ship.

Halfway out she met the business end of the shotgun coming in.

The situation was too far gone for panic. Even so, the steadiness of her voice amazed her. "Saul, you have no idea how bad things are going to get for you if you pull that trigger."

Seconds, sliced into tenths and then into hundredths, crawled past. She knew her heart was racing, but the individual beats pounded a slow march in her ear like a funeral drum. And every beat was precious because any one of them could be her last.

And the gun didn't fire. And the gun didn't fire. And then the gap between the muzzle and the end of her nose began to widen as Saul Sperrin backed cautiously up the muddy bank. And still the gun didn't fire.

And then it did.

At first Hazel couldn't work out if she'd somehow escaped injury or been so devastatingly blasted that her ability to process pain had shut down. She opened her eyes again, but the muzzle flare had been so close and the surrounding night so dark that all she could see was the afterglow impressed on her retina.

Then she thought that in adjusting the angle of his shot to include Ash, who was still half buried beneath her, he'd contrived to miss her altogether. Or nearly — she was beginning to feel the sting of individual pellets in outlying areas. Ash was lying fearfully still beneath her. If that was what had happened, any moment now Sperrin would reload and rectify his error. He was probably doing it already. If you know how, it's a matter of seconds to reload a shotgun. There wasn't a chance in the world she could finish scrambling out of this car and make a run for it before he could shoot again.

But you don't just wait. Even when living is no longer an option, there may be some choice about how you die. Hazel didn't want to die stuck in this window like a rat up a drainpipe, like an unfortunate lover surprised by the untimely return of the husband. She kicked and wriggled hard and — like a baby struggling to be born — got first her shoulders and then her hips through the narrow gap, and then there was nothing to stop her. She rolled across the verge, kept rolling across the gritty road, and flung herself into the deep shadow of the opposite hedge. The tangled overgrowth wouldn't stop a blast from a shotgun, but it might prevent the gunman from seeing her clearly enough to shoot.

She got her knees underneath her — everything seemed to be in working order — and turned back toward the car to meet the next assault. But there was no more gunfire, and after a moment she realized why. The footsteps were retreating. Silhouetted by the headlights of his own car, the man was dad-dancing and swinging his weapon like a club. Hazel heard him yelping.

A shotgun is useful for many things. Defending yourself against a close-quarters attack isn't one of them. The lurcher was too close and too fast; the best he could do was swing the stock at her, and she had no difficulty diving under the blows, fangs-first. Another moment and the car door slammed shut; then the engine roared and Saul Sperrin was fleeing the scene, unsure how much he'd achieved but unwilling to hang around any longer to find out.

Hazel staggered to her feet and just stood in the road, panting, for a moment. But he wasn't coming back — she heard the car accelerate until the distance swallowed its voice. She'd survived — not quite unhurt but substantially uninjured. The dog, too, up on her back legs against Hazel's car, seemed to have given better than she got.

Which left Ash. Hazel hurried to the car, already groping in her pocket for her phone. People do survive shotgun wounds. If she could get an ambulance here quickly enough . . .

He was sitting sideways, with his feet in the water, by the time she got there. "Are you all right?" he asked anxiously.

"Yes," she said. "You?"

"I think so."

Hazel reached for the interior light, but it seemed to be true. Like her, he'd collected a few stray pellets but nothing that couldn't be dealt with by means of tweezers and a bit of local anesthetic.

"Patience?"

"She's fine, Gabriel. I don't think he touched her. She drove him off." She barked a sudden laugh that was more than half hysteria. "We owe our lives to a dog!"

Ash smiled and reached through the open window to fondle Patience's ears. Happy now, the dog responded with a wave of her long white tail. "Why do you think I brought her?"

CHAPTER 17

Hazel had one pellet in her left cheek, two in her upper left arm, one in her other left cheek. None of them had gone deep enough to warrant even a local anesthetic. She lay facedown and gritted her teeth as they came out.

Ash was suffering similar ministrations in another cubicle. Detective Inspector Norris was waiting for them in the corridor, along with Patience. The A&E charge nurse had tried to stop him bringing a dog into the department, but Norris waved away her objections imperiously. "It's a guide dog."

She stared at him in patent disbelief. "That *isn't* a Labrador."

"What are you, some kind of a racist?" The policeman held her eye until she gave up. At his side, Patience put her nose momentarily into his hand before curling up at his feet.

Ash emerged first, Hazel moments later,

both of them walking with the particular care of people whose battle scars would be displayed only to the closest of friends. Norris supplied each of them with a cardboard cup of strong coffee and sat them down. Though he made no comment, he noticed that Hazel was sitting on only one half of her chair, Ash only on the other half of his. "All right. What happened?"

They told him. It didn't take long. The facts were simple enough. They ran into difficulties only when he started asking why.

"Why?" he demanded of Hazel. "Why in the name of all that's holy would you do such a stupid thing? You're a trained police officer. All right, you're still a probationer, but you've been doing this job long enough — and, I was told, well enough — to know we don't base our standard operating procedure on the Disney Channel! If *nothing* had gone wrong — if you hadn't ended up in a ditch with someone firing a shotgun at you — it would still have been an incredibly stupid thing to do, to march into a gypsy camp in the middle of the night and start asking questions about someone we think is a killer. I mean, Constable, whatever made you *think* that was a good idea?"

Hazel blushed to the roots of her hair. When he put it that way — and in all fairness it was a good way of putting it — she knew he was right. Only inexperience and the desperate bravado that comes of feeling you've been sitting on your hands for too long could explain it. She'd embarked on an unnecessarily bravura course of action without consulting the senior investigating officer, or even telling him what she proposed until she was already committed. That fact that they'd both — no, all three of them — walked away pretty much unscathed could only be attributed to overtime on the part of that special angel who watches over children and idiots. She hadn't a single thing to say in her own defense.

But Norris had asked her a question, and she reckoned she owed him an answer. "I thought it was a chance that would pass if I didn't grab it. I didn't expect to find Saul Sperrin; I hoped to find someone who'd seen him recently, who could tell us what part of the country he was in. I thought if we turned up in squad cars, nobody would talk to us, but if I just wandered around chatting to people, someone might. I thought it was one of those occasions when being in the right place at the right time counted for more than careful planning." She raised her head to look at him. "And that was naïve, wasn't it? I'm sorry, sir. I thought I could help. I'm sorry if I've compromised your investigation."

"And so you should be." But his tone was mollified. Of course it had been naïve. Of course it had been wrong. But he seemed to remember a situation not so very different that had confronted a young copper at Tilbury docks maybe twenty years ago, and how he'd chosen to respond; and he'd been wrong, too, but his superiors — after giving him a right royal ear bashing — had hinted that they'd rather have a young officer with too much zeal, too much willingness to get stuck in, than one habitually hiding in the bunker when the balloon went up.

"And the other thing I don't understand," he went on, "is why, having run you off the road and fired a shotgun at you, Sperrin didn't stick around long enough to finish the job."

"I don't understand any of it," said Hazel. "Why he'd come after us when it would have been so much safer to stay away. Why he put us in the ditch when it would have made more sense to follow us, find out who we were. And why he thought it was a good idea to shoot us. Whoever we were, whatever we knew, he was always going to be safer putting distance between us than taking us on. Caution served him well enough for thirty years, so why suddenly go on the offensive? If his son's body had turned up, he couldn't have thought we were the only ones who knew about it. And if it hadn't, then why feel so threatened?"

The DI nodded. Hazel had summarized his own puzzlement pretty accurately. "Mr. Ash?"

"I know why he didn't finish the job," said Ash. "My dog went for him."

"Your dog." Norris looked at Patience; Patience looked at Norris. "Well, maybe," he said diplomatically. "But if I'd steeled myself to commit a double murder, and the shotgun was in my hands, I'm not sure I'd be put off by the prospect of being nipped by a dog."

Nipped? echoed Patience indignantly. *Nipped?* Do I *look* like a Pekingese?

"That's easy to say when she's sitting quietly at your feet getting her ears stroked," said Ash. "Ask the guys in your Dog Branch how many hardened criminals stand their ground with one of their dogs hurtling toward them."

"It's a bit different," suggested Norris. "Those are trained dogs, and the ungodly know it. You can't fire a gun with forty kilos of German shepherd hanging off your arm."

That's true, said Patience sweetly. It's

pretty hard to concentrate with twenty kilos of lurcher swinging on your nuts as well.

"Well, for whatever reason," said Hazel, "he cut and ran. Where would he go? Not back to the fair — he knows we'll look for him there."

"He knows *I'll* look for him there," said Norris pointedly. "And I know I won't find him, and I won't find anyone who's seen him, and I probably won't find anyone who knows him. If he's any sense, he'll be on his way back to Ireland to disappear again."

"Or," said Ash pensively, "he might think that while you're busy watching the road to Holyhead there's a window of opportunity to find out how much trouble he's actually in. What we know, what's happening at Byrfield. He might decide to sneak in for a closer look."

Hazel felt a small anxious buzz behind her breastbone. She hadn't thought of that — that Sperrin might follow them back to base. She'd thought they were safe when he drove away. But Ash was right. What concerned Sperrin was the discovery of his son's body, and that could only happen at Byrfield. If he didn't run, Byrfield was where he'd go instead.

Norris nodded slowly. He'd heard two opinions of Gabriel Ash. He was beginning

213

to recognize which was right. "You ought to get back to Norbold now. You've contributed as much as you usefully can, and maybe" — another pointed look at Hazel — "a little more. I'd be happier with you off the scene now. If anything comes up, I know where to find you."

But it wasn't that simple, not for Hazel. It wasn't that she thought Ash was overstating the danger, and it wasn't that she doubted DI Norris's ability to solve the sad little mystery of the grave by the lake. And if Sperrin went to Byrfield, they shouldn't be there when he arrived. But the plain fact was, while Ash could leave now, Hazel couldn't.

"I can't do a runner and leave my father alone in the gate lodge. If Sperrin goes there looking for a couple in a bent and muddy hatchback, the first person he asks will send him to my dad's home."

"Would Mr. Best tell Sperrin where to find you?"

Hazel had to smother an astonished laugh. Of course, Norris's only experience of Fred Best was as a small older man carrying gardening tools or a ladder. "Of course not! That's not what worries me. What worries me is that he could get hurt *not* telling Sperrin where to find me."

Ash said, "Could we persuade him to come for a few weeks' holiday in the Midlands? He's very welcome to my guest room."

Hazel had seen Ash's guest room. In fact, she'd stayed in it for a week, and rendered it quite comfortable by the time she was leaving. It was now the only part of the big house in Highfield Road that didn't seem to be stuck in a time warp. But she also knew her father.

"I can ask him," she said doubtfully. "I don't think he'll come. It would seem to him like running away."

They all thought about that for a moment. Ash hadn't known Best very long, but he couldn't see him doing something that seemed like running away, either. "She's right," he told DI Norris. "We can't leave now."

The policeman knew when he was beaten. "Then be careful until we track Sperrin down. Don't go out alone at night. In fact, don't go out alone at all. Call me if you even *think* there's someone nosing around."

"Keep Patience with you," Ash said to Hazel. "She'll raise the alarm long before you know there's anyone there."

Hazel nodded. Privately she thought Ash held a generous view of his dog's abilities,

215

but any dog is worth having if you're worried about intruders. And, given the way they'd parted, Sperrin might indeed be unwilling to tangle with this one again.

The promise of dawn was paling the sky by the time Hazel's car had been towed out of the ditch and nursed, rancid and cantankerous, back to Byrfield. Hazel wouldn't wake her father with this; she crept upstairs for a couple of hours in her bed. Ash meant to walk up the drive to Byrfield, then thought better of it. It was a bit soon to be doing exactly what the detective inspector had told him not to do. Instead he kicked off his muddy shoes, put a towel under his damp posterior, and did his best to get comfortable on the cottage-size sofa — a task in which he was not aided by a white lurcher having no trouble at all getting comfortable on him.

CHAPTER 18

Fred Best heard the story over an early breakfast. Even before that, he realized there'd been trouble when he had to slide sideways into the bathroom past a rack of wet clothes.

He didn't comment on the wisdom of his daughter's actions, although one of his eyebrows did. When Hazel tried to suggest he should leave Byrfield for a while, the other rose to join it. She let the suggestion die half born.

Instead she said, "Norris needs a description of Saul Sperrin. We were no use at all — I never saw him clearly enough, neither did Gabriel. Do you remember him?"

Fred Best shook his head. "No, he was long gone before we moved here. I suppose we know now why he stayed away. There will be people in Burford who remember him, but he'd be better talking to Diana. Maybe she has a photograph."

The same idea occurred to Edwin Norris. At just about this time he was knocking on Diana Sperrin's door.

He didn't mean to tell her everything that had happened. But it occurred to him that she, too, could be in danger, and she needed to know that. Perhaps she would take the opportunity to go away for a fortnight. So he described the events of the previous night.

"There's no reason to suppose he'll come here," he said. "He has a good reason to stay away from you. On the other hand, it's sometimes hard to predict what people will do when they think their back's against the wall. Is there anywhere you could go for a few days?"

"Of course there is," said Diana briskly. "But I've no intentions of going there."

The more he saw of this woman, the harder Norris found it to read her. Shock and grief could explain most of that. They show in different ways in different people. In Diana they showed as a kind of distance, as if she was separating herself from what had happened. Every time he saw her she seemed colder, more withdrawn. Whatever paroxysms of anger and distress had shaken her, she'd kept them to the privacy of her own back room. She was, of course, accustomed to dealing with events alone. She'd made an unwise marriage with a man who'd stayed just long enough to father her two children, then disappeared, leaving her to raise them. So far as Norris could determine, the only significant thing he'd done in his sons' lives was end one of them.

"One of my officers" — that was stretching the truth — "asked about Sperrin at a gypsy camp ten miles from here. After she left, someone ran her off the road and fired a shotgun at her. We don't have a positive ID, but it's hard to think who else would do that. Can you give me a description of your husband?"

"I haven't seen him for thirty years."

Norris nodded. "Some things don't change. How tall is he?"

"About my height." Diana Sperrin was tall for a woman but still quite short for a man.

"Hair color?"

"Dark. But he'll be in his mid-sixties now, he's probably gone gray."

"Build?"

"Wiry. But again . . ."

"Thirty years changes people," agreed Norris. "But not always, and not in every way. He may have got fat. He probably hasn't got significantly more muscular. Did he know one end of a shotgun from the

219

other when you knew him?"

"Oh yes," she said with conviction. "He shot rabbits when he was asked to. And snared them when he wasn't."

"And you haven't thought of anything that would help us find him?"

"Inspector Norris," she said, her strong jaw coming up almost belligerently, "if I'd known how to find my husband, don't you think I'd have done it when he took my son? Don't you think I'd have done it at some point in the thirty years since?"

The detective nodded. "I'm sorry for what happened. Sooner or later, we will find him."

"I dare say you will," said Diana resentfully. "Now he's taken a potshot at one of you."

There was no way of keeping what had happened from Sperrin's son, and Ash didn't think it right to try. The man was entitled to know what was going on. It affected him more closely than any of them.

Or would have done if he'd believed it. "Whatever happened thirty years ago," he said roughly, "what possible reason could my father have for shooting at you?"

"We gave him a reason," Ash said quietly, "by going to that camp and asking about him. No one else had anything to gain by following us, let alone trying to kill us."

David Sperrin stared pugnaciously at him. "If he did what he's supposed to have done, why would he be within a hundred miles of this place? All he has to do is live in Ireland under an assumed name and he's safe. If it's worked for thirty years, why would he do anything different?"

Hazel had come up to the house when her father came to work. She poured herself a cup of coffee. "Maybe he thinks thirty years is long enough."

Sperrin turned on her like a machine gunner. "So he chooses just now, when the body's been found, to look up friends and family?"

"He may not have known we found Jamie," said Hazel reasonably. "And the other thing is, he may have been back before. But nobody was looking for him, so nobody realized."

"Do you look like him?" asked Ash. "Neither of us got a good look at the guy last night. But he wasn't a big man, and he seemed fairly quick on his feet."

I told you why that was, Patience said complacently.

"I don't look much like Mum, so I suppose I must," Sperrin admitted reluctantly.

Small and dark. All Hazel could have said about the man with the gun was that he was neither a midget nor a giant. He might have been David Sperrin's double — he might have been David Sperrin — and she wouldn't have known. It had been too dark, and there had been too much going on.

A little later Ash walked Patience as far as the shop in Burford. Byrfield's housekeeper had given him a list of supplies that were running short now she was feeding the five thousand. She'd meant to drive into the village later, but she appreciated his offer and refrained from adding a stone of potatoes to the order.

News of the previous night's events had already run around the village. Ash felt himself the object of curious looks. This was not, per se, a situation he was unfamiliar with, and at least the villagers didn't shy beer cans after him.

They did shy questions. He offered as little information as he could consistent with common courtesy, citing the ongoing investigation. The shopkeeper, an elderly woman with a froth of white hair and the apple cheeks of the terminally jovial, was deliberately slow filling his order so she could keep chivying him for details. Partly in self-defense, he came back with some questions of his own. Then he and Patience walked home. Patience did not carry the newspaper. She was not that kind of dog.

"You were a while," said Hazel, helping to put away the shopping.

"I got waylaid by the old lady in the shop."

"Amelia Perkins," sniffed the housekeeper, whose name was Mrs. Morrison, moving the bread from where Hazel kept it to where she kept it. "Known to one and all as Nosy Perkins."

Ash chuckled. "I can't imagine why."

"Because she thinks owning the only shop is the same as owning the rights to know what everyone in the village is doing, has done, and is thinking of doing." Mrs. Morrison spoke with the quiet steel of someone who didn't like to have her activities observed.

"How long has she been here?" asked Hazel, absentmindedly putting the breakfast rolls into the cupboard from which Mrs. Morrison had just removed the bread. "Did she remember Saul Sperrin?"

"For a little over a hundred years," said Ash, exaggerating slightly, but that was the impression she'd given. "And as a matter of fact, she did. She says David's wrong, he doesn't look like Saul at all. She says he was quite a tall man, with red hair."

223

"Then her memory isn't all she thinks it is," snorted Mrs. Morrison, "because he had black hair. I wouldn't have said he was tall, particularly, though he was well-enough built. Stout, even."

"You've been here for thirty years?" asked Ash, his eyebrows expressing gallant surprise.

"Longer," said Mrs. Morrison, not without some pride. "I came here as maid when I was sixteen. And that's" — she did the sum, didn't want to share the result — "long enough since."

"Did Mr. Morrison work on the estate, too?" asked Ash.

She was a tall, rather angular woman with an austere expression that collapsed like a falling soufflé when she was amused, as now. "Bless us all, there *is* no Mr. Morrison, and never was. It's a professional title. Cooks and housekeepers are always Mrs. It's considered more respectable, particularly if the gentleman is unmarried. Of course, some people will always talk. And sometimes," she confided, moving the breakfast rolls without comment, "there's good reason to talk. Nothing like that here, of course. His lordship's late father was a gentleman through and through."

"I wish people wouldn't keep saying that,"

Hazel said later, when they were alone. "As if Pete'll never be the earl his father was."

"*You* told me what a decent man the" — Ash couldn't remember the numbers — "last earl was."

"I know I did. And it's true. But every time one of us repeats it, somehow it belittles Pete. And Pete's a good man, too. And his father's been dead for nine years."

"What was he like?" asked Ash. "Or rather, *who* was he like — Pete or Vivienne?" He hadn't met the younger daughter.

"The girls. He was rather short and square, and very down-to-earth, and very kind. Imagine Viv in plus fours. I don't know who Pete takes after. He has his dad's personality — thank God he doesn't have his mother's! — but he's much taller, and fairer. Maybe he's a throwback to those early warrior earls. His dad was a farmer through and through. That's where Pete got his love of the land."

Ash smiled. "I take it you favor your mother."

Hazel nodded. "She was from farming stock, too, though not in this part of the world. She came from Lancashire. In the wedding photos, she's bent at the knees so she doesn't loom over my dad. The funny thing is, I never thought of him as a small man until I realized *I* was looming over him as well. I don't think any of his squaddies thought of him as a small man, either. At least they always decided they'd sooner face the enemy than turn around and face him."

Ash chuckled. Hazel looked curiously at him. "What about you? Mummy's boy?"

He laughed out loud. They'd reached that comfortable stage of friendship where they could say almost anything to each other and it wouldn't cause offense if no offense was intended. "I think I'm more like my father. He was a tax inspector — a numbers man. I think that's why I'm always trying to analyze things."

I never knew my father, Patience said piously.

"You must have been a laugh a minute as a kid," Hazel said with a grin.

Ash looked rueful. "I don't think I was ever a kid. I was good at math. I found geography interesting. I was prone to panic attacks at the approach of any kind of ball, and for some reason winning the chess league three years running didn't make me popular, either. I didn't like being a child. I promised myself that when I had —"

And there he stopped. Stopped dead, as if his throat had been cut. Hazel knew what he'd been about to say, knew, too, that for just a moment he'd forgotten. Forgotten what he'd lost. It hardly seemed possible. For four years it probably hadn't been. But life goes on, and normality tries to reestablish itself, however challenging the odds, and for Ash that meant forgetting, just for a moment, that he'd once had two sons and now they were gone.

Even six months ago the reality of that had been so overwhelming that it never left the forefront of his mind. And now, just for a moment, he'd forgotten. The guilt slid between his ribs like a knife. But it was progress of a kind.

Hazel watched him with compassion. "Gabriel — is this a good place for you to be? Would it be better if you took Patience home now?"

He managed a painful smile. "Because there, of course, nothing reminds me of my family."

They sat in silence for some minutes. Hazel said nothing more, just sat with him, keeping him company. She hoped — she had no way of knowing for sure — that there was some comfort in that for him. She didn't know what else to do.

And then she did. "Tell me about them," she said. "Your sons. What they were like. What they did. Who they were."

227

For a moment, as the expression froze on his face, she thought she'd hurt him terribly. But it was just astonishment. In four years almost no one had spoken of them in his presence. It was the place where angels feared to tread. For fear of twisting the knife in the wound, people had hurt him the other way, by almost pretending they'd never existed.

When the surprise passed and his expression softened, Hazel saw she'd guessed right. There was a warmth in his deep-set eyes. There would be tears there, too, soon, but that didn't matter. If a man can't cry for his lost children, what is the world worth?

"Gilbert's the oldest. He'd be eight now. Would be — will be." There was no point struggling with the tenses: Ash knew that Hazel understood that no one knew if those boys were dead or alive. "He takes after me. A lot goes on inside his head. He thinks things out, analyzes them, plans his moves. He likes finding things out. He was just learning to read when they disappeared. He was racing ahead, because he'd realized how much he could get from books once he could read them."

He smiled. "A year before, his default position was 'I'll ask Daddy.' Every time he needed an answer and either no one else knew or no one had the time to explain, he'd just nod wisely and say, 'I'll ask Daddy.' Then, as he came to understand my limitations, it was 'I'll get Daddy to find out.' But once he was reading, it was always 'I'll look it up.' Why the moon changes shape, why things fall down, not up, why grass keeps growing if you cut it but daffodils don't — 'I'll look it up.' He didn't understand everything he read, but he was getting there. He was definitely going to be a scientist of some kind.

"Guy was different in every way. He's much more like his mother — outgoing, gregarious, a people person. You could tell that while he was still in his pram. By the time he was two, he'd worked out that you catch more flies with sugar than vinegar. While other two-year-olds were throwing tantrums, mine was polishing his charm. And by God, it served him well! You couldn't be angry with him. He'd look at you with those huge dark eyes, and you'd know he was laughing at you, and you couldn't help laughing, too. I don't know what Guy would have grown up to be. An entertainer, possibly. Or a politician. Something where the ability to tell barefaced lies is a major advantage."

The tears were coming freely now. He dashed them away with his free hand. "Oh God, Hazel, I miss them. I miss them so much."

She reached across the table to squeeze his hand. "Of course you do." There were tears on her cheeks, too.

"I *loved* being a father. That came as a huge surprise to me. It was something I hadn't expected. Not so much having children — that's pretty natural, after all — but taking so much joy in them. It was as if I'd found the thing I was really good at, the thing I was put on earth to do. To be a father. To be the best father in the history of the world." He managed a damp chuckle at her expression. "I know, the odds are I wasn't any better at it than most men, but I *felt* I was. Those boys made sense of my existence in a way that even professional success hadn't.

"And then they were gone. I wasn't a father anymore. Or a husband, or a professional. I was none of the things that had shaped my life, given it substance and value. It really is no wonder that I fell apart, is it?"

"No, Gabriel," whispered Hazel, "it isn't."

"Thank you," he said. "For asking about them. You have no idea how good it feels to be able to talk about them. To feel that my head isn't the only place where they still exist. That they haven't been entirely obliterated by what happened."

There was nothing Hazel could say to that. But then, there was nothing that needed saying.

The second batch of DNA results came in on Friday morning. DI Norris called Hazel as soon as he'd read the report. It didn't take long to absorb its contents. It only confirmed what the first batch had established. "Your friend who shall remain nameless, though not necessarily untitled, is no relation to the child by the lake."

Although Pete Byrfield had known he was off the hook, except possibly with his mother, for two days, Hazel appreciated the call. "Thank you. I'll tell him." She hesitated. She had no right to ask. But then, he was under no obligation to answer. "The tests on the child — he really did have Down syndrome?"

Strictly speaking, Norris should have wished her good day and hung up. Somehow it seemed a little late for that. "Yes. The DNA showed the extra gene."

"But David said there was nothing wrong with his brother."

She seemed to hear Norris shrugging. "He

231

was five when the kid went missing. How much was he going to remember?"

Hazel remembered what she'd said to Ash, that she'd only realized her father was a small man when she found herself talking to his bald spot. "I suppose that's true. Children take things pretty much at face value. It's only later that we start wanting to classify them. Big, little, perfect, imperfect."

"There's that," acknowledged the DI. "And then, kids' memories work differently to those of adults. Small children can forget completely things that we as adults find hauntingly memorable. It's why they make such difficult witnesses — not because they're likely to lie, not even because they can't cope with being questioned, but because they just don't file memories in such a way that they can pull them out again."

"I suppose sometimes that's a good thing." She was thinking of Ash's sons. If against all the odds either of them had survived to be raised by another family somewhere, it was better, for them, that they didn't know where they'd come from, about the trauma that had ripped their family apart.

Norris made no comment. "Are you going to be sticking around, Best?"

"Yes." She didn't elaborate, and Norris

didn't ask her to.

"In that case, do you want to make it official? I can get you a temporary transfer."

That surprised her. It was an unexpected compliment, that he wanted her on his team. But after a moment she shook her head. "I'm sorry, sir, I don't think I can. I need to be here, not in the inquiry room. Also, strictly speaking, I'm considered unfit for duty."

"Mm." Norris sounded unconvinced. He may have been thinking about the events of Wednesday night, and wondering what she got up to when she *was* fit for duty.

CHAPTER 19

David Sperrin didn't know what to do with himself. An archaeologist prevented from digging is never a happy sight, but this one had more on his mind than rain, bank holidays, and problems with the paperwork. He should have been with his mother, but Wool Row was the last place he felt he'd be welcome. Instead he hung about Byrfield, unusually clean and drinking too much coffee.

And everyone else, in deference to his odd status as the newly bereaved brother of someone who had died thirty years before, was giving him too wide a berth. They meant it kindly. They thought he needed space. He didn't; he needed company. He needed people to argue with.

Byrfield would probably have guessed this, and volunteered for the task. But Byrfield was out in the fields, catching up on work he'd neglected when he'd been preoccupied with his own dysfunctional family.

Once again, Hazel found herself re-arranging the deck chairs on the *Titanic*. She made a jug of lemonade, took Sperrin out onto the lawn, and sat him down under one of the biggest surviving elms in England to drink it. "I can't imagine how you're feeling. I don't suppose *confused* does more than scratch the surface."

Sperrin snorted. Like the man himself, it was a sound angry on the outside and vulnerable underneath. He seemed almost grateful to have someone telling him where to go and what to do. "It doesn't make any sense!"

"It doesn't seem to make much, does it?" agreed Hazel. "Of course, it'll make more when we know everything."

"Why would my father kill Jamie? Why would he try to kill you?"

"The first may have been an accident," she suggested. Until there was evidence to the contrary, it was the best thing for him to think. "The second an act of panic."

"He had no reason to connect you with anything that happened here," objected Sperrin. "You didn't even live here when he left."

"I wasn't actually alive when he left," murmured Hazel. "But you're right, of course. And nothing I said at the horse fair should have warned him. I don't know how he knew we were a threat to him."

It wasn't the only puzzle that was consuming Sperrin. "This is *all* wrong," he muttered, no longer looking at her, but inside himself, sieving his memory, trying to reconcile what he thought he knew with what Detective Inspector Norris thought *he* knew. "How can it be Jamie that we found? He didn't have Down syndrome. There was nothing wrong with him."

"You were very young," she reminded him gently. "Young enough that, to you, he was just your big brother. Would you have been aware if he had health problems?"

"Maybe not," he retorted, "but my mother would. You're not telling me that for more than thirty years she's never thought to mention that he had Down's? That would be . . . bizarre! He was her golden boy — the clever one, the good one, the one who'd have made her proud if our dad hadn't whisked him off to the travelers in Ireland. Astrophysicist, brain surgeon, something like that. All my life, Jamie's been the example I've failed to live up to. And you're telling me he was some kind of a simpleton?"

"Not the words I'd have chosen," said

Hazel sharply. "He had an extra gene on one chromosome. It gave him a disability. It didn't stop him from being a loving son and a fun-to-be-with older brother."

"But the things she said!"

"David" — she sighed — "there are no baby books that tell you how to feel when the child you've been waiting nine months for turns out to be different to other people's. It's a shock. Overnight, your expectations have to change. That unspoken contract, that we look after our kids when they're young and hope they'll look after us when we're old, goes out the window. A disabled child is likely to need care for the rest of his life, and that may mean the rest of yours.

"People react in different ways. Some people — surprisingly few, when you consider what it's going to mean — decide they can't cope and walk away. Some go to the other extreme — put all the love they're capable of into this damaged scrap of humanity, as if trying to compensate for that first devastating bit of bad luck.

"That's how your mother reacted. She was left to raise a disabled child alone — she had to love him, or the resentment would have destroyed her. So she poured everything into him. And yes, maybe that left less than there should have been for you. And maybe, in loving him despite his imperfections, she effectively blinded herself to them. After he was gone, of course, it was easy to remember only the best bits. Easier than it would have been if she'd still been caring for him. I'm sorry if it meant you had a difficult childhood, David. But think what *she* went through, and get over it."

She'd done it again: left someone with the sensation of having been savaged by a hamster. Sperrin stared at her, literally openmouthed, for half a minute, which is a long time for the universe to hold its breath. Then his jaw clamped shut like a steel trap and he was on his feet and striding down the drive toward Burford before Hazel got over the shock of what she'd just said and hurried after him.

"Where are you going?" she demanded breathlessly when she caught up.

"Where do you think?" His face was dark with anger and set in hard lines; there was something urgent and mechanical about his pace, like a toy soldier marching to war.

"Don't have this out with Diana just now! Not when you're angry and upset. Calm down first. Don't make it harder than it has to be."

For another hundred yards she thought

he was going to ignore her. Then, just short of the gate lodge, his pace began to slacken, his determination to waver. He finally came to an uncertain halt at Fred Best's front door. "Jamie's dead? That really was him we found?"

Hazel nodded. "Yes. There's no room for doubt."

"And he's *been* dead for thirty years." Sperrin stared at her as if he believed she was keeping something from him, something that might finally make sense of this. But she couldn't help. All she could do was stand beside him as gradually he came to terms with it. "Thirty years," he said again in a kind of wonder; and she knew that the absence of tears on his cheeks didn't mean he wasn't crying.

Hazel saw David Sperrin as far as his mother's house, but she didn't go inside. There were things he needed to say to Diana, and perhaps things she ought to say to him, and neither of them needed an audience. Hazel could only hope Sperrin would leave the cottage in Wool Row with some kind of understanding, not even so much for his mother's sake as for his own.

Across the road and a little farther into Burford, a white dog was sitting on the pavement outside the Spotted Pig. Hazel waited a moment and Ash came across to her, Patience trotting at his heel.

"What are you up to?"

"Nothing." But they'd known each other for a couple of months now, and he didn't really expect that to satisfy her. When her gaze didn't flicker and her eyebrows showed no signs of descending, he sighed and explained. "It's just . . . there's something odd here. Nobody's seen Saul Sperrin for thirty years, but the moment you start asking about him he's right there, armed and ready to kill. It just doesn't seem that likely."

Hazel shrugged. "It was a horse fair. One of the few places in England there *was* a decent chance of running into him."

"It was a horse fair ten miles from a place where people knew him. Not other travelers, but people who owed him no favors. The last time he was in Burford, he kidnapped his son and the child ended up dead. David's right: Why *would* he risk coming back here? You can't buy horses in Ireland anymore?"

The fair brows finally lowered and knit thoughtfully as Hazel considered this. "Well, *somebody* ran us off the road and shot at us. I can't think of anyone it's *more* likely to have been. Can you?"

He didn't answer that. He was thinking aloud. "And then, *why* come after us with a shotgun? If he didn't buy your story about the horse, why not just disappear? He's stayed off the radar for thirty years; he could do it again. And if he thought maybe there *was* a horse and he'd follow us to find out, why try to kill us before we got wherever it was we were going? And did he just happen to have a shotgun in his car? I mean, at what point did he think he was going to need that?"

And now Hazel had no answers. These events had seemed to follow a certain logic as they were happening. But they didn't stand up to analysis. He was right: There was something else going on. Or something different.

"What were you doing in the pub?"

"I've been trying to get a picture of Saul Sperrin from people who were around thirty years ago. People who'd have met him, or at least seen him in the village, and formed some kind of an impression of him."

"And some of the regulars must have been here forever," Hazel agreed. "Did they remember him?"

"Oh yes."

"And what did they say about him?" This was just a little like pulling teeth.

241

"It wasn't what they said, exactly," said Ash, frowning. "Or it was, but that wasn't the significant thing."

"Gabriel," exclaimed Hazel impatiently, "will you for pity's sake spit it out!"

He nodded, aware he was making a mess of this. "What Mrs. Perkins in the shop remembers, and what Mrs. Morrison the housekeeper remembers, and what the old men in the pub remember are all different. They're describing different men."

Hazel shrugged, obscurely disappointed. "You always get that with eyewitnesses. They remember different aspects of what they've seen — different things that made an impression on them. You have to put the various accounts together and look for common threads. Always — not just after thirty years." She sniffed. "I'd have thought you'd know that."

"I do know that." Ash hid a tiny smile. It amused him when she talked as if she'd been doing the job for years. "And that's what I thought it was, to start with. Some people remembered Sperrin as being taller or fatter, or having or not having red hair. But no two people remember *any* two things the same. The more people I talk to, the more descriptions I get of him. No one human being could match all of them."

Hazel was beginning to share his puzzlement. She knew he wasn't making this up. He didn't invent things — he hadn't that kind of imagination. He could be putting two and two together and getting eight. Or the people he'd spoken to might have been teasing him — he hadn't the imagination to notice that always. Or maybe it meant something.

"So what are you thinking? That some of them are remembering someone else?" Inspiration glimmered. "Maybe Diana had other men friends. She'd only have been around thirty then. Maybe when Saul let her down, she looked for company elsewhere, and some of the neighbors are remembering those men rather than Sperrin."

"That's possible," agreed Ash. "By everyone's account, Sperrin was never around much. I don't think he ever really lived in the village. Maybe people just assumed the man coming out of Diana's front door was her husband, when sometimes it wasn't."

Hazel waited, but he volunteered nothing more. She breathed heavily at him. "But that isn't what you're thinking, is it?"

"Well — no," he admitted.

"And is it a secret, or are you going to tell me?"

"It's going to sound pretty crazy," Ash warned her.

Nobody she knew — nobody she cared for — came so close so often to getting a slap. "Gabriel, ever since we met you've been saying pretty crazy things to me! And the craziest thing of all is how many of them have turned out to be true. So yes, I might think you've finally lost your marbles, but I'm going to listen anyway. So talk."

He bit his lip. He nodded. Then drew a deep breath and said, "I'm beginning to wonder if Saul Sperrin is a real person at all."

CHAPTER 20

"You're sure about this?" asked Hazel anxiously. But they were already walking back toward the cottage at the end of Wool Row.

"No, I'm not sure," said Ash honestly. "You could be right, that there were a lot of men and Sperrin was just one of them. But that's not what people are saying. They're all saying they remember Saul Sperrin, but they're all describing him in radically different ways."

"And that means he doesn't exist?"

"I don't know what it means," confessed Ash. "But it isn't normal. Even after so long, you'd expect people to tell you more or less the same things. To remember the same significant events: the time he got drunk and smashed up the bar, the shillelagh he always produced on St. Patrick's Day, the time he turned up driving an ex-military half-track — something like that.

But so far nobody's told me anything that anybody else has said. It's as if . . ." He closed down, continuing the sentence inside his head.

Hazel tired of waiting. "As if *what, Gabriel?*"

Ash said slowly, "As if they went to the Nuremberg rallies and missed hearing Hitler. They know he was there, they know *they* were there, they assume something must have distracted them at the critical moment, but the fact is they missed something they think everybody else saw. So each of them has put it together in his own head, from what he's been told, from what he thinks he knows, and each of them has created a memory that thirty years on he can't distinguish from the real thing. A false memory.

"They don't think they're lying. When I ask about Saul Sperrin, this is the picture they get and they think they're remembering him. But because the foundation for that memory is inside their own heads rather than something they actually witnessed, everybody's recollection of the man is different. Nobody claims to have known him well. I'm not sure any of them ever actually saw him."

Hazel was staring at him, literally openmouthed. "Can that really happen?"

"Oh yes," he replied without hesitation. "There's something in the human psyche that just longs to join in. The 'Me, too' impulse. Tell someone half the town saw a UFO, and there's a good chance he'll say 'Me, too.' He might have been inside bathing the dog, he might even have been in the garden and seen nothing, but if something that looks like a bandwagon goes rattling down the street, a lot of people feel the urge to jump on. They don't feel like they're lying. They think if a lot of people reported the UFO then there must have been a UFO, and if they were around that night they could have seen it, and if they *could* have seen it then it's almost as if they *did* see it. The more often they're asked to talk about it, the surer they become that they saw the same as everyone else.

"Only I think — I *think* — maybe *nobody* saw the UFO this time. That they're *all* saying 'Me, too.' And this long after, they've no idea they're doing it."

By an act of physical will, Hazel closed her mouth. She dragged her eyes away from his face long enough to look where they were going. Her voice, when it came, wasn't much more than a squeak. "And you're going to put this theory to Diana Sperrin?"

"At this point, it seems the logical thing to do," said Ash, with that trademark quiet obstinacy that you could take for humility if you weren't concentrating. "She knows. Nobody else does."

"But . . . but . . ." Hazel had to make herself focus on one problem at a time. "If it wasn't Saul Sperrin who shot at us . . . ?"

"Who was it?" Ash nodded. "That's certainly a question we need an answer to. But it's not one Diana can help with."

"No," agreed Hazel weakly. "Then . . . ?" And then she saw what he'd seen, and her eyes flew wide again. If there was no Saul Sperrin, he not only couldn't have run them off the road on their way home from the horse fair; he couldn't have killed his elder son, either. "You think *Diana* killed Jamie?"

"I don't know," Ash said again. "That's what I want to ask her."

If Hazel hadn't been so comprehensively floored by the direction his theory had taken them, she would have known that she had an absolute duty to stop him before he knocked on Diana Sperrin's door. The hypothesis might or might not have merit — knowing him as she was coming to, perhaps it did — but it was for the police to pursue. She should have swung him around by the arm immediately, marched him back to Byrfield, and, if necessary, sat on his head while she phoned DI Norris. She knew that. She just didn't have time to recognize that she knew it before Ash had let himself in at the gate and was knocking on the door.

David Sperrin opened it so quickly, he must have been about to leave. He looked pretty much the way Hazel felt. Ash steered him gently back inside. "I need to talk to you. Both of you."

Diana put her head around the kitchen door. "Are you still . . . ?" Then she saw the visitors. She froze, holding on to the door as if for support. Patience ambled calmly past her, immediately identified the most comfortable seat in the kitchen, and hopped up.

Diana was rallying fast. She fixed Ash with a hawkish eye. "I don't think I have to talk to you."

"No, you don't," he agreed without hesitation. "You *will* have to talk to Detective Inspector Norris."

"I already did."

"I know. But I don't think you've told him everything."

It was hard to judge from her expression, her chin raised, her eye still imperious, whether she understood. But David didn't. He looked at his mother, then at Ash, then back at Diana, more puzzled each time. "Mum? Do you know what he's on about?"

"No," she said shortly. But if it had been true, she'd have been curious, too.

Ash paused, as if unsure how to begin. Then he said, "Somebody tried to kill us last night. Me and Constable Best. She'd been asking some gypsies about Saul, and we assumed that he was the one who'd come after us."

He was watching Diana's face. Hazel saw nothing there, a determined mass of nothing, but Ash had been doing this longer than she had and perhaps he had learned to read nothing.

He nodded. "I don't think that now. I've come to ask you because I know you know. Apart from the man who shot at us, you're the only one who does know for sure whether it was Saul."

"I never left the house last night," said Diana loftily. "And no one came here. How would I know who shot at you?"

"I don't think you do," said Ash. "But I think you know it couldn't have been Saul Sperrin. Don't you?"

She shrugged negligently. "I've no idea where he is or what he gets up to."

"That's not entirely true," said Ash.

David Sperrin was moving quickly, and

predictably, from confusion to anger. "What the hell is all this about? What are you accusing her of? You think *she* took a shot at you?"

Hazel shook her head. "No. It was definitely a man. We thought it was your father. Now Ash doesn't think it could have been."

"Okay." Sperrin considered. "Well — isn't that good?"

"Mrs. Sperrin," said Ash, "do you have a passport?"

"What?" That surprised her. "No! Where would I go?"

"Or any official documents in that name?"

"*What* name?" demanded David, left behind again.

"Mrs. Saul Sperrin. A medical card? National Insurance number? A marriage certificate?"

Diana laughed out loud. "Good grief, is *that* what this is all about? You think you've caught me out in the terrible crime of being an unmarried mother? Of living in sin with a man I wasn't married to, thirty years ago? God bless us all, I'm astonished to learn that anybody still cares!"

David understood that well enough. He even managed to look affronted. "You were never married?" he demanded. "You mean to say I'm . . ."

"A bastard, dear? Yes indeed. Aren't you pleased? You've always worked so hard at it."

"And Jamie?"

"A love child," Diana said firmly. She made the distinction sound like a slap.

"Bugger me," said David weakly, sinking onto the battered sofa. Patience moved over obligingly.

"Was that it?" Diana turned her pale searchlight gaze back to Ash. "Was that what you wanted to know? Can I go and do something useful now? Like arranging a proper funeral for my child."

"Of course you must do that," said Hazel firmly. "And if you want us to leave, we will. We have no authority here, either of us. It may not feel like it, but we really are only trying to help."

"By pointing out that a man I haven't, in any event, seen for thirty years never bothered to marry me?"

Ash's tone remained polite. But it had developed a hard edge that Hazel had never heard there before. "Miss Best did not, in fact, say we're trying to help *you*. Miss Sperrin — that is your name, isn't it? The name you were born with?"

There was a fractional pause, then Diana nodded. "Yes. So?"

"You registered your sons in your name, not their father's."

"Yes."

"Who was their father?"

Her strong jaw came up again. "You know who. Saul . . ."

"Saul who? Not Sperrin — that really would be a coincidence. Or a problem."

"And yet," said Hazel, more to Ash than to Diana, "when I asked after Saul Sperrin at the gypsy camp, they seemed to know who I meant."

Ash shook his head. "They were doing what everyone's been doing for more than thirty years — going along with a fiction. Swanleigh wanted to seem helpful while he worked out if there was some way of getting the horse for himself. He'd no idea who you were talking about. But if he'd said that, you'd have left and he'd have missed his chance."

"But *somebody* followed us from the fair."

"Somebody followed us," agreed Ash. "We don't really know how long he'd been following us, so we don't really know where he followed us from." He looked at Diana again. "The only thing I'm reasonably confident of is that it wasn't David's father. I don't know who the father of your sons was, Miss Sperrin, but I'm pretty sure it wasn't an Irish traveler called Saul."

Tight-lipped, she said, "And I say it was."

Ash shook his head again. He always looked in need of a haircut. "No. There's no evidence that Saul Sperrin or anyone like him ever existed. You invented him. People who think they remember him are just remembering things you've said to them. That he was a traveler. That he kept disappearing back to Ireland." He drew a long breath. "That he kidnapped your son James."

There are bombs now that will destroy every living thing without inflicting damage on the infrastructure. The buildings go on standing. The services go on serving. Only the people who created it all are dead. For a long moment it was as if Gabriel Ash had dropped that kind of a bombshell. Nobody moved. Almost it seemed that nobody breathed. The only sound was the low murmur of a kettle on the range.

"Miss Sperrin — did you bury Jamie up by the lake? Was it you who put together that little cist, with the paving slabs to protect him from the earth and his favorite toys around him? It had to be someone who loved him. Was it you?"

There was another long pause. Not because Diana Sperrin was preparing a lie —

Hazel was sure of that. She'd done all the lying she was going to do. Many strange and unexpected emotions left their trails across her expression, but the strangest of all, and to Hazel the clearest, was satisfaction. She looked like a woman who knew she'd done the best with the hand she'd been dealt. It hadn't been a good hand, and the game had gone on far too long, but she had the satisfaction of knowing that she couldn't have done any better with what she'd had to work with, and neither could anyone else.

"Yes," she said simply.

CHAPTER 21

Hazel Best had seen corpses with more color than David Sperrin. She had no doubt that if he'd tried to stand up, he'd have fallen.

This might have been what Ash had been expecting. It might have been what Diana had expected, sooner or later. Even she herself had had a few minutes to come to terms with the idea. But Sperrin had seen none of it coming. A few days ago he'd been a man with two parents and a brother, even if two of them didn't see him and the one who did didn't like him much. Now he was a man who'd been an only child for thirty years, who'd never — except in the biological sense — had a father, and whose sole remaining family had just admitted to . . . what, exactly?

"Mum — what are you *saying*?" Something of the frightened child was audible in his deep man's voice. "That *you* killed Jamie?"

His mother regarded him with disdain. "Of course I didn't kill Jamie. I loved him. I would never have hurt a hair on his head."

"Then . . . *how* did he die? An accident?"

Diana delayed answering for so long that Hazel thought she was refusing to. Then she said, "That's right — an accident."

"Then . . . why did you *bury* him? Why this *pretense* of the last thirty years?" He remembered the cards on the mantelpiece. "You *knew* he wasn't writing to you! You sent birthday cards to *yourself*?"

Hazel got in first. "Diana, you need to talk to DI Norris, and even before that you need to talk to a solicitor. I don't think you should say anything more until you have."

Diana Sperrin shrugged haughtily. "It doesn't matter. I have nothing more to say. Inspector Norris can talk till he's blue in the face, but there's nothing more I wish to tell him. And for that I don't need a solicitor."

It wasn't a good decision, but it was hers to make. Hazel nodded and went outside to make the call.

David Sperrin's voice was low with shock and what sounded almost like resentment. "You never told me he was defective."

257

That stirred his mother to fury in a way that even Ash's meddling had not. "Jamie was *not* defective! He was perfect. From the day he was born to the day he died, he was the perfect child — loving, giving, sunny as a summer afternoon. So it took him longer than most to learn to tie his shoelaces — so what? *You* couldn't tell the time until I got you a digital watch!"

When DI Norris got back to his desk on Friday afternoon, following a court appearance that should have taken ten minutes but in fact took forty-five because, inexplicably, the magistrates wanted to hear the accused's apology for a defense, he found that his in-box had — as it so often did during even brief absences — replenished itself in the manner of the widow's cruse. He lifted out the top three items. Experience had taught him that this was the maximum he was likely to deal with at one go, and taking any more would only discourage him.

One of them puzzled him, so he tackled it first. He recognized the logo because he'd had a fax from the same source earlier in the day, but he hadn't been expecting another. He read the covering note, then studied the data it covered. Then he read it all again.

By now a glimmer of understanding was beginning to dawn. He wasn't sure if the information advanced or was even relevant to his case, but it certainly lifted the corner of a curtain.

He sat back in his chair, mulling over the fax, and a slow smile began to spread across his face. "Well now," he observed to himself with a certain complacency. "Who's been a naughty little aristocrat?"

That was when his phone rang. He heard Hazel out in a silence that somehow grew deeper the longer it persisted.

Finally he said, "All right, I'm on my way. Keep them all there till I arrive."

Before DI Norris arrived at the cottage, Pete Byrfield did. Hazel, who'd answered the door, stared at him in astonishment. "What are you doing here?"

"Damned if I know," said Byrfield. "Inspector Norris just phoned, asked me to meet him here." He seemed genuinely mystified but not — now that he knew the dead boy was no brother of his — worried. "What are *you* doing here?"

She did a bit of condensing. "I came with Ash. He worked out who it was who buried Jamie by the lake. It was his mother."

The twenty-eighth earl looked as if she'd

hit him about the head with a sockful of wet sand. "She . . . Diana? *Diana* killed her son?"

"I don't know," said Hazel. "She says not. But she won't say what happened, except that she was the one who buried him."

"She told you that?" Byrfield sounded stunned.

"Gabriel put it to her straight, and she was too proud to lie. So I called DI Norris."

"And he called me. But why?"

Hazel shrugged. By the standards of this week it was a comparatively minor mystery. "He'll be here soon. He'll explain then."

"How's David?"

"Shell-shocked."

DI Norris didn't come alone. There were three of them, including a uniformed woman constable, in two cars. He cautioned Diana immediately and took her out to the squad car. Waiting uneasily in Diana's front room, after perhaps fifteen minutes the others heard the car drive away and then Norris returned.

He glanced around as if to check that he'd got everyone he wanted. Then he waved a generous hand to invite them all to sit. There was a shortage of chairs. Hazel ended up perched on the arm of Ash's chair.

Patience ended up on the floor.

The detective inspector began. "I've come by some information that I feel I should pass on to you. It most directly concerns you, Mr. Sperrin, and Lord Byrfield. It also, because of the way I came by this information, concerns Constable Best. And since I know that anything I tell her is going to reach Mr. Ash, I propose to share it with the four of you. It isn't evidence of a crime, only a misdemeanor."

He paused a moment to arrange his thoughts. "Lord Byrfield, I've been a CID detective for many years. But actually, our tea lady could have worked out who supplied the DNA sample that arrived under the name of Best. Constable Best tried to be discreet, but it was pretty obvious that the only real candidate was you. It had to be someone who didn't know who the boy was, who was afraid he might be a relation, and who stood to lose or gain something significant if he was."

Byrfield swallowed. "But he wasn't my brother — he was David's. Wasn't he?" Confusion was making him doubt what he'd been told.

"Yes, he was," confirmed DI Norris. "But tell me this. That day you went to the laboratory. Your sister drove you?"

That surprised all of them. All Byrfield could do was answer. "My sister Vivienne went with me. In fact, I drove."

"She gave a sample as well."

"Yes. The lab technician suggested it would — I don't know — help with the baseline something or other. . . ."

"That's right," said Norris, the calm in his voice somehow reassuring, though what he was saying was still far from clear. "So they analyzed the two samples. They were only supposed to send your results to me. And when I got them, and they showed no blood relationship between you and the dead boy, I had no further interest in you, and I told Constable Best as much."

"Yes. Then . . . ?"

"Then someone at the lab made a mistake. They thought that the two samples that had been taken together should have been sent to the same place, and when they saw this hadn't been done, they thought they were rectifying an error. This morning I got the results of your sister's test."

"And?" Other ghosts were creeping in around the corners of Pete Byrfield's eyes. "What did they find? Is she ill? Should she be here, too?"

"Lord Byrfield — she isn't your sister. She's Mr. Sperrin's sister. And Jamie's."

CHAPTER 22

The detective inspector had imparted much worse news in his time and he breezed on, largely unconcerned. "Now, this is only of interest to me insofar as it affects my investigation. At first I thought it didn't, and I wasn't going to tell you. Now I think maybe it does, and anyway, maybe you're entitled to know."

Pete Byrfield looked, Hazel thought, pretty much how Mrs. Lot must have looked after she glanced back to the cities of the plain: white and rigid. Behind the kind eyes his brain was whirring — so fast, bits were going to start coming off. Even so, he couldn't make any sense of it. What he was being told didn't add up. His voice, when it finally came, was a fragile plaint. "What are you saying? That Viv's . . . That my mother . . . *Her and Saul Sperrin?*"

"No, Lord Byrfield," said Edwin Norris patiently. "There is not now and never was a Saul Sperrin. He was a convenient fiction. And the reason Ms. Sperrin needed a convenient fiction was that she didn't want to say who *was* the father of her sons."

He waited and watched, and sure enough, after perhaps half a minute an answer began filtering down through Byrfield's expression. "You mean — Diana and my *father . . .*"

Norris sucked his teeth. "Well, yes," he said carefully, "and no."

"But . . ." Byrfield finally unfroze enough to shake his head, the light hair flicking in his eyes. "That can't be right. If David and I were half brothers, it would have showed up in the DNA."

Hazel had been doing the math, too, and got the answer first. Or perhaps Ash did, hence his sudden urge to lean forward and stroke his dog's ears, but Hazel was the one who accepted the need — the obligation — to explain.

"Pete," she said gently, "there's a reason DI Norris wanted to talk to you and didn't ask Viv to be here, too. This doesn't concern Viv and Posy."

The twenty-eighth earl was thoroughly confused again. "But he said . . ."

"You said it yourself," sighed Hazel, "your parents didn't have the happiest home life.

But both of them desperately wanted a son. Viv and Posy are your father's children. So is David, and so was Jamie. And, in the strictly biological sense, you're not."

It's a wise child that knows his own father. But Pete didn't just have it in writing: He had it in stone and in land, and there was the dusty chest in the box room where he kept the ermine. . . . He *knew* who he was. He had always known. "What?"

Hazel smiled. "You don't even look like the rest of them. Viv and Posy and David all look the same — short, strong, and dark. Like your father. And you're a fair-skinned beanpole. Did it never occur to you to wonder why?"

Byrfield shrugged, too, helplessly. "Some kind of a throwback . . ."

"Of course," she agreed. "That happens all the time. It can happen much more dramatically than that — black parents suddenly producing an apparently white child, or the other way around. Two half-forgotten genes meet and the results are . . . surprising. But that's not the likeliest explanation. The easiest way of introducing new characteristics into a family is by introducing new genes. And that's what the DNA says, isn't it?" She appealed to Norris, who nodded. "The last earl wasn't your father. Your mother brought you home as a souvenir from an away day."

Byrfield made a funny burbling noise that was more than half a laugh.

And Ash thought that the magic was at work again. Nobody else could have got away with it. Nobody else could have said that without causing deep offense. But Hazel Best wore the goodness of her heart on her sleeve, and people recognized and responded to her good intentions even in the most trying of circumstances.

"You're not saying they adopted me." Hazel shook her head. "Then . . . who *was* my dad?"

"Oh, that's easy." Hazel beamed. "The last earl. He gave you everything *but* his genes. He loved you every day of your life, and he went to his rest content that you were his son and heir in every way that mattered. If you mean who was your biological father, I don't know. It could have been anyone. You might even have come out of a test tube. Ask your mother, if you think you can trust the answer. But if I were you, I wouldn't get too hung up on it. Your dad considered you his son. Isn't that enough?"

"Hang on. Hang on," interjected David Sperrin. "Are you saying . . . Are you saying *I'm* the rightful earl of Byrfield?" The look of horror on his face was the exact antithesis of hope.

"I don't think so," said Hazel tactfully. "I think only legitimate children inherit. You could always take it up with the heraldic King of Arms or whoever."

"Good God, no," grunted Sperrin, subsiding in relief.

"But . . . but . . ." Pete Byrfield had the strong feeling he'd done somebody out of something. "So Dad and Diana had Jamie, and four years later Mother and Dad had Viv. Then Dad and Diana had David, and he and Mother had Posy. Then Mother and this two-meter Viking with the weak chin had me. Is that it?"

Norris nodded. "Looks like it."

"Good grief." But something like a smile was taking over his unimpressive features. "And you think you know people . . ." He looked helplessly at Sperrin. "I don't think we're related, are we? But you're my half sisters' half brother. You've got to be entitled to something."

Sperrin considered. "You could buy me that magnetometer."

"You really think that's a good idea?" said Byrfield. "Seeing how much trouble you can cause with just a shovel?"

They traded a grin, two men who had

267

always liked each other enough to face in good faith whatever problems these revelations would bring.

Ash was looking at Norris. "What changed your mind?"

"About what?"

"You said you were going to keep this to yourself. Then you thought it might have a bearing on your investigation. What bearing?"

He probably had no right to ask. Certainly DI Norris didn't have to tell him. Except that someone had shot at Ash because of these people and their complicated home lives. Except that, actually, that probably wasn't the case. . . . Norris gave up trying to work it out and just told him. "Motive," he said simply. "Could any of this have provided someone with a motive for murder?"

David Sperrin swallowed hard. "Do you think my mother killed Jamie?"

"She says not."

"What does she say happened?"

"Right now she's saying very little," grunted Norris. "That may change when we do a formal interview back at the station, though I'm not confident. She says she buried Jamie, and I believe her. She says she didn't kill him, and I'm inclined to believe that, too. But right now, that's all she's saying. I don't know what the circumstances were. I don't know who shot him, or why. I don't know if Ms. Sperrin was there when it happened or not. Of course I'll ask her all these things again, maybe several times, but I can't make her answer if she doesn't want to." He looked hard at David. "What about you, Mr. Sperrin?"

"I was five years old, Inspector! I don't remember a thing about it. I've always believed what I was told — that my father was a traveler and he took Jamie back to Ireland."

"That's not what I meant. I mean, do you think she'd tell you something she wouldn't tell me?"

Sperrin bristled. The shock had subsided enough now for his normal prickly personality to surface. "Even if she did, do you think I'd tell you something she didn't want you to know?"

"Not doing might be considered obstruction."

"I think I might tell you where to put your obstruction."

"Boys, boys," said Hazel, trying hard to mollify. "David — *is* there a realistic chance that your mother might confide in you?"

"In me?" The soar of his voice contained

the answer. "Why would she start now? She doesn't even like me."

"So the question is academic," said Hazel. "Diana isn't going to talk to David, so he isn't going to be able to withhold material information. You talked about a motive?"

DI Norris sniffed. She was right, but that didn't mean he had to like Sperrin's attitude. "Thirty years ago, when that little boy died, his mother had something to hide. If she hadn't, she'd have called us and called for an ambulance, and Jamie would have got his Christian burial and we'd have known how and why he died, and if anyone was to blame.

"If Diana's telling the truth, she denied us that opportunity when she buried him secretly at Byrfield. Your father . . ." He glanced at the twenty-eighth earl, then at Sperrin, then gave up entirely. "The last earl would have been master of Byrfield then, so it's possible they did it together. But either of them would have been free to come to me — well, my predecessor — if they blamed the other for what happened. To that extent we have to consider it a conspiracy."

A lot had been thrown at Pete Byrfield today. He'd been told that his father wasn't his father, his sisters weren't his full sisters, and even he wasn't who he'd always believed he was. Much of it had amazed, puzzled, even amused him, but none of it had angered him. But this did. Sparks crackled in his pale Viking eyes. "You didn't know my father, Inspector. For that reason, and that reason only, I'm prepared to forgive you that suggestion. But talk to anyone in the village. Talk to anyone who knew him — anyone who had dealings with him. Tell them you think he conspired to cover up the death of one of his children. They'll laugh in your face."

DI Norris made no reply. He swiveled on his heel until he was looking at David. "Mr. Sperrin?"

David swallowed. "I hardly knew him."

"I understand he helped you get to university. Why did you suppose that was?"

Sperrin looked bewildered. "I just thought he was a kind man. That he took his duties as lord of the manor more seriously than most, and he helped me because he could."

"Did he send any of the other village children to university?"

Byrfield's tongue hadn't lost its irascible edge. "Inspector, you *know* why he helped David. He was David's father. There's nothing sinister about it. He had a son he felt he couldn't acknowledge, but he could support

271

him. What are you suggesting? That David should have known? That he *did* know?"

Norris was still looking at the archaeologist. "Did you?"

David Sperrin passed a weary hand across his face. "I never suspected. Not for a moment."

"A lot seems to have passed you by," observed DI Norris critically. "Your brother's medical condition. His death. The fact that your supposed father was a figment of your mother's imagination, and that the kind man who lived in the big house was your real father. Are you always this" — he wanted to say *dim* — "gullible?"

"He was only five when Jamie died," Hazel pointed out, pursing her lips in discreet disapproval.

"Yes. And how old were you the last time your mother put a card on the mantelpiece and said, 'That's from your brother James'? I mean, didn't you recognize her handwriting?"

Sperrin shook his head in a kind of wonder. "Inspector, I can't help you. Maybe you're right — maybe I was very, very stupid. But I never suspected anything. She told me our father had taken Jamie, and I believed her. And I never thought to have a graphologist analyze the Christmas cards."

272

They regarded each other levelly for half a minute more. Then Norris didn't so much blink as turn a page. "Okay. Well, I don't think there's anything else you can tell me at the moment, is there? I'll probably want to talk to all of you again at some point, so I'd be obliged if anyone planning a foreign holiday would put it on hold. Except maybe you two" — his gaze traveled between Hazel and Gabriel Ash — "for whom it might be a very good idea."

"We can't do that, Inspector," said Hazel. One elevated eyebrow asked her why not. "Patience hasn't had her rabies shots."

"And that," said Norris with conviction, "might explain a very great deal."

"I don't know why he thinks *we're* mad," said Byrfield plaintively after the policeman had gone. "It's not like any of this was our doing. We're hardly to blame for the actions of our parents!"

"Whoever they were," muttered Sperrin.

Byrfield was watching him with concern. The nice thing about Pete Byrfield, Hazel thought, is that although he worries a lot, mostly what he worries about are other people. "We need to talk to a solicitor. If you like, we can talk to separate solicitors."

Sperrin peered at him uncertainly. "Why would we want to do that?"

"Because you need someone looking after your interests who isn't also looking after the Byrfield family interests." He drew himself up straight. "But the first thing is to get someone down to the police station to look after Diana. Whatever she does or doesn't want to tell Inspector Norris, she needs someone by her side, guiding her through. Our solicitor can do that." He glanced at Hazel, who nodded approval.

Byrfield turned his attention back to Sperrin. "Once that's in hand, though, you need to think about what this means to you. And you'll need someone by *your* side, guiding you, who hasn't been in my family's employ for the last thirty years. I can't imagine there'll be a conflict of interests. I'm determined there won't be. But I also don't want either of us wondering, further down the line, if we resolved matters appropriately. If you got everything you're entitled to."

"Like what?"

As far as Hazel could judge, Sperrin's astonishment was genuine.

"Like I don't exactly know," said Byrfield impatiently. "But you're my father's son, and I don't propose to see you excluded from the advantages that ought to bring."

David laughed out loud. "Pete, I'm a bastard! I thought I was the son of a feckless Irish traveler, it turns out I'm the by-blow of an English gentleman. That's interesting, but I don't think it'll have a material effect on my way of life! Look. He did all right by me. He got me to university when there was no other way I could have gone. He gave me pretty much everything I've got, and though it might not be what you'd have chosen, it *is* what I chose. I *like* rolling the turf back to see how people did things a thousand years ago. I have absolutely no interest in cows. You couldn't pay me enough to take over the running of Byrfield. Each to his own, my friend, and let's leave the lawyers to make money out of mugs."

Pete stood looking at him, as if wondering how much of it he meant, or would go on meaning, for some moments. Then he turned and headed for home. "We'll talk again, when the dust's settled. In the meantime, I'll get Parsons, or possibly Parsons, or, failing him, Parsons, to run over and see Diana." The front door of the cottage closed behind him.

After he'd gone, Hazel turned to David. "Are you all right?"

Impossible to tell if he was nodding or shaking his head. "I don't know what that means anymore. My brother's dead. And it seems stupid to start grieving now, because he's *been* dead for most of my life. And my mother knew. Knew? . . . She buried him! My father may have helped. Of course, my father isn't the man I thought he was . . ." He blew out a gusty sigh. "All right? I'm going with probably not."

"On the bright side," suggested Hazel, "you've got two half sisters you didn't know about."

"Yeah," he growled. "They're going to be thrilled about that." A thought struck him with sudden horror. "This doesn't mean I'm related to Pete's mother, does it?"

CHAPTER 23

They were walking back up the drive toward Byrfield. Patience disappeared into the rhododendrons, on the trail of a rabbit.

Ash was quiet. There was nothing unusual about this. But Hazel was learning to read his silences as you might read another man's body language. Sometimes he was silent because he was thinking, sometimes because he didn't want to think. Sometimes he was silent because there was nothing he wanted to say, and sometimes because there was nothing he *could* say.

This was a thinking silence. Hazel slowed her stride to match his. "You're wondering what happened to Jamie."

Ash nodded. "Yes."

"Do you think Diana killed him?"

He didn't answer immediately. Then he shook his head. "No. I think she'd have said so if she had. There's a vein of adamancy in that woman. I don't think her pride would allow her to hide behind a lie. She probably doesn't fancy doing time any more now than she did thirty years ago."

"I don't think that's why she lied then. I think she was protecting someone else."

"Henry?"

Ash nodded. "Maybe."

"Henry's been dead a long time now," Hazel pointed out. "He doesn't need protecting anymore."

"True. But that also means there's no one left to contradict anything she says. She could say Henry Byrfield shot Jamie, and it's unlikely Inspector Norris could prove any different. That would be the safest lie to tell, if she was prepared to lie. If it *is* a lie."

"You didn't know him." But Hazel no longer sounded as confident as she once had. It seemed none of them had known him as well as they thought they had. Except just possibly his wife. Everyone remembered the last earl fondly, and no one had a good word to say about the countess. But he'd had two children out of wedlock before she succumbed to the unknown Viking, and even then she may have been thinking more of the Byrfield title than of herself. One thing Hazel was sure of: Alice Byrfield had always been able to read a calendar. If there were reassessments to be done, maybe Pete's mother was due an upgrade.

Ash, too, was doing mental arithmetic. "It took eleven paving slabs to make that little grave. The closest they were likely to be was in the yard at Home Farm, a quarter of a mile across the fields. She might have been able to lift two at a time, but I don't think she carried them across rough ground. So if she was working alone, she made that trip thirteen times — with the slabs, with the tools, and with her child's body. It's just about possible she did all that in a single night without anybody noticing — and without anybody reporting the theft of eleven paving slabs in the morning — but it's much more likely that she had help. Henry Byrfield could have had them put on a trailer and tractored them down to the lake in broad daylight without anyone asking questions. He's about the only one who could."

It made more sense than anything else. "You think he was covering for Diana?"

"I think he was *helping* Diana. They must have agreed it was the best thing to do in the circumstances — whatever those circumstances were. Either of them could have called the police, but neither of them chose to. Either they were both responsible for

Jamie's death or neither of them was."

"Or it *was* Diana, but the old earl decided he had too much to lose by telling the police, and so the world, that he'd fathered her two illegitimate sons," suggested Hazel. The rancor in her tone surprised her.

Ash half turned to look at her, one eyebrow canted quizzically. "Everyone says he was a good man. He was a good father to Pete, though he probably knew he wasn't actually his son, and he made sure David got what he wanted. Do you think he'd have let Diana shoot his son, then help her cover up the crime for fear of embarrassment?"

Hazel didn't have to think long. "No, I don't."

"That's two reasons to believe Diana's telling the truth."

"But if she didn't kill Jamie, why won't she say what happened? Maybe it was nothing more than a terrible accident, but nobody's going to believe that while she refuses to explain."

Patience reappeared from the shrubbery with white fluff caught in her jaws.

"Pete's solicitor will talk her around," Hazel added in the hopeful tone of someone trying to sound surer than she feels. "He'll make her understand that the only way forward now is to tell the truth. To tell Norris exactly what happened, and throw herself on the mercy of the court."

Ash remained doubtful. "Diana Sperrin is a strong woman. I don't think she'd have acted as she did if she wasn't sure she could see it through."

"She may have thought she'd never be caught."

Ash disagreed. "She must have known she might be. She's had thirty years to decide what to do if this moment came. And this is the best she could come up with? No comment?"

"It *can* be a pretty smart strategy," Hazel felt bound to point out.

"If you're guilty. Not if you're innocent."

"But she *isn't* innocent," said Hazel reasonably. "She's committed at least one offense. She's admitted as much."

"She's admitted to burying Jamie, not to killing him."

"Maybe she doesn't know who killed him."

Ash dismissed that immediately. "Of course she knows. If she didn't, she'd want us to find out. She'd have wanted that from the start. She's protecting someone."

"Or someone's memory." The circular nature of the debate had brought them back to Henry Byrfield again. "Maybe it really was an accident," suggested Hazel, helpless to find another answer. "And rather than force Henry to explain to the police what happened, including his relationship with the dead child, she agreed to a clandestine burial. She'd invented Saul Sperrin ten years before, as a cover for her ongoing activities with the earl. The simplest thing was to invoke him again. To tell people he'd taken Jamie."

"It's not impossible," conceded Ash. "She's not a particularly conventional woman. A Christian burial and a stone in the churchyard may not have meant much to her. Granted that nothing was going to bring Jamie back, protecting her lover may have meant more."

"And having launched the fiction that Jamie was abducted by her husband, it was easier to keep it going than to stop it. Hence the thirty years' worth of cards she sent herself." Hazel frowned. "You can't call it outstanding police work, can you, when the forces of two countries are looking for a man who never existed. Did nobody think of checking the records for Saul Sperrin's birth certificate, or their marriage certificate?"

"It only seems obvious because of what we know," said Ash. "If someone came to you tomorrow accusing her husband of child abduction, would you begin your inquiries with the Registry of Births, Marriages, and Deaths?"

Hazel glowered. "I would now."

At least someone knew how to deal constructively with the new situation. Pete Byrfield made some phone calls, and in the late afternoon his sisters arrived, together, in Vivienne's car. He greeted them with a reassuring hug and ushered them upstairs to the countess's sitting room.

Hazel tried not to eavesdrop, but it wasn't easy. Byrfield was a small-enough house that a family row involving the countess and her three children would always rattle the stoppers in the crystal decanters. But only once were voices raised high enough to carry, and then they dropped quickly out of hearing again.

David Sperrin had never stood on ceremony at Byrfield. He'd traipsed in through whichever door was nearest and never minded the mud on his boots. Only now that it might seem he had a right to leave muddy footprints anywhere he wanted did he feel the need to ring the bell.

Byrfield met him with an impish grin. He'd known he was coming: He'd summoned him. He showed Sperrin upstairs, and pretended not to notice that Sperrin had showered and put on a clean shirt for the meeting.

"I like your friend Pete," said Gabriel Ash, leafing through a catalog of farm machinery that might as well have been upside down and written in Sanskrit for all he was getting out of it.

Hazel smiled. "Me, too."

The sound of loose ends flapping kept them all from sleep.

Edwin Norris conducted two interviews with Diana Sperrin. Although he was keen to resolve the matter — and perhaps even keener to understand it — he was punctilious about waiting for her solicitor to join them.

Because the Byrfield estate was a significant client, the senior Mr. Parsons took the duty on himself. But in fact, a newly qualified solicitor would have been more than equal to the task. Diana told him nothing she hadn't already told DI Norris, and proposed telling neither of them any more. It wasn't that she was difficult, or aggressive, or deceitful. She'd just said all that she intended to, ever.

Simple rage kept the countess awake. After

everything — after everything she'd put up with, everything she'd done! — it was all going to come out anyway. People would know. People in Burford would know. Tradesmen would know. She'd be a laughingstock.

The four Byrfield siblings — it's probably the only way to describe them — sat up all night, replenishing the coffeepot and the whiskey decanter at intervals, getting to know one another all over again.

Hazel found herself thinking like a police officer. She lay in the dark, in the familiar comfort of her old bed in her old room, and marshaled all the facts she could be sure of, and all the inferences she could reasonably count on, and tried to see through the drama that had occurred center stage to glimpse what might have been going on in the wings.

Ash retired to his room to leave the Byrfields alone, but he didn't go to bed. He sat in the chair all night, doing pretty much what Hazel was doing down in the gate lodge, but with a different set of facts.

Patience took advantage of the unoccupied bed and snored her way through till morning.

CHAPTER 24

At half-past seven on Saturday morning they met on the midpoint of the gravel drive. Hazel had been on her way up to Byrfield, Ash hurrying down to the gate lodge. They gasped out, "I need to talk to you!" pretty much in unison.

Ash was less fit, but Hazel had been running, so she let him go first. Apart from anything else, he looked like he might explode if he didn't.

"I've been thinking about this all damn night," he panted. "But I know who did it. At least I think I know who must have done it."

Hazel nodded energetically, her fair hair dancing. She'd paused just long enough to drag a brush through it, but all she'd done after that was tie it out of her way with an elastic band. "Me, too. You want to see if we've come up with the same thing?"

"Of course we have," said Ash dismissively, "it's the only thing that makes sense. If it wasn't Saul Sperrin shooting at us — for the very good reason that there is not now and never was a Saul Sperrin — then someone was trying to kill us for reasons entirely unconnected with Byrfield."

He'd managed to surprise her. They hadn't been thinking the same thing after all. Hazel had been too wrapped up in the thirty-year-old tragedy to wonder who had run them off the road and why. "Okay," she said, a little uncertainly.

"So what other cages have we been rattling?"

Hazel considered. "Most of the people I've annoyed recently are dead now. You?"

Ash blinked. But it was probably true. Until she'd met him she'd had no enemies. Now she hadn't again, but that was because Norbold's senior police officer and its last remaining gangster had both died in a closing act something like Hamlet's scant weeks before.

But if Hazel wasn't the target, Ash must be. He nodded slowly. "I think so, yes. I didn't at the time, but there's nobody else — nobody — who could still think I pose any kind of a threat. But he just might. And if he did, he might have arranged to have me followed. This week, that meant following both of us. And when he decided to remove the threat, that meant both of us, too. It was on the way back from the gypsy camp simply because that was the first time for days there hadn't been other people, potential witnesses, around."

Hazel went over it again in her mind, word for word, and searched his dark, excited eyes for clues, but it didn't help. She had no idea what he was talking about. "He who?"

"Stephen Graves!" said Ash impatiently. "The man I called on coming down here. The CEO of Bertram Castings."

Hazel still thought she must have misunderstood. "The bloke who lost his airplane?"

Ash nodded energetically. For a moment it looked like he wouldn't be able to stop. "In fact, he lost several. Yes, him."

Hazel knew that several missing airplanes didn't provide a motive for something that one missing airplane hadn't. "Gabriel — what possible reason could he have for wanting to hurt you?"

To Ash it seemed as clear as day. "To stop me asking questions!"

Hazel shook her head, mystified. "That's not what I mean. I mean, what reason could *he* have? He's a victim, like you. Well — not like you, obviously," she added quickly, "but someone who lost something to the same criminals who took your family. Why wouldn't he be cheering you on?"

"I thought he was. He gave me some more names to . . ." For the first time this side of midnight he was assailed by doubts. "Which he didn't have to do if he didn't want me going any further with this. So maybe it wasn't him. Maybe he called someone: 'Don't be alarmed if some idiot in an ill-fitting suit wants to ask you about the piracy, he's been here and I think he's probably harmless.' Maybe he called all the people whose names he gave me. But one of them wasn't a victim — he was a conspirator.

"We knew someone in England was assisting them," he hurried on. In fact, they had never known anything of the kind. It was one inference that could be put on something that a target criminal had possibly said to a corrupt policeman. Ash had clung to it like a life belt because he'd had nothing else to keep him afloat; and Hazel refrained from reminding him of this because he still hadn't. "Maybe one of those people, maybe just someone working in one of the offices. A dispatch clerk, someone whose job it was to get the permits together — someone like that.

"Whoever it was, he got worried that

questions were being asked again. That I might pay him a visit next. He made some calls of his own, and they traced me to Byrfield and set someone to watching me. In all likelihood the decision had already been taken to shut me up, but the opportunity didn't present itself until we were driving around the back roads of Cambridgeshire in the middle of the night." Ash looked at Hazel, white-faced. "I almost got you killed."

"*You* did nothing of the kind," Hazel retorted sharply. "You didn't put us off the road, and you didn't fire a shotgun at us. Gabriel, you may have done all sorts of wicked things in your life" — she didn't think so, but she hadn't known him long enough to be sure — "but you're no more responsible for what happened to us than for what happened to your family. Don't feel guilty over things that aren't your fault. It's unproductive and it's self-indulgent. We'll find whoever's to blame and we'll see him in jail. And if this *is* connected with the loss of your wife and sons, we'll find out. We'll learn everything he knows. Then we'll follow where the trail leads us."

Ash was staring at her as if seeing her for the first time. Hazel didn't often take command like this — what her mother had called "Putting her foot down with a firm hand" — and when she did, people who'd thought her a nice, amiable, easygoing young woman tended to do a double take. Their startled expressions were an ongoing source of satisfaction to her. She said nothing, but watched with a degree of complacency as his mind struggled for a foothold on the suddenly shifting ground.

"Er — so I'm heading back there. To Bertram Castings. Find out who Graves talked to after I saw him."

Now Hazel's expression turned cool. "What about the Byrfields? And Diana, and David? You're going to just walk away — leave them to sort their problems out themselves?"

Someone else might have reminded her that sometimes people are best left to sort their problems out for themselves, that the line between helping them and meddling is so thin you can get paper cuts from it. But Gabriel Ash had a life worth living for the first time in four years thanks to Hazel Best's compulsive helping disorder, so even if it was true, she wasn't going to hear it from him.

"What more can we do? The only one who can sort it out is Diana, and she doesn't want our help. Hazel, I have to follow this

291

up! I can't just sit here when someone fifty miles away knows someone who knows something about my family! You must see that."

It was impossible not to see, not to understand, how much this mattered to him. Only sometimes she thought it would be nice if he could acknowledge that other people's pain mattered as well. She cared about Pete Byrfield, had even come to care about David Sperrin, and their drama was onstage right now. She believed she could help here, even if all she was doing was making coffee at regular intervals.

On top of which, while Ash had been having insights into the attack on them, Hazel had been having insights into the death of Jamie Sperrin. Or at least the significant things that had and hadn't happened immediately afterward.

She took a step back and nodded. "All right, then. If you need to go, you need to go. I dare say Mrs. Morrison will have the number of a taxi firm."

Ash stared at her in astonishment. "You aren't coming?"

"No. Not this time, Gabriel. I need to talk to David again. And then the pair of us need to talk to Diana. It can't wait."

His lips formed the word *But.* Some

instinct warned him not to give it voice. Of course she hadn't the same sense of urgency about his quest. It was a kind of impertinence to assume that she would have. After four years of living in such isolation that, when he started taking Patience for walks, his neighbors thought he was a squatter, he'd allowed himself to become dependent on this young woman — too dependent. Of course she was going to resent it, sooner or later. He'd already wrecked her career; now he was monopolizing her time and imposing on her goodwill, to the point of telling her that what troubled her was less important than what troubled him. He, too, stepped back. There were now two good paces between them.

"You're right. I'm sorry." His eyes were down around her feet somewhere. "Of course you ought to stay. But I have to go."

"Then go."

The housekeeper called for a taxi. But it was early in the day and they were a long way from anywhere — the soonest the cab firm could oblige was nine-thirty. Byrfield was a big house, but too small to avoid somebody's gaze for two hours, so he found Hazel and told her.

She breathed heavily at him. "Take my car, why don't you? Anywhere I need to go, someone can drive me."

If she'd offered earlier, probably he'd have said yes. Now he was feeling too guilty. "I'll wait for the taxi. Have you seen David yet?"

Hazel shook her head. "He'll be down for breakfast soon."

But Sperrin didn't appear for breakfast, and when, concerned for him, Hazel checked his room, he wasn't there, either.

Knowing Diana's cottage was currently empty, he might have gone there. But Hazel struck off through the farmyard and diagonally across the water meadow, and found him down by the lake. DI Norris still had the little grave cordoned off. Sperrin had found himself another grassy hump between the woods and the water, a natural one this time, and was sitting cross-legged on it like a slightly scruffy woodland sprite, staring across the lake with unseeing eyes.

He didn't hear her approach, started at the sound of her voice.

"It's a nice spot, isn't it?"

Sperrin's voice was low. "I used to think so."

"You will again," she predicted confidently. "It'll be the place you come to think about Jamie. Which is, after all, the role graveyards have always played." She paused, watching him. "David, I can only imagine how much of a shock all this has been to you. And I'm sorry for your loss."

Sperrin gave a sort of impatient snort. Hazel thought the object of his impatience was himself. "That's kind of the point, though, isn't it? I haven't actually lost anything. My brother's been dead for thirty years. I hardly remember him. Everything I think I remember, I heard from my mother, and we all know how reliable she turned out to be. I didn't even know he was . . . disabled." Hazel had no doubt that, if this conversation had been about anyone else, he would have used a different word.

"I suppose that's what childhood is," she said. "Taking things, and people, at face value. He was your big brother. You remember him as being pretty good at that. So perhaps he was."

He cast her a glance with just a hint of gratitude in it. "Do you think she killed him?"

"Ash doesn't think so. He reckons she'd have said so if she had. That she'd have wanted to justify her actions rather than deny them."

"Then why won't she tell us what happened?"

Hazel veered off at a tangent. "What do you remember of the day he disappeared?"

"Jesus — I was five years old!"

"Yes. But it was a big thing to happen, it must have made an impact. What's the first time you remember being aware that he wasn't around anymore?"

Sperrin thought back. And she was right, there was a memory. He remembered sitting beside the fire, wrapped in a blanket, instead of being put to bed. He remembered a male voice in the house. He wasn't used to the sound of men's voices.

"What's your last memory of Jamie?"

That was harder. Most of what he thought he remembered from his childhood were things that, in fact, he'd been told by his mother. But suddenly he had an image in his mind that he knew was a genuine memory. "Playing Frisbee."

Hazel smiled, too. "You used to play Frisbee together. In the garden?"

"I suppose so." He struggled to push out the parameters of his recollection. "It seemed bigger. Of course, I was small. And cowboys and Indians." A grin spread slowly. "That required a certain amount of ingenuity, because Mum didn't approve of toy guns. Thought they might corrupt us or something. But it's amazing what you can do by pointing your finger and shouting 'Bang' loudly enough."

"I think," Hazel said carefully, "your brother, Jamie, had a nice life. A short one, which ended far too soon, but still a nice life. I think he was loved by his mother and watched over by his father, and he had a little brother who played Frisbee and illicit cowboys and Indians with him. I think his life was probably pretty sunny."

Sperrin went through one of those mercurial changes of mood that were characteristic of him, from sunshine to sudden deep shadow, from fond remembering to bitter recrimination. "And then someone blew his head off and shoveled him out of sight beside a pond."

Hazel felt his hurt and sympathized. But it was important for him to recognize that some of what had been done had been done with love. She shook her head. "You saw the grave, David. You know the care that went into making it. When she buried Jamie, your mother loved him as much as she ever had. I think your father helped her. They loved and cared for him, and I think they tried to do their best for him in difficult circumstances."

"But why?" he demanded. Behind the frustrated anger he wasn't far from tears. "Why" — an unsteady hand encompassed the lakeside scene — "*this*? A DIY burial.

Why couldn't they tell people what had happened? Why is my mother still keeping it a secret?"

"I don't know," said Hazel carefully, "but I think she's protecting someone."

"Who? Saul Sperrin? Henry Byrfield? One of them never existed, and the other is past paying for anything he did! There's no one else she cares about enough to cross the road for, let alone to go to prison for."

"I think there might be," said Hazel.

CHAPTER 25

DI Norris had known hardened criminals who couldn't hold their tongues like Diana Sperrin. She sat in his interview room, composed and smiling faintly, like a cross between the Mona Lisa and the sphinx, saying nothing.

No, that's not quite right. She wasn't afraid of speaking. She wasn't concerned that the policeman might trick her into saying something she didn't want to. She responded politely when he asked after her well-being; she engaged with him in a little casual conversation. She just didn't add anything — anything at all — to what she'd already said about losing her child. Norris knew that she wouldn't if they stayed in this room until one of them died.

Usually he was irritated by any interruptions to an interview. This time it came as a relief when someone tapped on the door and said there were people outside looking for him.

"Who?"

"David Sperrin. And Constable Best."

He knew they hadn't just swung by to say hello. They must have a good reason for the desk sergeant to risk Norris's ire. "I'll see them in my office. Bring Ms. Sperrin a cup of tea, will you?"

"Coffee, please," she said demurely.

The DI assumed that Sperrin had come to plead for his mother's release. Norris couldn't think what else he might have to say — unless it was that he'd known about the contents of the grassy mound all along, and Norris didn't believe that. He'd been too young when it all happened, and too shocked when it all came out.

But it seemed Sperrin wasn't here to intercede on his mother's behalf, either. He looked around warily but offered nothing by way of explanation for his presence. In fact, Norris quickly concluded that he wouldn't have been here at all but for Hazel Best.

He peered over his glasses at her. "Solved it then, have you, Constable?"

There was a glow in her face that told him she longed to say yes. But even twelve months as a probationary constable had taught her to take nothing for granted. "I wouldn't go that far, sir. But if she isn't co-operating . . . ?" She raised a fair eyebrow.

Norris lowered both of his. "That's putting it mildly."

"Then there may be nothing to lose and something to gain by letting me interview her."

"Letting *you* interview her?" He could hardly have sounded more affronted if she'd asked him to sign over his pension as well.

"I *am* a serving police officer," she reminded him reproachfully. "And I think Diana Sperrin may tell me what happened, although she's prepared to grow old and die before she'll tell you. Particularly . . ." She let the sentence trail away.

"Particularly?"

"If I can take David in there with me."

That really was too much. Edwin Norris had been a policeman for too long to think that by the book was the only way of doing things, or even necessarily the best way. But he'd also seen a lot of good cases thrown out — by juries but still more often by the Crown Prosecution Service — because procedure had been short-circuited at a critical juncture. He could hear defense counsel now, quite possibly Mr. William Burbage, QC, with his kicked-spaniel eyes and his peculiarly irritating nasal twang, inquiring as he cast significant glances toward the jury box: "And was the purpose of this some kind of emotional blackmail, Detective Inspector Norris?"

"Over my dead body," he snarled. "This is a murder investigation, Constable Best, it is not Amateur Night at the Flying Ferret. You, I can just about justify. He" — Norris glared at Sperrin as if it had been his suggestion — "sits out here with a cup of Sergeant Brooks's tea, unless and until I have something to ask him."

"All right," Hazel agreed. It was, she reflected privately, easy to seem accommodating when she'd already got everything she'd come in here with any hopes of getting.

Diana Sperrin looked surprised to see her. "Hazel?"

"This is Constable Best," said Norris woodenly, more for the tape's benefit than for anyone else as he resumed the interview. Then he sat back and waited.

Hazel leaned forward. "I think I know what happened. I may be a bit sketchy on some of the details, but the important things — the things that made you do what you did, thirty years ago and since — those I'm pretty sure I have right. Do you want me to tell DI Norris, or will you?"

Diana didn't move. She hardly blinked. She regarded Hazel levelly, while behind her eyes the creative mind was whirring. *Did* she know? Little Hazel Best, daughter of Byrfield's handyman? *How* could she know? How much could she prove? Or was it already too late to be worrying about that? "You don't know what happened," she said flatly. "You may think you do, but you don't."

"You know," said Hazel pointedly.

"Yes."

"Henry Byrfield knew."

A much longer pause. Then: "Yes."

"And David knows."

For a second Diana's eyes kindled. Hazel thought it was less because the secret she'd kept for three decades seemed under threat, more a conditioned reflex to the sound of his name. Then her lip curled dismissively. "David knows nothing. He was five years old."

"Children see as much as adults," said Hazel. "They don't seem to remember as much as adults because they file it differently. It's a bit like computers — it's all in there somewhere but you have to know which buttons to press to get it out."

Diana's lips tightened to a hard line. Her eyes were defiant. She said nothing. Silence had served her for thirty years; it was always going to be her strategy of choice.

Hazel sighed. So she was going to have to do it, and take the risk that she was wrong. It wouldn't be the first time. Even complete humiliation wore off after a while.

She said, "Jamie was ten, wasn't he, and David was five. It was a nice time for all of you. Jamie's little brother was getting big enough to play Frisbee with him. And you finally felt you could afford to take your eye off them for more than a minute at a time. Jamie was older, but you'd been waiting for David to grow enough to keep him safe. I'm sure you gave them lots of instructions. 'Don't play on the road. Don't go near the lake. Stay away from the tractors.' And then you let them head out and enjoy the freedom of the Byrfield estate. After all, they were entitled."

Hazel paused, head on one side, waiting for a response, but Diana offered none. She hardly seemed to be listening. It may have been because she knew how the story ended, or because she could see that Hazel had already strayed from the one true path.

Edwin Norris was attending closely. But he offered no comment, either.

Hazel went on. "You must have wondered later if you'd loosened the apron strings too soon. David was a smart, self-reliant child, but five is still only five, too young to be held responsible for his own actions, let alone those of his vulnerable older brother. But Jamie was going to be vulnerable however long you waited, and sooner or later you were going to have to take the risk. They were getting bored with the confines of your back garden. When you judged the time was right, you let them out to play cowboys and Indians in the woods."

"I didn't like them playing —" Diana stopped herself.

Hazel smiled. "With toy guns. I know — David remembers. I have news for you: They played cowboys and Indians anyway. And they played Frisbee. And they stayed off the road, and away from the lake, and didn't get in the way of the tractors, and you thought they were safe. I expect you checked them every ten minutes at first, then every half hour. Finally you started to worry only if they were late for meals." She looked across the Formica table at the older woman. "What happened then?"

Diana Sperrin's determined chin came up. "You said you knew."

"I know what the outcome was," said Hazel quietly. "I know who you blamed. In spite of that, I know what you did to protect him. You denied your older son a proper funeral so that your younger son wouldn't grow up labeled as the boy who shot his brother."

DI Norris sat up straight, like a puppet whose strings have been jerked. "David? *David* killed Jamie?"

"He pulled the trigger," said Hazel wearily. "But he was five years old — years below the age of criminal responsibility, years too young to have been anywhere near a shotgun, and years too young to have been entrusted with the care of another child. Any child, much less a disabled one. No one would have blamed David. The responsibility lay with his parents."

Diana stiffened, too, the power of resentment like a rod straightening her spine. But the anger didn't flush in her face. Her cheeks paled to the color of stone. "Oh, you smug, self-righteous little prig! What can you *possibly* know about it? Do you have children?" Hazel shook her head. "Then wait till you have before you criticize me. Wait till you have two of them, and one has the sweetest nature in the world and no common sense, and the other always wants to be doing, doing, doing. Wait till you haven't had a proper night's sleep for ten years. And you can't go out unless you take them with you, and if you take them, you need eyes in the back of your head because one of them's going to run off at every opportunity and the other is going to make friends with the most shifty-looking wastrel he can find.

"And you can't get away from it even for a weekend. Their father can't take them — his wife doesn't know they're his. You have no family of your own, and even if you had the kind of friends who'd be willing to keep a challenging child overnight, it's just too difficult. Would they forget he can have sweets one at a time but not a whole bag at once because he'll keep stuffing them in his mouth until he chokes? Would they understand when he picks every flower in their garden because he wants to give them a bouquet? When he draws them a picture in felt-tip pen on their new flock wallpaper?

"Jamie was a lovely, lovely little boy. But to keep him safe and out of trouble, the state would have needed a team of five carers. I had to do it alone. Because he was still a child, and you're expected to look after your children, I didn't qualify for much help. It was like running a marathon every day. Like running a marathon with a boulder in your arms."

It was more that she'd run out of breath

than of things she wanted to say. Norris took advantage of the pause. "Ms. Sperrin — are you saying that's why Jamie died? Because you were exhausted? Because there weren't enough hours in the day, and you thought David was old enough to keep Jamie out of trouble for a bit, and it turned out you were wrong?"

Diana composed herself first, then nodded. "Yes." Her voice was distant.

"What happened?"

"I don't know."

"Yes, you do," said Hazel softly.

Diana was looking at her as if she was the enemy. "I don't know what happened. I wasn't there."

"David was there," said Hazel. A hardness was creeping into her tone. "David will remember, if we force him to. Is that what you want? For some therapist to dig down through thirty years of scar tissue to the moment when a five-year-old boy caused his brother's death? Something that simple self-preservation required him to forget, so he never knew why his own mother despised him. You tried to protect him from that once — now you want to dump it on him? You haven't punished him enough?"

"It was his fault!" The words seemed

308

wrung from Diana Sperrin as if she'd been racked.

"He was five years old! *Nothing* is *anybody's* fault when they're five years old!"

"He pointed . . ." But she'd fought too hard to keep it, even now she couldn't bring herself to share the secret.

"What?" asked DI Norris sharply. "He pointed the gun at Jamie? What gun — where did it come from? Who gave him the gun, Ms. Sperrin?"

Two little boys, in shorts and torn T-shirts and scabby knees, playing in the golden light of a rural English summer, bathed in birdsong and the smell of cut grass. Byrfield was making hay all along the top meadows, the rumble of the tractors a distant backdrop to their game. Rooks in the high elms kept up a constant mocking commentary.

The Frisbee was looking a little the worse for wear. Just counting today, it had been stuck in a tree and brought down by a well-aimed stone, recovered from a cowpat and washed off in a ditch. The rim was starting to break up, and it no longer flew as true as it once had.

Which did nothing to spoil its owners' pleasure. You could have heard them from two fields away. People who think that squealing is the prerogative of little girls never heard these two. They played like the day would never end but minutes were going out of fashion.

As the hay making moved on from one field to the next, leaving little tepees of bales to catch the drying wind, the rabbits chased away by all the activity ventured out of the headlands. In the wake of the rabbits came a man with a gun.

Henry Byrfield looked at the sons he could not acknowledge and the heart broke within him. He knew he'd married the wrong woman. He'd done what his family expected, what his position required, but the money she'd brought with her, welcome as it was to ensure the liquidity of an estate that was asset-rich but income-poor, did not then, had not since, and never would make up for the tyranny of a loveless marriage. She had given him two daughters he loved; she might even give Byrfield an heir this time. She was pregnant again, doggedly determined despite the previous disappointments; although the twenty-seventh earl entertained unspoken, unspeakable doubts about his own role in the forthcoming happy event.

What she had never given him was any sense of being wanted or needed at his own fireside. Almost before the wedding cake was eaten he'd known she was never going to be what he longed for: a companion, a comforter, someone to care for him and be in his corner. He was still a comparatively young man: he wanted some fun out of life. Unable to find it at home, he'd gone elsewhere.

He wasn't proud of that. He knew he'd behaved badly. He hoped and believed it was desperation rather than wickedness that turned him down a route he would not willingly have chosen. But Diana Sperrin was fun to be with — artistically unpredictable, stimulating intellectually, exciting in bed, a friend by the fireside. And in due course the mother of his first and second sons.

All right, even a doting father would admit that Jamie wasn't an unqualified success. But he was sweet and charming, and Byrfield never saw him bumbling happily hand in hand with his mother around the village without experiencing a pang of love. And David, when he arrived, quickly established himself as a presence to be reckoned with, and Henry Byrfield thought he hadn't done so badly after all.

This summer he'd started seeing them about the fields and along the edge of the wood, their mother lengthening the reins as they managed to stay out of trouble. It provided Byrfield with opportunities to see them that he'd never had before.

Of course he'd visited the cottage, discreetly, by the back way after dark; and in daylight he'd made a point of finding business in the village when Diana was shopping, or painting in her front garden. He would pause by the gate, or in the shop doorway, and raise his hat politely and pass the time of day — not too much of it, not enough to be remarked upon — while his eyes drank in the contents of the pram or pushchair.

And he'd never known, never been sure, if his wife suspected or not. He'd done everything he could think of, short of ending it, to keep the affair from her. But Alice was an intelligent woman. And sometimes the way she looked at him . . .

Here and now, though, there was the chance to spend time with his sons. Show them the squirrels in the wood. Show them the many birds of Byrfield, and where each nested, and tell them which song belonged to which. Any landowner might do the same for a couple of village children who loved the hedges and fields as much as he did.

Today he had come out for rabbits, but he was also watching for the boys, and his heart skipped to see them. They were playing with the Frisbee, the older boy running clumsily and dropping it more often than he caught it, the younger making up for his lack of stride with sheer determination.

The gun was broken over Byrfield's arm and he had a brace of rabbits tied at his waist. The boys came over to see them, stroking the soft fur. Henry Byrfield remembered going out with his own father thirty years before — the fields had seemed bigger then, the rabbits bigger and without number — and the thrilling day the gun was put for the first time into his nine-year-old hands. "Time you were doing this, old man. . . ."

Most of the arguments still put forward against evolution are so blatantly spurious, so intellectually bankrupt, that they don't warrant the time of intelligent human beings in refuting them. There's one exception: that if nature truly favored the proliferation of the most suitably equipped, women would have four arms by now, and eyes dotted around their heads like a spider. They already have a keen sense, which no man can match, of when something is a really bad idea.

Henry Byrfield was not a stupid man. He was not a rash or careless man. He weighed the wisdom of what he was proposing to do before starting. He knew that James, although physically a year older, was mentally much younger than he himself had been on that magical day. But he also knew the child was good at doing what he was told. And he believed that while many things that growing boys and young men do would not be available to him, the richest life that could be provided for the child would be one that was as normal as possible. He thought he could give Jamie a taste of shooting without putting him or anyone else at risk.

He leaned forward and said gently, "Would you like to have a go, Jamie?"

The boy's face shone like a sunflower and he nodded.

Predictably, David interjected, "Me, too!"

But his father was having none of it. "You're too young. I'll show you when you're older. Now, stay behind us." The younger boy scowled and thumped down on the grass, picking sulkily at the broken edge of the Frisbee.

Byrfield cradled his arms round Jamie, holding his hands on stock and barrel. He held the child tightly against him to absorb the recoil. "You'll have a big bruise on your shoulder tomorrow!" When he was satisfied, he loaded two cartridges, picked out a likely tussock on the hillside, and guided Jamie's finger to the trigger. "Squeeze gently."

It was the loudest noise either of the boys had heard up close. David jumped up from the grass and craned around his father's legs to see the result. Jamie started to cry.

Concern verged on panic in the twenty-seventh earl's eyes. Wailing children had never been his area of expertise. "It's all right, Jamie — it just makes a big bang. Did it startle you? You'll get used to it. Look, let's do it again. . . ."

But Jamie Sperrin had had enough. His shoulder hurt and his ears rang, and he wanted his mother and the safety of his home. He tried to pull away from the man's grasp.

Byrfield held on to him — partly because he didn't want to have to explain the child's distress to his mother, partly because he really didn't want them to part like this, with Jamie frightened of him. Then he became aware of how this would look to a chance observer: a grown man forcibly detaining a wailing child. Someone else's child . . .

"All right, all right," he said hurriedly, "we won't do it again. Look, I'll put it down. . . ." He broke the shotgun and laid it on the grass.

Jamie was still sobbing and sniffling, but

the thing that had frightened him was on the ground, and he allowed himself to be comforted against the man's waistcoat. His fingers found the fur of the dead rabbits, caressing their silky coolness.

In tending to his older son's distress, Henry Byrfield had allowed himself to forget that there were two children with him. And that the younger one was *not* known for biddability and obedience. He only remembered when he heard the unmistakable snap of the gun closing, the distinctive though not particularly loud sound that turned an awkward burden into a lethal weapon.

"David shot Jamie?" DI Norris's gaze on the woman across the table was intense. "Is that what you're telling me? That your five-year-old son picked up Henry Byrfield's gun and shot his ten-year-old brother?"

Diana Sperrin had aged years in the telling. "Yes."

CHAPTER 26

Hazel wanted to slap her as she'd rarely
wanted to slap anyone before, even Ash.
"And you've never forgiven him. A five-
year-old child, who picked up a shotgun
someone was stupid enough to leave lying
around. Who didn't understand the difference between real guns and pretend ones,
and pointed it the way he and Jamie pointed
their fingers and said 'Bang!' *It wasn't his
fault.*"

"That's what Henry said . . ." And there
Diana's voice trailed off.

"What did he say?" asked Norris.

"That David was pointing the gun right at
Jamie's face. That he was grinning. That he
said 'Bang!' and pulled the trigger."

Hazel's heart turned over inside her. What
do little boys play? Soldiers, cowboys and
Indians, aliens and starship troopers. They
point their fingers in one another's faces
and say "Bang!" Then they fall over and lie

317

still for a moment. But then — and this is important — they get up again. The five-year-old David had thought it was the same with the real gun, except that the bang was louder. He'd had no idea — how could he? — how much damage it would do.

Norris said, "Was Henry Byrfield hurt?"

"A couple of pellets in his arm," said Diana dismissively. "I helped him get them out."

"Did neither of you think to call an ambulance?"

Anger kindled in the woman's eye. "You think there was some point? For a ten-year-old boy who'd taken a shotgun blast in the face? He was dead before all the bits hit the ground."

It was undoubtedly true. But the brutality of the statement, coming from the child's mother, knocked the wind out of Edwin Norris like a knee in the gut. He cleared his throat. "Who decided that you should bury him yourselves and say he'd been abducted?"

"We both did."

But Hazel didn't believe that. "No," she said with conviction. "Henry Byrfield was a good man — a kind and decent man. He didn't blame a five-year-old boy for what had happened — he knew who was respon-

318

sible. He wanted to go to the police. Didn't he?" When Diana refused to answer, she said it again. "Didn't he?"

"Yes!" snapped Diana Sperrin. "He thought it was the honorable thing to do." She managed to make it sound like a weakness.

"But you didn't?" asked Norris.

"I didn't see what it would achieve," Diana said through gritted teeth. "There was nothing we could do for Jamie. Except bury him with love, and we didn't need any help with that. If Henry had called the police, everything would have come out. Why was this middle-aged man playing with two little boys in a field? Because he was their father, of course. We'd have had to say so — anything else would have been worse.

"That would have been the end of his marriage. His wife would have left Byrfield, taking her daughters, her bump, and her money with her. I'd have had to leave, too. Small communities can be very intolerant of those who don't obey the rules. And David would have grown up notorious as the boy who blew his brother's head off. And for what? To put the record straight? It was too high a price to pay, for all of us."

"So you buried Jamie by the lake."

Diana nodded. "That night. Henry

319

brought the paving stones from the farmyard in the bucket of the tractor. I got some
things together for Jamie, to make him
comfortable." She glared at Hazel, daring
her to comment. But Hazel said nothing.

"And after that you called the police and
said Jamie had been abducted by his father,"
said Norris.

"It seemed the easiest solution," said Diana. By now she just sounded very tired.
"I'd told people I was married, that the
boys' father drifted in and out of our lives,
and they believed me. They even thought
they'd met him, some of them. Nobody,
including the police, was surprised when
you couldn't find him. A traveling man like
that — where would you start looking? After
six months I was the only one still pushing
for him to be found, and I was only doing it
to keep the police from wondering why I
wasn't."

"And you never told David?" Hazel's
voice was low.

"That he'd murdered his brother? Of
course not," said Diana coldly. "At first he
was too young to keep his mouth shut. By
the time he was old enough to be trusted,
he'd no recollection of what happened. He
saw me opening the greetings cards, and he
really thought they were from Jamie."

"It wasn't murder," said DI Norris. Maybe it was pedantic, but it was important to set the record straight. "A child that age is legally incapable of committing murder. We'd have prosecuted Byrfield, and you're right: It would all have come out then. David might have been taken into care for his own safety. Or maybe not. There's a presumption that children are better off with their mother unless there's a clear-cut reason to move them."

"Would hatred be considered reason enough?" asked Hazel disingenuously.

Diana summoned up the strength to glare at her. "I have never laid a hand on either of my sons."

Hazel's expression was uncharacteristically chilly. "No. You just made one of them pay every day for something he doesn't even remember doing. You forgave Byrfield, but you never forgave David for what happened. You didn't even tell him what it was he'd done that was so bad that his own mother could barely look at him. Don't you dare sit there and claim you were protecting David. You acted as you did to protect Byrfield, and yourself. But Henry Byrfield died nine years ago. You could have said something then, if only to your son. If only so he'd know why you resented him so."

"I didn't . . ." Another of those sentences that Diana began and then abandoned.

Edwin Norris pressed her. "You didn't what?"

"I didn't want to resent him. To freeze him out," said Diana Sperrin. For the first time Hazel thought she detected a trace of regret in her tone. "At first there were things to do, things to deal with, which meant keeping a lid on my feelings. Demanding that people go out looking for my missing son when I hoped they'd never find him. Insisting that he was alive in Ireland when I knew he was dead under the grass by the Byrfield lake. I told David the same thing as I told the police. I told him over and over again, and kept him from talking to anyone until I knew he had no recollection of anything else. Yes, I was hard on him. I had to be, for all our sakes.

"Later, when the search had been all but abandoned, when life was almost normal again, I could have reached out to him. Told him everything was all right — was going to be all right. Told him I l-loved him" — she stumbled on the word — "and we'd have to get each other through this because neither of us had anyone else. But it was too late. The anger I felt, the sheer bloody anger, had corroded my soul, and the scar tissue had come between us, thick and dense and impenetrable. Resentment doesn't cover it. You're right: I hated my son for what he'd done, and time did nothing to heal it, only set it hard. Why didn't I tell him when he was old enough? I think it was because I didn't feel he deserved to know."

"Have you any idea how much you hurt him?"

"He hurt me!" cried Diana Sperrin, a wail of torment wrung from her, as if these events had happened just hours before.

"The difference is," said Hazel through gritted teeth, "you were a grown woman and he was a little boy. A confused little boy who couldn't think why his mother had stopped loving him."

"But he was the *wrong* little boy! I wanted Jamie. I wanted Jamie back. I only ever wanted my beautiful Jamie."

"The people you meet when you haven't got your gun," said Edwin Norris mildly as he walked Hazel back to her muddy car. "How is it that some people manage to get it *so* wrong? Are they actually trying?"

"Diana? I think she tried very hard," said Hazel. "I think she tried so hard to be a good mother to Jamie that there was nothing left for David." She met his gaze. "Will

323

you tell him? I should really get on my way now."

Norris nodded grimly. "How much does he know?"

"I don't know. He's almost as hard to read as his mother. I don't think he remembers any of this. But given the things I was asking him about, he must have his suspicions. We shouldn't leave him wondering."

"I'll talk to him when I go back inside," DI Norris promised. "I'll need to at some point, we might as well get it over with. And then he'll probably need to talk to a therapist."

"I think they both will," said Hazel ruefully. "*Separate* therapists. Who will then need to talk to *their* therapists."

"Diana's will have to form an orderly queue behind me and her legal representatives," said Norris grimly.

"You mean to charge her, then."

"Of course I mean to charge her! Another day or two," he muttered, "and I might have some idea what I mean to charge her with."

"Well, don't annoy the shrink too much," murmured Hazel. "*You* might need him, too, before you've finished with the Byrfield family."

They shared a bleak chuckle as they crossed the car park.

Norris held the door for her while Hazel settled herself gingerly onto her damp car seat. He said, "Are you planning to go back to work in Norbold?"

Hazel nodded. "When I'm signed off fit."

Norris blew a silent whistle. "So this was you off your game, was it?"

Hazel appreciated the compliment. But she wanted to be honest with him. "I know these people. I grew up among them. It gave me an advantage."

"Yes," agreed Norris, "and so did having a head on your shoulders. I was going to say, if you fancy a change of scene, I'd be glad to have you here."

She hadn't expected that. But immediately she could see the advantages. Being closer to her father. Seeing more of Pete Byrfield. Getting out of a posting that would always have grim memories for her, and where she would always be as welcome as the specter at the feast.

And that was the problem. It would be the easiest, most comfortable solution. And once you start taking the easy way out, it gets harder and harder to do anything else.

"Thank you," she said, and meant it. "I won't forget that offer. Someday I'll come back and see if it's still open. But the first thing I have to do is the last thing I want to do, which is go back to Meadowvale Police Station and pick up where I left off. Nothing that happened there was my fault. I won't have it look as if I have something to run away from."

Edwin Norris clasped her hand warmly; and then, on an impulse, ducked his head through the open window and kissed her soundly on the cheek. It wasn't professional. It wasn't PC. But it was a gesture of friendship and support, and in a wicked world it's a brave soul who rejects either. Hazel grinned at him and nodded, and felt the pleasure of knowing she had an ally.

"Good enough," he said, straightening up. "I'll be here. So where are you going now?"

Hazel sighed. "Grantham. I'll collect Ash from the armaments place. He only just had the taxi fare to get him there. Lord knows how he was thinking of getting home."

CHAPTER 27

Saturday morning was a good time to find Stephen Graves in his office. With the factory silent and the workers absent, it was his chance to catch up on paperwork.

He was surprised to see Ash again so quickly, but received him no less courteously than before. "Does this mean you're making some progress?"

"Perhaps," said Ash carefully. Patience had curled at his feet in Graves's office but was refusing to look at him. He'd had to smuggle her onto the taxi bundled up in his coat, and she blamed him for the indignity.

He couldn't afford to worry about that. He needed to concentrate on his questions, and Graves's answers. "Who did you talk to after I left here?"

The CEO of Bertram Castings recoiled as if he'd been struck. "No one! Who would I have talked to? What do you think I am?"

"I think you're someone who knows this

industry a lot better than I do," said Ash honestly. "You gave me a list of names of other people I could talk to — people who'd had shipments hijacked, some of them since I lost touch with the situation. It occurred to me you might have called some of them to let them know I'd be in contact. Did you?"

Was that a flicker of relief at the back of the man's eyes? Was it the perfectly normal response of someone who thought he was being accused of something finding that he wasn't? Or just a glimmer of understanding where before there had been bewilderment?

"No," said Stephen Graves.

"You didn't talk to any of them? Or to anyone in any of their offices?"

Graves thought a bit longer, then shook his head. "No. I thought you'd prefer it that way."

Ash nodded. "Yes. Thank you."

"Why do you ask?"

Ash had debated with himself on the way over — he would have discussed it with Patience if the taxi driver had known he had two passengers — how much he should tell Graves. In the end he decided there was no reason to treat the man as any kind of a threat unless he gave some indication that he might be one. "Something happened not long after I left here. Someone ran me off the road and fired a gun at me." He saw Graves's eyes flare wide and forestalled his next question. "No, nobody hurt. But it was a serious attempt on my life. And my social circle is so narrow these days that probably the only people who want me dead right now are the pirates who hijacked your arms shipments and kidnapped my family."

He paused, but Graves made no attempt to respond, so Ash carried on. "Now, I don't think they're keeping tabs on me from the Horn of Africa. It means I was right: They have contacts very much closer to home. People feeding them information about what shipments to expect and where to look for them. Which explains how a Midlands drug baron could know something about my family's disappearance. And also how the kidnapping was arranged. It wasn't done over the phone from Somalia."

He was still watching Graves carefully to see if any of this resonated with him. He was not blind to the possibility that the man in front of him was himself the spy. He'd been talking to Graves not long before Cathy and the boys vanished, and then again not long before someone put him in a ditch and shot at him. Set against that were the losses, in cash and in business confidence, sustained by Bertram Castings as a result of the pirates' activities. On the *other* other hand, whoever the local agent was, he might have made more out of selling his information than Bertrams or any of the targeted companies could have paid him in a month of Sundays.

Ash had that feeling between his shoulder blades that suggested he was at least thinking about this in the right way. That didn't mean that Graves, or anyone at Bertrams, was involved in the hijackings, just that someone like him, someone in the office of one of these companies, probably was.

In a perfect world, Stephen Graves would have clapped his palm to his forehead and remembered talking incautiously to a shifty-eyed competitor he'd never entirely trusted. Or else his own eyes would have gone shifty and avoided Ash's gaze, and that would have been significant, too. But life is never that simple. Graves looked shocked, but no more than anyone might who found himself surrounded by wicked criminality. He had a wife and children, would have been less than human had he not pictured himself in Ash's position. Of course Graves looked shocked. Poker players talk about "tells" — individual quirks by which opponents give away unconsciously the strength of their hand. Perhaps it holds for poker, but it doesn't in real life. The best investigator in the world cannot tell when a good liar is lying. The liar doesn't tend to look up to the left, or down to the right; he — or she, for lying is an equal-opportunity occupation — doesn't scratch his nose or play with his glasses. He may seem vague, but so may an honest witness struggling to recall details; he may pile on too much detail, but so may an honest witness with a good memory who thinks this is what will help crack the case. The only reliable way to detect a liar is to listen to the words. Because if the events he's recounting wouldn't have happened that way, they didn't happen that way.

So while Ash was watching Graves's face for reactions, he was also listening intently for the words that would give him away. And he didn't hear any. This may have been because, so far, Ash had done most of the talking. It may have been because Graves knew that the less he said, the less he would have to explain. Or it may simply have been that the man was as stunned by developments as he appeared to be. With all his experience, Ash couldn't tell. He needed Graves to open up. What he talked about hardly mattered as long as he started talking. There are people who can't find a gap in the conversation without trying to fill it. Such people are an interrogator's dream: They can't keep a secret to save their lives. If you ever want to rob a bank, don't do it with someone who finishes your sentences. You'll definitely go down, and no one will help you finish your sentence then.

"Mr. Graves," said Ash, "I need you to help me here. I think we're within striking distance of the truth. I think what's happened proves it. Someone you know, or who knows someone you know, is passing back intelligence that makes it possible for African pirates to keep hijacking British arms shipments and to keep getting away with it. I think it possible, likely even, that you know something that would tell us who. Maybe you don't *know* that you know, and I don't know what questions to ask.

"So will you just talk to me? Tell me about the industry. Tell me how it all works — the difficult bits, the tedious bits, how much government interference you have to put up with, if there are ways of getting around it. I swear to God, I am not interested in your VAT returns. But I need more background information. I'm sure I asked you a lot of this four years ago, you and the other people who'd been targeted, but a lot's happened since then and I may have forgotten some of it. Will you humor me? Will you talk to me as if I was writing an article for *Big Guns* or whatever your industry magazine is called?"

"*Big Guns*?" said Stephen Graves faintly.

"It's not called that?" Graves shook his head. "Whatever."

So, overcoming an initial hesitation, Graves talked and Ash listened. He talked Ash through the events that had led to their first meeting. He described three further lost shipments in the intervening years, in forensic detail that suggested he'd spent many a sleepless night going over what he might have done, or not done, or done differently to make things turn out otherwise. He described all the losses in the British arms industry that had been or could be attributed to these pirates, going back some six years and including several Ash was unaware of. He described the makeup of his own company, starting with his professional background and concluding with the service history of the night watchman.

Then he did the same, in almost as much detail, for his competitors' companies. It was a small, tight-knit world in which, despite strenuous efforts to protect commercial secrets, everyone knew everyone else's business.

He talked for an hour, almost without prompting. At the end of that time, Ash didn't believe he'd caught him out in an untruth. Stephen Graves was either an honest man or a skillful liar.

Left with nothing more to ask, all Ash could do was thank him for his time, wake Patience, and leave.

A familiar and still muddy car was waiting in the Bertrams car park — in, Ash couldn't help but notice, the space reserved for the company chairman. Hazel didn't get out or even wave; she just sat waiting for him. Watching to see what he would do. As if he had options. He swallowed the last of his pride and walked toward her. "Car for Ash?" he mumbled with a faint, ingratiating grin.

"Actually, no," said Hazel coolly. "I thought Patience might like a lift."

The dog waved her scimitar tail in agreement. Or perhaps just at the sound of her name.

Ash considered. "How about if I sit on the floor and promise not to shed or chew the upholstery?"

Staying angry with him would be like holding a grudge against a child. She popped the lock on the passenger side. "Get in." And when he had, and Patience was sprawled gracefully on the backseat, Hazel said, "Well? Did you get what you came for?"

Ash considered. "I don't know."

One day, she thought, I'll actually do it. I'll deck him. "Is there someone we could ask? Perhaps Mr. Graves could tell us."

Ash gave a little muffled chuckle. "That's pretty much what I've been wondering. If there's something Mr. Graves could tell me and isn't doing. He's told me all there is to know about the arms industry — manufacturing, sales, regulations, loopholes in the regulations, the makers, the sellers, the buyers. I'm not sure he's told me anything useful. And I don't know if that's because he doesn't know anything about the pirates or because he knows enough not to let me *know* how much he knows."

It took Hazel longer to understand that than it had taken Ash to say it, but she got there in the end. "So what do you want to do now? Go home?"

"You're not going back to Byrfield?"

Hazel shook her head. "All done, for good and ill. I *will* go back, before very long, to see how everyone's coping with the new situation, but there's nothing more I can do there right now. These people need to talk to one another. I'd just be in the way."

"How did it all end?"

Hazel yawned. "Can I tell you later? I *am* ready for home."

Ash bit his lip. "Actually, could we stay here a little longer? Half an hour — an hour at most?"

Hazel looked surprised. "We could. Why would we want to?"

"I'd like to see what Stephen Graves does next."

"Why should he do anything?"

"He may not. Or he may want to tell someone I've been back to see him."

Hazel looked around her. "I suspect they have telephones in Grantham."

"Telephones can be hacked. Telephone calls can be overheard. If you had something to discuss urgently with someone, and absolute discretion was the only way to ensure you stayed out of jail, I don't think you'd want to phone at all. But if you had to, you wouldn't use your office phone, your home phone, or your mobile. I want to see if Mr. Graves wants to talk to someone so discreetly that he feels the need for special measures."

"Such as?

"If he goes out to buy a new phone. If he goes to an Internet café, or a public phone, or a house that isn't his to make the call."

"How will you know?"

"I know where he lives."

Most of the time it was easy to forget that Gabriel Ash was an intelligent, astute man who had once been highly regarded in national security circles. Then he said something like that, and a little shiver traveled down Hazel's back. *I know where you live:* the oldest, and still the most chilling, threat in the book.

Ten minutes passed, then fifteen, then twenty. Relenting, Hazel told Ash what had happened at the police station.

He seemed less surprised than she had expected. "How did David take it?"

"I don't know. DI Norris was going to tell him after I left."

"It's a hard thing to hear."

Hazel nodded somberly. "And yet, at some level, he already knew. Norris isn't so much telling him what happened as reminding him. Anyway, he was five years old. He *must* know it wasn't his fault."

"He shot his brother dead. I'm not sure common sense will be much comfort to him," said Ash. "His whole world's gone to hell in a handcart in the last few days. Let's just hope that, when the dust has settled, he'll get more support from his new family than he got from his old one."

"I'm sure he will," said Hazel, who'd known the Byrfields most of her life. "Pete and the girls will see him right. They're decent people. They'll make sure he gets everything he's entitled to, and everything he needs." There was a long pause while she thought. Finally she said, "You know, Pete wasn't far from right after all."

Ash nodded slowly. "He was afraid his parents had killed his older brother. And it turned out one of them was indeed responsible."

"Yes," agreed Hazel. "But that isn't quite what I meant. He thought the child died to protect Byrfield — the estate, the land — and he was right. Keeping Byrfield safe for the next generation was the only reason the twenty-seventh earl wasn't with the woman he loved and the mother of his sons. If he had been, Diana would never have allowed him to take a gun anywhere near them." She shivered, as if a cold breeze had crossed the car. "Pete said that land holds you in an iron fist. Henry Byrfield lost his son because of the compromise he made to keep his land."

Ash said nothing. Perhaps his thoughts were somewhere else. Patience got up, turned around, lay down again.

Then she sat up, gazing across the car park. The front door of Bertram Castings opened and Stephen Graves came out, locking up behind him, and walked quickly to his car.

Hazel glanced at her watch. "Late for lunch? Or has somebody dropped a match in a bucket of detonators?"

"Can we follow him?" asked Ash, watching intently.

The beckoning mirage of putting her feet up with a trashy magazine at home receded into the desert of duty. "Of course we can."

The car ahead made for the center of Grantham. "He isn't going home," observed Ash.

"Where does he live?"

"A little green-belt village to the west of town." Graves was leading them in the opposite direction, more or less back the way they'd come.

"It could still be a late lunch," said Hazel. "Or maybe he wants to use a cash machine."

"Maybe," said Ash diplomatically.

But he wasn't surprised, and actually neither was Hazel, when the car in front passed through the center of Grantham and out the far side. The signs indicated destinations to the south and east — Peterborough, Norwich, Cambridge. Graves picked up the

A1 and they followed.

Ash risked a sideways glance at Hazel. "Are you all right with this? I mean, I've no idea how long it's going to take. But we aren't going to be home for tea."

"It doesn't matter." She looked at him and she was smiling. "Gabriel, it doesn't matter. Neither of us has anything to rush back to. We'll go where he goes. If you think he can cast some light on what happened to your family, we'll follow him to Hull, hell, or Halifax. But if it turns out it's his day to visit his maiden aunt in Saffron Walden, you can buy me dinner before we head back."

He nodded gratefully. Out of the corner of her eye Hazel saw him mentally patting his pockets. "Only . . ."

"Ah, yes. You spent all your money on the taxi, and you can't go to an ATM because you don't know the pin for your credit card." Ash had the grace to look embarrassed. "We have *got* to reintegrate you into the twenty-first century. Meanwhile, *I'll* buy us dinner before we head back, but you're going to owe me big-time."

"I already do," mumbled Ash.

"Bigger than that."

On the open road, Hazel left two cars between her own and Graves's, confident she wouldn't lose him if he pulled off or pulled over. And indeed, when he signaled approaching Peterborough, thinking journey's end was in sight, Hazel did the same. But Graves just wanted petrol. Not knowing how much farther they were going, Hazel filled up as well. In the shop, she also bought milk, sausage rolls, and chocolate — emergency supplies in case the pursuit went on into the evening. As an afterthought, she picked up a box of dog biscuits as well.

She was paying when Stephen Graves came into the shop. Under the pretense of checking her change, she watched to see what he would buy. But apparently he wasn't intending to be on the road all night: all he bought apart from his fuel was cigarettes.

Hazel let him leave before her, to give him no reason to notice her or see who was waiting in her car. Only as he drove off did she hurry the last few paces and jump behind the wheel, with Ash muttering, "We're going to lose him" in an anxious whine.

"It's a dual carriageway," retorted Hazel briskly, "we're not going to lose him because he has a hundred meters' head start." With no appearance of haste, she nevertheless closed the distance back to the two cars it had been before.

Signs invited them to consider the possibilities offered by Huntingdon and St. Neots. But Graves stayed on the main road to Cambridge, so Hazel did, too. Spires began to appear among the trees. "You know," she said lightly, "we're going to feel pretty foolish if he's playing silly beggars with a twenty-year-old undergraduate at Queens' College."

"It's a long way to come for a mistress," remarked Ash. "I'm fairly sure you can get one closer than" — he craned to look at the mileage — "seventy miles from home."

"Who knows what a man will do when he thinks he's in love?" Hazel chuckled. And even the silence that followed didn't warn her she'd strayed onto dangerous ground.

It took Ash a couple more miles to respond. "Is that what you think I'm doing?" he asked in a low voice. "Acting like an idiot because I think I'm still in love?"

His reaction to her throw-away humor jolted Hazel to the core. Every time she thought she was getting to know this man, one or the other of them did or said something to highlight a chasm of understanding that yawned as wide as and perhaps even deeper than ever. She had never meant to hurt him. Once again, however, she'd managed to do it anyway. Was the fault hers? Was Ash unduly sensitive — and if so, was it something he could, or could be expected to, help? He was as he was, a product of his history. She didn't need to be sitting here beside him. Perhaps it would be better to leave him to find his own way to salvation. She didn't think so. But perhaps she was wrong, and always had been.

"Gabriel," she managed to say, "I didn't mean that. I didn't mean anything *like* that. Because (a) we weren't discussing you, we were discussing Stephen Graves. And (b) even if he has a mistress in Cambridge, what has that got to do with your search for your wife? He has a bit on the side, you have a family. There's no point of comparison, and it never occurred to me to try to make one."

He seemed not to believe her. "But it's a valid question, isn't it? Am I chasing phantoms? And if so, is there a right time to stop? Will I know if that time comes? Has it already come, and gone?" There was a barred note of challenge in his voice, as if he wanted her to say yes so he could shout her down.

Hazel shook her head. "No one can answer that but you. If you want my opinion, it's that an hour and a half into a pursuit across the east of England is not a good time to be wondering. When we left Grantham, you thought there was something to be learned from following this man. Nothing has changed: If there was then, there still is. We've come this far, let's see where he takes us. If you're serious about maybe calling it a day, we can talk about it after we get home."

It was an eminently sensible response from an eminently sensible young woman, and it deprived Ash of the argument he had been working himself up for. He didn't know why he was angry with her. He wasn't even sure it was her he was angry with. But he knew that he was angry. And that was new, too, and if it took Hazel by surprise, it astonished Ash. It was years since he'd dared to feel angry.

There was something liberating about it. He'd every reason to shout and even scream. If his therapist had been here, she'd have reminded Ash that if he hadn't done it before and he wanted to do it now, that was because he was finally feeling safe enough to let his emotions off the leash. Safe in himself, safe with those he was with. But Laura Fry wasn't here; she was in her office in Norbold. And this wasn't something that could wait until his next appointment.

"Stop being so damned reasonable!" he snarled. "I asked what you think — not what you think I want to think you think!"

Reasonable was Hazel's middle name. It was what made her good at her job. It was, she believed, a big part of what made her a valuable human being, and she was damned if she was going to apologize for it. But her tone hardened just enough that it should have rung warning bells. "Gabriel, what's this all about? I am not your enemy. I've tried hard — bloody hard, at times — to be a good friend. I wasn't criticizing what you're doing. If I had anything to say about that, I'd come straight out and say it, not pretend I was talking about something else. I thought we knew each other well enough that you'd know that."

He did. At least the rational core of him did. The intelligent, intuitive part of him, which had made him good at his job, knew she'd been more than a friend to him; she'd been an anchor, a candle in the dark. It knew she bore him nothing but goodwill, and that he didn't want to shout at her. That side of him wanted to stop, right now, and throw itself on her mercy once again, and hope that once again she'd touch his hand and quietly talk him out of the dark place.

But the liberated, angry part was reckless and stormed on. "We *don't* know each other! You don't know anything about me. You think I'm crazy, wasting my life chasing a dead woman and two dead boys. You thought I was crazy the day we met, and nothing that's happened since has made you revise that opinion."

"I never thought you were crazy," said Hazel, with a sort of forced calm and a certain economy truthwise.

"Of course you did! You all did, everyone at Meadowvale. You called me 'Rambles With Dogs'!"

She had to admit that much was true. Most of Norbold's police force didn't know his real name and wouldn't have thought to ask. "Well . . . you know . . . You *do* talk to Patience the way most people talk to other human beings."

He couldn't deny it. He didn't try to deny it. "What *you* don't know," he retorted triumphantly, "is that *she talks back!*"

On the backseat the white lurcher rolled her toffee-colored eyes. Ooooh shit, she murmured, you've done it now.

Afterward Hazel tried to convince herself that he'd been joking. He'd picked a fight with her for no better reason than that he was tired and discouraged and thought he was on a fool's errand, and then he'd tried to defuse it with a silly joke. It hadn't come out as a joke because he hadn't been getting much practice. But right now, and also later, if she was honest with herself, she knew that he meant it. He talked to his dog, and he thought she talked back.

What she might have done next is anybody's guess. The sensible thing would have been to ask her sat nav to find the nearest hospital with an emergency psychiatric unit. Or at least to have performed a 180 at the next roundabout and taken him home. But she didn't, and the reason she didn't was that before she could reach even that obvious a conclusion, two cars ahead of her Stephen Graves indicated left and turned toward Cambridge.

Two car lengths isn't long enough to come up with a whole new strategy. She did what she'd come here to do. She followed him.

CHAPTER 28

"He's heading for Midsummer Common."

Hazel looked at Ash in surprise. It was the first thing either of them had said since he dropped his bombshell, and he spoke as if the last five minutes simply hadn't happened. As if he hadn't lost control and ranted at her as if he hated her, and then knocked her sideways by admitting that he heard voices. Only it hadn't been an admission, exactly. There was nothing guilty or confessional about it. He'd thrown it in front of her as a challenge. As if it was a trump card, daring her to better it.

She couldn't — *couldn't* — reopen that conversation. Better to go on with this one. "Er — you know Cambridge?"

"Cathy was at Clare."

"What did she read?"

"Economics."

For some reason that surprised Hazel. All she'd known of Cathy Ash till now was as a wife and mother, and victim. Somehow she hadn't pictured her as a high-achiever as well.

Ash didn't notice her blink. Perhaps he was too busy looking for the fence-repair kit. "What about you?"

"BSc with qualified teacher status," she said, expressionless. "And then police studies at Liverpool."

"He's turning."

Graves was turning into one of the prime bits of real estate in Cambridge, an area of modern apartments with views over both the Common and the Cam, a short walk from the city center. Hazel stayed on the main road when the car ahead pulled into a residents' car park.

"Let me out," said Ash urgently. "You can't stop here, and I don't want to lose him."

"You keep your eye on him," said Hazel tersely, "and let me worry about parking." She pulled into a residential parking bay on the opposite side and fifty meters farther up. She pulled something out of her glove compartment and wedged it against the windscreen.

Ash peered at it as he got out. It was a printed card: **Doctor on call.** "But you're not . . ."

She looked at him exactly the way Patience might, and he didn't finish the sentence.

"Which building?"

Graves was still climbing the steps as they crossed the road. The glass doors swung closed behind him.

Beside her, Hazel felt Ash gathering himself to run; she held him with a touch. "Let him get out of sight."

"We'll lose him!"

"We'll find him again." As the elevator swallowed the businessman, Hazel walked briskly into the lobby and fixed the concierge with an authoritative eye. "Constable Hazel Best, Norbold Police. Give me the number, please, of the apartment where Mr. Graves is heading."

Even an active member of the police in a distant town would have had limited powers in Cambridge; and what she produced in support of her authority was not, in fact, her warrant card, but her pass to use police sports facilities. But it had the badge on it and it had her name on it, and most members of the public don't see enough police documentation to discriminate between one thing and another, particularly when someone is standing over them radiating the right to be there.

The concierge was a responsible middle-aged man who took his duties seriously; and one of those duties was to help the police to protect his residents. Graves was known to him as a visitor, but he was not a resident, so the question of divided loyalties did not arise. He barely hesitated before answering. "Ms. Regan's apartment — four oh five."

"Is Ms. Regan in?"

"I don't believe so, no. She moved out a week ago. Mr. Graves has a key. Er . . ." He was still trying to be helpful. "Shall I phone ahead?"

"On no account." Hazel tempered the admonition with a quick smile; then she headed into the second elevator, dragging Ash along with her. "See? Now we know where he's going, we don't have to get close enough for him to see us."

"What do we do if Ms. Regan really *is* his mistress?" asked Ash.

"Ask what he's doing there after she's moved out," said Hazel.

The elevator reached the fourth floor. Hazel got out first, in case Graves was still in the hallway. He wasn't — no one was — but the sound of a door closing told her where he had gone. Polished brass numerals on the door confirmed it.

"How do we get in?" whispered Ash.

She had to remind herself that although

he'd been involved in national security for years, he'd worked mostly behind a desk. What seemed blindingly obvious to her might be a minefield of new experiences to him. She said patiently, "We ring the bell."

Stephen Graves was not expecting visitors. He took the precaution of using the peephole before he opened it. What he saw was a fresh-faced young woman in an open-necked shirt proffering a folded piece of paper. "Message for you, sir."

It could have been anything, important or not. *She* could have been anyone, including a member of the building's service staff. He opened the door to find out.

Graves had been alone in the apartment. Now suddenly he wasn't alone anymore, and one of the two people who'd come in so quickly that they'd crammed him up against the wall was about the last person in the world who should have been here.

"A— Ash!" he stammered, fighting for calm. Ricocheting off the narrow walls, his uncertain gaze found Hazel. "And . . . who are you?"

Hazel's voice dipped significantly. "I'm a police officer, Mr. Graves." Then she waited while he worried about that.

Finally he managed to say, "You followed me."

"Yes," said Hazel flatly. "We did."

"Why?"

Hazel let a little impatience creep into her tone. "Come on, Mr. Graves, don't let's waste any more time. You've been less than frank with us, haven't you? Well, the time has come to tell us exactly what you know — *all* you know — and we'll see if there's a way you can walk away from this."

It was as if someone else was talking. She hadn't learned this in police studies. She thought she'd picked it up from the late-night transatlantic cop shows for which she entertained a secret weakness. Doing her own job on the streets of Norbold, she would never have dreamed of playing fast and loose with procedure. But here it was different. She had no lawful authority to throw the man up against his girlfriend's wall and put the fear of God into him, and in a way that made it easier. If she was acting as a private citizen, why should she be bound by police regulations? Hell, they'd sent her on gardening leave because they thought the stress had got to her. Maybe they were right.

Graves made a valiant attempt to restore his dignity, pulling down his jacket and straightening his tie. He looked at Ash as if he'd caught him kicking a puppy and said loftily, "I don't know what it is that you think I'm keeping from you. I've done everything in my power to help you, long after there was any chance that it would do any good. This is the thanks I get — to be hounded and harassed and treated like some kind of criminal?"

His haughty gaze shifted to Hazel. "I want to state, for the record, that I am not involved in any criminal activity, nor have I ever been, and if you're basing this accusation on anything Gabriel Ash has told you, you should know the man spent two months in an insane asylum! Now, are you ready to leave, or shall I call my solicitor?"

For a moment Hazel felt her resolve wavering. But it was already too late for that. Backing away with a muttered apology wouldn't get her out of this. Only if Ash was right, and they could prove it, would she come up smelling of roses rather than fertilizer — and not even the nice stuff that comes in bags.

She breathed heavily at him. The trick, she knew instinctively, was to make him feel the way she'd been made to feel by Sergeant Mole, who'd supervised her initial training. Sergeant Mole, whose measured footsteps made grown men and women hide in cupboards, whose lifted eyebrow had been known to cause hysterics, the curl of whose lip reduced intelligent people to gibbering wrecks. He'd never been known to lay a hand on anyone. He didn't need to. He just had to look at you *that way,* and let your painful awareness of your own inferiority do the rest.

Hazel Best wasn't Sergeant Mole. And Stephen Graves wasn't a raw police recruit already wondering whether he'd bitten off more than he could chew without choking. But by God, she was going to give it her best shot.

She let her head move fractionally from side to side in a rigidly controlled expression of bitter disappointment. Her voice had gravel in it. "Mr. Graves, do you think — do you really think — that I'm here because Gabriel Ash thought it was a good idea? Do you really think that's all it takes to launch a police operation? That you can whistle up a squad car like ordering a pizza, and pursue someone across half of England on the off chance that they'll be surprised enough to tell you something useful? *Have you any idea of the paperwork involved?*"

Graves blinked. Hazel had a sense that the ground under his feet seemed less firm than it had a minute before. "So . . . what's this all about?" he said at last.

"You know what it's about," growled Ash. "I told you — no one else, just you — that I was taking up the case again, and five days later someone fired a gun at me!"

"Mr. Ash," said Hazel sharply, "remember what you were told. You're allowed to be here for one reason only, and this isn't it. We will get to the truth, and we'll do it sooner rather than later. But it's my job to ask the questions, not yours."

From the look he gave her, Ash was almost as taken aback as Graves was. Except that he knew she was making this up as she went along, and Graves didn't seem to suspect it. At least not yet.

"So, Mr. Graves," she went on, "are you going to cooperate with our investigation? We know you're involved. You can deny it till you're blue in the face, but we know it and we can prove it. Is that what you want — for us to prove it in court? Remembering that people have died as a result of this piracy? You probably shouldn't count on getting a sympathetic jury.

"But it's your call. You *can* phone your solicitor" — it was all she could do not to call him "your mouthpiece": those damned films again! — "and we'll take this down the police station, and from then on everything's official and by the book. Or we can use this window of opportunity to see if there's some other way of proceeding. If you were a victim of these events, like Mr. Ash and his family, now is the time to say so. If you're acting under duress, if the pirates have a hold over you that's prevented you from being open and honest with us until now, this is when you tell us. Later will be too late."

In the tense silence that followed, with Graves staring at her in shock and horror and Ash with a kind of startled admiration, Hazel tried to remember exactly what she'd said. Had she lied? Had she said anything that would compromise a prosecution when this was handed over to real CID officers? She hoped not. She thought all the actual words were true, even if the impression she'd been trying to create with them was a fiction.

And in one way it mattered less than it might otherwise have done. Getting Graves into court, getting convictions against him or anyone, was a secondary consideration. The main purpose of this — of all of it: of today's drive, of everything Ash had done since he got his face out of the dirt where events had ground it — was to find out what had happened to Cathy Ash and her sons. Making someone amenable would be a bonus; the prime purpose was to learn the facts. If Stephen Graves knew them, or knew someone who did, and could be induced to talk, it mattered more that he told the truth than that they could make charges against him stick. Ash needed to hear the truth. What he did in consequence — if he did anything, if there was anything to do — was tomorrow's problem.

So she held Graves's stricken eyes, and she didn't blink, and she let her own gaze harden and narrow until it must have felt like a drill boring into his forehead. "Well?" she said impatiently. "Have you anything to tell us? Or do we start making phone calls?"

Still the man couldn't bring himself to decide. Hazel sighed, reached for her phone. "All right, then. Just don't say you never got a break. . . ."

It was the final straw that broke his resolve. Stephen Graves had no way of knowing if it would be better to confide in this young policewoman and hope she'd be able to help him, or say nothing and hope there was a gap between what the police knew and what they could prove that he could vanish through. But she was here, and Ash was here, and that meant it wasn't all smoke and mirrors. They'd tied him to this thing. Doing nothing — holding tight and hoping

— was no longer an option.

"All right!" he said rapidly. "All right. I'll tell you what I know. But you have to understand, I'm not part of it. Not from choice, and not for money. I was told what I had to do, and that if I didn't do it, or if I talked about it afterward, someone would die." He looked beseechingly at Ash. "I know you know how that feels."

CHAPTER 29

Whatever Hazel was expecting, it wasn't that. "A hostage?" She heard her voice soar. "The pirates took someone of yours hostage, too?"

Ash was beyond pale. His skin was gray. But he was fighting to hold himself together, this close to answers he'd been seeking through four long, hard years. Hazel could hear the clamped-down tension in his voice, but the questions he was asking were the right questions. "Someone off one of your transports?"

Graves shook his head. "No. Someone I didn't even know until . . . It's hard to explain. Look, can I tell you what happened? How it happened? Then you'll understand. I'm not trying to get out of anything. I don't know — I honest to God don't know — where I stand legally. Duress? Yes, certainly. They said they'd kill her if I didn't keep my mouth shut.

"She's just some woman. I didn't even know her before this started. But they were clever, you see. They let her talk to me. They let us talk over a period of months, and you build up a kind of relationship. And it was as if this was the one person I could do something to save. All the others, including the men flying my shipments, were gone and couldn't be helped. But this one woman was alive, and would stay alive if I cooperated, and would die if I didn't. Somehow that mattered more than everything else.

"You're going to tell me," he said, anticipating Hazel's interjection with perfect accuracy, "that I could have saved a lot more people by going to the police with the information I had. And maybe you're right. I'm not sure — I only know what they allowed me to know, I couldn't tell anyone where they are or how to find them — but maybe I could have prevented some of the later hijackings. And I know: people died every time. People working for me, some of them. And I can't tell you how sorry I am — for them, for their families, for my colleagues in this industry who thought those deaths were their responsibility, when in fact they were mine.

"I could have stopped that. I could have

blown the whistle, and trusted to the police to protect me and mine. I *should* have done that. But they'd have killed her. This one woman, who begged me to help her, who I'd managed to keep alive this far."

He took a deep breath, the first he'd managed since deciding to talk. Then he went on in a slightly more measured fashion. "I tried to do it. I kept trying. I picked up the phone more times than I can tell you. Sometimes I even got as far as dialing. I almost told you, Gabriel, when you came to see me — last week, and then again today. It would have been the easiest thing in the world, and also the hardest. I knew — I've always known — it was the right thing to do. But you see, I knew her by now. She trusted me. I couldn't betray her. It was easier to condemn a lot of people I'd never met than this one woman, sitting in a locked room somewhere in Somalia, guns pointed at her head, struggling to survive every day in the hope of a rescue that never came. I couldn't bring myself to buy other people's lives with hers."

"What did you do instead?" Hazel asked softly, afraid that even at this late stage he could be jolted back into silence. "Give them advance warning of your shipments that were heading into their part of the world? Tell them when you heard about other people's shipments?"

Graves hung his head. "Yes. That's exactly what I did. Payloads, routes, destinations, refueling stops. The level of onboard security. It wasn't worth their while to take on heavily guarded shipments — but nobody can afford that level of security all the time. When there's been no trouble for a while, the security is scaled back. That's what I told them — when it was safe to take on a particular plane and when it wasn't."

"But surely to God," exclaimed Hazel, "*nobody* refuels in Somalia! Nobody's that much of an optimist."

Graves shook his head. "Of course not. But the world hasn't just got smaller for you and me — it's got smaller for the Somali pirates as well. In small, fast surface craft they'll board ocean-going ships three hundred miles offshore. But they have aircraft as well — planes and helicopters. With those, all central Africa is within their reach."

"Then why not overfly central Africa?"

"We try to. The problem is, a plane capable of carrying that much fuel is prohibitively expensive to operate. Our customers resist spending that kind of money. And then, what do you do if your end user is in the danger zone? You take all the precautions you can, you remind yourself that most flights get through without any trouble, and you go for it. Usually you're lucky. Sometimes you're not."

"It isn't luck," growled Ash, "when someone is passing your flight plans to the enemy."

"No," whispered Graves. The weight of his culpability had bowed him. He looked up hesitantly. "What will you do?"

"What do you *think* we're going to do?" demanded Hazel. "The first thing we're going to do is tell everyone involved in this industry to put on hold any plans they've mentioned in your hearing. Then we're going to have you talk to experts in this field with a view to getting as much information as possible about where these pirates are located and how they can be stopped."

"And the woman?"

Hazel hardened her heart. "It'll be someone else's decision, but I don't think we can afford to prioritize her safety. Not with aircrew going missing every few months. In order to protect her, you've sacrificed innocent people. That can't go on. I'm sorry for her, desperately sorry. But it's too high a price to pay for one woman's life."

"Who is she?"

Hazel didn't have to look at him; she could tell from the timbre of Ash's voice what he was thinking. "Gabriel — don't."

"I know," he said quickly. There was an urgent rasp in the words. "I know all about odds. I know what the odds are against its being Cathy. But the thing about odds is, even at a thousand to one, there is that one. Even at fourteen million to one, *somebody* wins the lottery." A fragile smile flickered across his face. "It could be me."

Hazel shrugged. He needed to know. Even though knowing would tear him up all over again. She said to Graves, "You heard the man. Who is she, this woman whose life is worth dozens of other people's?"

Grave shook his head apologetically. "I don't know. They've never told me her name. They must have told her not to tell me. They call her . . ." He glanced furtively between them and swallowed. "They call her the cash cow."

Cold fury bubbled up behind Hazel's breastbone. She mightn't be Gabriel Ash's wife, this nameless woman sitting in a locked room in Mogadishu, but she was someone's wife, someone's mother, someone's daughter. And the men who had snatched her from that life — hauled her off a yacht, or a tourist beach, or a safari coach, waved their guns in her face, put her in immediate and ongoing fear of death — had the temerity to insult her as well. The cash cow. She kept them safe, and she kept the trade on which their piracy depended flowing, and they called her that.

Hazel had never wanted to kill anyone before, not even the man she *had* killed. She'd done what was necessary to keep other, better people alive, but she hadn't wanted to end his life the way she wanted to end theirs. The pirates. The term didn't make her smile anymore. There was nothing funny about them. They were thieves and terrorists and killers, and they kept this woman as a kind of human shield. They might have had her for years and they probably intended to keep her for years more, until despair killed her. And if they'd been where she could reach them, she'd have killed every one of them with any weapon that came to hand, or failing that, with her hands alone. The only word for that was *hatred.*

"Are you going to arrest me?" asked Graves timidly.

"Not my decision," said Hazel roughly, and accurately. "You'll certainly be interviewed under caution. Then it'll be up to the Crown Prosecution Service."

"They'll kill her."

"You don't know that."

"They said they'd kill her if I stopped helping them. They said they'd kill her if I stopped talking to them. They said if I went to the police, they'd kill her."

Hazel was too tired to lie. "Then they probably will."

Graves stared at her. "You're all right with that?"

"Of course I'm not all right with that!" Hazel retorted fiercely. "But there's nothing I can do to prevent it. They're operating in a lawless state thousands of miles away, and even if we knew where they were holding her, there'd be nothing we could do to help her. The people we *can* help, the lives we can save, are the people flying those two or three planes a year that go missing. And the people your weapons are killing who'll go home to their wives when the shipments can be sure of reaching their authorized end users again."

The sound of a computer filtered in from an adjoining room. Graves's eyes flared wide. "I think that's them."

Fear knotted a cold hand about Hazel's entrails. She wasn't ready for this. She wasn't capable of dealing with this. But there was no one to hand it over to, and no time to find someone. She swallowed hard. "What makes you think so?"

"Because that's why I come here! I can't talk to them in my office, can I, and I can't talk to them at home. There's a computer here that I use. It's set up to receive satellite video calls."

"Who lives here?"

Graves shook that off. "A friend. She's gone abroad for a while. I keep an eye on the place for her." His chin came up in a kind of terrified defiance. "Should I take that or not?"

"What'll happen if you don't?"

"I don't know," Graves said. "I always have. They let me know when I need to be here, and I wait for their call."

Every instinct Hazel possessed was telling her that he shouldn't take the call. That they had to buy time, and use it to pass the matter over to the proper authorities. She wasn't even sure who the proper authorities were, but the Cambridge police would either know or find out. It would probably involve the Home Office and the Foreign Office as well. Decisions at the highest level. And none of them, *none,* to be taken by a twenty-six-year-old probationary constable on sick leave because right now her judgment was considered suspect.

What *would* they do, the pirates, if their call went unanswered? Call again, obviously, try to reestablish contact. Their business depended on it. But what would they do about the woman? Would they keep her alive because the source of their information had built up a useful rapport with her? Would they hurt her to make Graves feel guilty? Or would they kill her to show him they meant what they said? There would be other women they could use to keep him in line — if he was willing to compromise himself for one stranger, he'd probably do it for another.

All this passed through — no, *raced* through — her mind in much less time than it takes to read it. The computer in the next room demanded attention again, but only once. She had to make a decision, and good or bad, she had to make it now. She wished she knew more about this kind of operation. She wished, desperately, she had someone to advise her.

With the force of a thunderbolt came the realization that she *did* have someone to advise her. Someone with experience of exactly this kind of operation. Someone whose government had thought highly enough of his abilities to vest him with the job of closing it down.

Someone the pirates feared so much they'd destroyed his life in order to keep him off their backs.

Hazel half turned to Ash, hesitantly. The time-dilation effect of the emergency made her voice sound slow and echoey. "Gabriel . . ."

"Answer it," said Ash without hesitation.

"Are you sure? If we don't, they'll have to call back. By then we could have an expert here to take it. . . ."

"*I'm* the expert on this," Ash said tersely. He said to Graves, "Answer it. Don't tell them we're here."

Graves nodded but still checked with Hazel for confirmation. "Officer?"

Inwardly, Hazel squirmed in an agony of indecision. She trusted Ash's intellect. She didn't entirely trust his emotions, and somewhere in his mind he still thought that the woman whose life they were gambling with could be his wife. Maybe he was right anyway. Maybe he was terribly wrong. Hazel had no way of judging. Nothing in her training had prepared her for this. Perhaps nothing could have done.

"I don't know," she admitted, and whether or not the men heard it, she detected the tremor in her own voice. "God help me, I don't know."

"I do." It was almost as if everything that had happened in the last four years had been leading Gabriel Ash to this moment. As if the horrors he'd suffered, and had to confront, and had finally to move past had been steeling him. For four years he'd spent a significant part of every day considering how he would face the men who had taken his wife, if ever fate presented him with the opportunity. There was probably no way that contact could have been made that he had *not* contemplated. All the murderous hours he'd spent sweating his way through one scenario after another turned out after all to have had some kind of a point. He *was* prepared. The grief, the agony, the madness had all contributed to the staggering fact that, here and now, he knew what to do.

"Answer it. Do what you normally do, say what you normally say. Don't let them know we're here. But keep them talking — or her, if it's the woman. Out of sight of the webcam, jot down everything you see. Everything in the room, everything anyone's wearing, every symbol that comes up on the screen. Never mind whether it makes sense to you. Put a pad beside the monitor, don't move your hand too much, but jot down everything you see. We can use it later to work out where they're calling from."

There was no time left, least of all for an argument when she had no confidence that he was wrong. Hazel nodded. "Do it."

Stephen Graves did as he was told: followed the protocol exactly as he had all the previous times he'd done this. He keyed in his user name and password. They needed to know it was him they were talking to.

As always, there was a delay. An image tried to form, broke up, tried again, so bleached by distance and the marginal quality of the equipment that it was almost monochrome. Seconds passed. There was nothing unusual in that, only today the seconds stretched till their sinews groaned.

Once the decision had been made, Hazel had quickly taken up a position to the right of the monitor, out of view of the webcam, not even her shadow showing — she'd checked. From here, bent awkwardly because there hadn't been time to pull up a chair, she had a tangential view of the screen and also of the pad where Graves's right hand was already sketching letters and numbers and symbols. This was her field, at least it had been once, but she didn't even try to analyze them now. There would be time for that later. Right now the priority was to keep Graves on track — support, encourage, help him out if he stepped into the quagmire. With only a tiny sideways glance he could see her face, lip-read her silent instructions, and no one in Mogadishu would have any reason to guess.

Ash was on the other side, also invisible to the computer's camera, paying for his privacy with an on-screen image even poorer than the one Graves was seeing. Of course it was coming a long way — no one had Somalia at the top of their agenda when they were designing their satellites' orbits; in addition, there were undoubtedly measures being taken at the other end to keep the signal untraceable.

In spite of all that, a picture was forming. A face — a woman's face. Still too grainy to read much of an expression into it, and nothing whatever in the background — plain, colorless walls. Words came over the speaker, and a moment later her lips began to move. "Stephen? Stephen, are you there?"

"I'm here," Graves said quickly. "Are you all right?"

A pause long enough to become uncomfortable, but it was only because of the distance the signal had to come. As soon as she'd received his transmission, she'd answered it. "I don't know. Things are happening. I don't know what it means. I think

they're going to move me again. Stephen —
try to help them. Whatever they want, try to
do it. They say you're my only chance."

She was an Englishwoman. It took Hazel
a couple of sentences to be sure, because of
the sound quality, but she had no doubt
now. Well, if she was English, even if she'd
been living abroad, it should be possible to
find out who she was. There would be a
record somewhere of her disappearance.
Just how much help that would be, Hazel
wasn't entirely certain, but it seemed to her
to matter. The woman must have family and
friends somewhere, people who'd want to
know that at least for now she was alive.

She concentrated on the imperfect picture
of the woman's face. It's harder than anyone
ever imagines to positively identify a picture
of someone you don't know. Hazel made a
note of all the things that might help. Age,
she thought, somewhere between forty and
forty-five — though the life she'd been
forced into would put years on anyone, so
she could be younger. Thin, but that was
only to be expected. Fairish hair, light skin;
eyes looked washed-out, so probably blue
or gray. Wearing a T-shirt you could buy in
any bazaar anywhere in the world. It wasn't
much to go on.

She was concentrating so hard on doing

her job that, incredibly, for a moment she had forgotten who else was here doing it with her. Remembering with a start, wondering how he was dealing with this, she looked guiltily across at him.

Ash was transfixed by the image on the screen. She might have been Medusa, with the power to turn men to stone, rather than an exhausted, terrified woman begging a man she had never met for help he couldn't now give her. Ash's lips moved, but it was like the transmission from Mogadishu — the sound was out of sync and came moments later. "Cathy?"

Hazel didn't believe for one moment that it was Ash's wife they were looking at. The man was trying to see what he wanted to see above everything in the world, and it had been four years, and the picture was poor enough for him to project even his most desperate hopes onto it. Another moment and he'd see he was wrong, and then the disappointment would take him like an avalanche, crushing him.

But something was going to happen before that, and arguably it was even worse. He was shifting his position to get a better view of the screen. Another second, less, and he'd be where she could see him. And if the woman could see him . . .

Hazel mouthed urgently at him, flagging her arms to get his attention, waving him back out of the line of sight. Ash saw nothing but the computer screen, and the grainy, jerky picture of a woman that he was trying with all his might to force into the image of his lost wife. He leaned closer. *"Cathy?"* he whispered again.

And then it was too late. She'd seen him. Her pale eyes flicked sideways from Stephen Graves, and her mouth fell open with shock. Her pale, dry lips tried three or four times to form a word before anything came, and this time it wasn't just the lip-sync problem. She looked as if she'd been sideswiped with a length of two-by-four.

And then she said, *"Gabriel?"*

ABOUT THE AUTHOR

Jo Bannister began her career as a journalist after leaving school at sixteen to work on a weekly newspaper. She was shortlisted for several prestigious awards and worked as an editor for some years before leaving to pursue her writing full time. She lives in Northern Ireland and spends most of her spare time with her horse and dog, or clambering over archaeological sites. Her thriller, *Death in High Places,* was nominated for the RT Reviewers' Choice Best Book Award.

The employees of Thorndike Press hope you have enjoyed this Large Print book. All our Thorndike, Wheeler, and Kennebec Large Print titles are designed for easy reading, and all our books are made to last. Other Thorndike Press Large Print books are available at your library, through selected bookstores, or directly from us.

For information about titles, please call:
(800) 223-1244

or visit our Web site at:
http://gale.cengage.com/thorndike

To share your comments, please write:
Publisher
Thorndike Press
10 Water St., Suite 310
Waterville, ME 04901